VICIOUS CREATURES

VICIOUS CREATURES

A NOVEL OF SUSPENSE

ASHTON NOONE

SCARLET
NEW YORK

VICIOUS CREATURES

Scarlet
An Imprint of Penzler Publishers
58 Warren Street
New York, N.Y. 10007

Copyright © 2022 by Kristine Saretsky

First Scarlet Press edition

Interior design by Maria Fernandez

Library of Congress Control Number: 2022902993

ISBN: 978-1-61316-338-2
eBook ISBN: 978-1-61316-301-6

10 9 8 7 6 5 4 3 2 1

Printed in the United States of America
Distributed by W. W. Norton & Company

PROLOGUE

The dead boy lay in the glade for three days before somebody said something. Glazed eyes open wide, face tilted toward the sky. Adam Albright was a senior at Reachwood High School, ready to graduate with the rest of us at the beginning of summer. His parents buried him in the suit he was supposed to wear, class ring glittering gold on his finger.

We all knew he was there, of course—long before they carried his body out of Reachwood Forest. Limbs cold and rigid, a hole in his chest open to expose the flesh and bone below. Dried blood streaked his skin mud-red. Leaves and white flowers circled his brow, as proud as a crown. For three days, we had ventured into the forest to visit his body and leave offerings like small apologies.

We wore black to his funeral mass, gathering as close as shadows in the church pews. Before they left his body in the ground, we tossed flowers across the lid of his casket like some kind of bright shroud.

We never told anybody what we did.

TODAY

CHAPTER 1

I never wanted to come back home.

Reachwood Forest still waits here over a decade later. Trees cut through the suburb, growing too close together in the steep ravine. Tangled branches cast shadows deep enough and dark enough to make me shiver and roll up my window. Nothing has really changed. The streets still bear the same names, leading up to the opulent houses at the top of the hill. The same wealthy families still live there, overlooking the neighborhood and the forest below.

"Are we going to be there soon?" Marjorie fidgets with the sleeves of her jacket. Nearly fourteen-and-a-half years old, but she hasn't learned how to be patient.

"We'll reach it in a few minutes." My hands grip the steering wheel tight. Marjorie slouches down in her seat as the manicured lawns pass by outside.

"What's wrong?" she asks when I pick at a half-healed scab on the inside of my wrist, teasing at its raw edges. The quick twinge of pain brightens the edges of my vision.

"Nothing. I'm just wondering what everyone will think."

Thirty-three years old, nearly broke, in the middle of a contested divorce and retreating to my childhood home with my daughter until I get back on my feet again. I can hear the whispers already as the scab cracks open, exposing the soft new skin beneath the surface.

"Who cares?" Marjorie says. Her nails tap against the screen of her phone as she texts the friends she left behind at home. "It's not like they know anything about you anymore."

I steer into the still-familiar driveway and park the car. Marjorie leans forward in her seat to study the house we haven't visited since she was a baby and asks, "This is it?"

"Yeah. We're here." I flinch as my phone vibrates on the dashboard.

"It's so small—not like our house." Marjorie curls her hands in her lap. Her fingers pluck at the soft-knit hem of her pastel sweater. "I want to go back."

"I know. I want to go home too, but we've got to get through this, okay?"

Marjorie doesn't say anything. We sit together in silence as a song plays on the radio. Some bubblegum pop ballad I probably liked back when I was still in ninth or tenth grade.

The house hasn't changed. Two stories tall, it rises from the dirt to throw its shadow over the car. Not a single leaf out of place in the neatly trimmed hedges lining the driveway. The lawn stretches out in front of us, clean-cut and immaculate. Flowers unfurl in brilliant bursts of color in the garden.

"I thought Grandma and Grandpa were paying you to fix this place before they move away." Marjorie shuffles her feet. "It looks okay to me."

"They hired someone to keep the yard looking nice. It's probably a mess inside," I say, picturing my parents' faces as I unbuckle my seatbelt. Marjorie frowns when I pick at the scab on my wrist again. The new wound oozes clear fluid.

The empty house sits like an open secret in front of us, windows wide enough to allow any curious eyes a glimpse of the rooms and hallways inside. The song on the radio ends and the announcers switch to the latest local news. Another child lost in the forest—vanished from the path. Sometimes the missing children return home again.

Sometimes they never come back.

"Come on." I open the door. My phone vibrates again and I ignore it, shoving it into my jacket pocket.

The yellowing leaves on the trees rustle as I pull the first suitcase from the trunk. Marjorie pouts as she drags another bag from the back seat. She drops it to the ground with a thud and says, "You take this one. It's too heavy."

"Fine." The laceration on my wrist stings as I haul the bag up the driveway. I tilt my head down to hide my face from any prying eyes peering out at us from inside the neighboring houses. Not eager to let anyone know I've returned home yet. To begin the spread of rumors that could eventually reach my childhood friends.

They might start to ask questions.

Marjorie grabs another suitcase and hurries after me, carrying it up the porch steps and dropping it down on the mat. She taps her feet while I search underneath the flowerpots until my fingers close around the spare key. I unlock the front door and Marjorie disappears inside the house, leaving me to retrieve the last of our belongings from the trunk.

◦—•—◦

"Marjorie?" I call out after I drag our bags into the foyer and pile them high on the stone-tiled floor. "Where are you?"

"Over here." Marjorie's voice travels through the empty rooms. I follow the sound down the hallway. Old photos still decorate the walls—my teenage face smiles as I walk past. Or maybe it's a grimace. The warmth never quite reaches my eyes.

"What are you doing?" I ask when I find her. She's standing by the window in the kitchen, staring out into the dark. My throat catches as I glimpse the forest pressing against the edges of the yard outside. Sharp-needled fir trees thick enough to blot out the sun, moon and all the stars in the sky.

The place where Adam died.

"Just looking at everything," Marjorie says. Her breath fogs the pane.

"What do you think?"

"I still think it looks like shit." She spits the words. "We should have stayed at our place."

"You know we wouldn't be safe there."

"But we will be here?" Marjorie asks. My mouth twitches as her eyes focus on the forest again. A warning forms on my tongue, but I swallow the words down before I can say them out loud. Marjorie would just ignore it. Better to stay silent.

"It's been a long day. Get ready for bed—we can unpack everything tomorrow," I say finally. Marjorie follows me to where the bedrooms wait at the end of the hallway, twisting the beaded friendship bracelet that circles her wrist. A present from her best friend when they were both seven. She's carried it with her for half of her life. Guilt curls inside my stomach—I've uprooted her from the only home she's ever known.

"Remember, this isn't forever." I clear my throat. "Your grandparents are letting us stay here until I get everything together. We'll move back home as soon as the divorce is settled."

"Why are they letting us stay here? I barely even know them." Marjorie pauses in the middle of the hall.

"That's only because your father didn't want them to visit."

Not quite a lie.

"They could have at least tried to see us. They're your parents." Suspicion shadows her face, like she knows I'm not telling her everything. And it's true—I never told her about how my parents stopped speaking to me in the months leading up to Marjorie's birth over fourteen years ago. Ashamed of the accusations hurled at me soon after Adam's murder. My teenage pregnancy that tarnished the picture-perfect image of our family even further.

"Well, they're helping us out now." Exasperation rasps at the edges of my voice.

"They didn't even wait to make sure we got here safe." Marjorie folds her arms and scowls. Almost an exact reflection of me—strawberry blond hair and blue eyes. Faint freckles dust her cheekbones and the bridge of her nose.

"They're out shopping for a new house. We'll see them tomorrow," I say. My stomach drops at the thought of seeing my parents again. Maybe they felt the same way and decided to stay away tonight. Leave us alone inside their empty home.

"So what? They should have waited for us."

"I don't want to talk about this anymore." I sigh and push open the bedroom door. "This is your new room—I'll see you in the morning."

Marjorie walks inside without another word and slams the door behind her. Silence settles over the house again.

⁃⥊⃓⁃

I return to the bedrooms an hour or so later, moving past familiar doorways—a bathroom, a linen closet. Two bedrooms sit at the end of the hall. When I crack the first door open to check on Marjorie, I blink.

My old room.

The same narrow bed rests below the window and the same lavender paint decorates the walls. The air smells stale and heavy, like no one has visited here since I moved out soon after my high school graduation.

Marjorie has claimed the space, curled up tight beneath the sunflower-patterned sheets that used to cover me. The shallow sound of her breathing fills the small room. I close the door quietly, afraid to wake her from her fitful sleep.

Dragging my heavy suitcase into the spare room, I sit on the edge of the bed and cough when dust floats up from the covers. My phone vibrates as I rummage through my bag for pajamas and a toothbrush. It buzzes again and I ignore it, padding barefoot down the hall to change and brush my teeth.

I undress in the dark, not wanting to glimpse the bruises my ex-husband left mottled across my body. A surgical incision still heals on my wrist. A scar splits the thin skin on my palm and another rests as ragged as a bite mark against the hollow of my neck.

The taste of mint toothpaste lingers against my tongue when I return to my bedroom. I retrieve a bottle of strong painkillers from my suitcase, shake one of the little white pills onto my palm and swallow it dry.

I take a deep breath before I finally check my phone. My hands quiver as I scroll through my notifications. But there are no new messages from my ex-husband—just three missed calls from my parents and a text from Mother: *Ava, are you at the house yet?*

Yes. I type back.

"Mom?" Marjorie knocks on my bedroom door. I stow the orange prescription pill bottle away again beneath the tight-packed clothes.

"What?"

"Can you stay with me tonight?" She enters the room, gnawing on her bottom lip with the tip of one pointed tooth.

"Sure," I say and shove my suitcase into the dark space underneath my bed. I follow her back to my childhood room and unroll the spare futon on the floor beside her bed. Before I crawl under the covers, I draw the curtains tight to block out the sight of Reachwood Forest waiting outside. These windows are so wide.

Anything could look inside while we sleep at night.

CHAPTER 2

"Have you talked to your friends yet?" Mother asks the next morning as she hangs the few clothes I've brought with me in the guest room closet. Alison Montgomery, the reigning gossip queen of the Reachwood Community Association—she hasn't changed in the decade I've stayed away. Face fully made up even this early in the morning, not a strand of blond-dyed hair out of place. Maybe she had plastic surgery done at some faraway clinic to stop aging.

"No. I don't really want anyone to know we're here." I shake my head. Guilt darts quick though her eyes and I ask, "Did you tell anybody?"

"Not really. Well, I might have mentioned it to a few people," she admits as I trace the raised scar that lines my palm. The faded memory of a childhood injury. "I just thought they'd be happy to see you."

"How are they doing?" Curiosity stirs inside of me. My friends and I had all drifted apart after our high school graduation. Retreated inside ourselves during the investigation into Adam's death, leaving calls unanswered and text messages unread. I fled to nearby Portland at the start of that summer, just over a week after his body was discovered. Threw myself into a new relationship with my now ex-husband almost immediately in a desperate attempt to forget everything.

"They've all done well for themselves. Victoria owns the most expensive house in the neighborhood now," Mother says. She trails in my footsteps as I walk toward the front door, where the rest of my bags still lie in a haphazard pile on the floor.

"Oh." My throat tightens. I glance out the window at the houses lining the street in neat rows, brick exteriors almost identical. The forest rises behind the buildings. Trees grow untamed in the ravine that cuts through Reachwood, separating the old neighborhood that was built over a century ago from the suburban sprawl that eventually spread out from the city to engulf it.

My eyes flit to the top of the hill, where the families who founded the original town still live inside expensive mansions. The Albrights, Harts and Gallaghers. Descended from the prospectors who pursued rumors of a new gold rush through the mountains of Oregon over a century ago. The only three families to remain here after the original settlement walked into Reachwood Forest one day and vanished without a trace. They struck a fortune when they discovered a vein of gold in the forest soon after the mass disappearance. Their descendants have enjoyed the wealth and privilege it afforded them ever since.

Victoria must still live up there somewhere. Although she used to want to leave this place more than anything.

"She married Cyril after you left," Mother says. Her gaze sharpens on my face. Eyes expectant, as though she's waiting for some kind of reaction. "Did you know that?"

"No. She never told me." I chew on the corner of my lip, remembering how I would have followed Victoria anywhere when we were still teenagers. We haven't spoken to each other in years. Not even during my few brief visits back to Reachwood to show Marjorie to my parents when she was still a newborn.

"Cyril runs the Reachwood Mining Company now," Mother explains as I carry the bags down the hallway. The favored son of the Hart family, it doesn't surprise me that he inherited control of the gold mines from his father. It shouldn't surprise me that he married Victoria, either. The only daughter of the Gallagher family, the marriage would be the perfect arrangement to unite the wealth of their two powerful dynasties.

"Nathalie and Matthew have done well for themselves, too. They got married a few years ago. He still plays in the NBA, and she runs some kind of technology company." She lists their achievements like I have done nothing. And it's true—after I had Marjorie, I never went back to school. Too busy caring for my new baby and catering to the increasing demands of my ex-husband to find the time to study.

"Great." I force a smile onto my face as I drop my suitcases on the bed.

"Adam's family still lives here too, actually." Mother sorts more clothes into my closet. "They never moved, not even after everything they've gone through."

"I didn't think they would. I mean, they practically built this neighborhood." I hesitate, working up the courage to ask my next question. The one that's been haunting me ever since I arrived home. "Do they still talk about him? You know—about what happened."

I shiver at the memory of his dead body lying in the grove.

"Of course they all still talk about him." Mother fiddles with the wedding band that adorns her ring finger. Maybe crafted from some of the same gold that my father spent years of his life transporting from the Reachwood mines. "Even though the case went cold years ago."

"Oh." I can't think of anything else to say as Adam's face appears in my mind again. The eldest son of the Albright family, he inherited their fair hair and pale eyes.

"Ambrose stayed to take care of their parents. I think he has a son around Marjorie's age." Her eyes narrow when I pull my bottle of painkillers from their hiding place at the bottom of my suitcase. The white pills rattle in the container as I carry them into the bathroom and lock them away safe in the medicine cabinet.

"Are you sure you need those?" Mother asks.

"What do you mean?" I frown. My wrist still hurts, although it's been almost a month since my ex-husband broke it. Grabbed it and twisted so hard the bone fractured in half. Fixed with surgery, but the persistent nerve damage still gnaws at me every day. The medication is the only thing that drives it away.

"You know what you used to be like, Ava."

"You never stop reminding me," I snap the words as I slip past her in the doorway.

"You skipped lunch, too." Mother follows me back down the hallway and into my bedroom, so close she almost treads on my heels. Her breath tickles against the back of my neck.

"I just wasn't hungry. Don't worry."

"Do you even know how long you're going to stay here?" she demands as I set my last suitcase down on the bed. Maybe she wishes I had never divorced my ex-husband—that I had stayed with him instead and attempted to repair our marriage. After all, he hadn't always been like this. But his grip on his temper had lessened over the years we spent together. Now there was nothing left to salvage.

"I haven't heard anything from my lawyer," I say and open my suitcase, refolding my wrinkled jeans before I stack them in a neat pile inside the dresser. "We'll leave as soon as the divorce is over."

"We'll pay you to help us move out, but I hope you haven't spent your entire inheritance," Mother says. Her lips thin at the mention of the wealth I received after my grandparents died in an unexpected accident. Still a sore spot, even over a decade later. She didn't speak to me for weeks after she found out they made me the sole heir of their estate. The only benefactor of their sizeable life insurance policy and wrongful death settlement. "They left you everything so you could take care of Marjorie. Sometimes I think they shouldn't have—it would have taught you more responsibility."

"I didn't spend it," I protest, although my bank accounts sit almost empty. Drained from staying home to raise Marjorie and paying for my ex-husband's expensive tastes in everything. "Anyway, did you find a place yesterday?"

"No. I didn't like any of the houses they showed us," Mother says and slides open the window. A crisp breeze blows into the room, carrying the rich smell of dirt and decaying leaves. Somewhere outside, a dog barks. The insistent sound carries into the house as she asks, "You're really not planning to visit your friends?"

"I haven't decided yet."

"You should give them a call. I'm sure they'd all like to see you again. In the flesh. You only visited once or twice and you never even tried to see them." A touch of judgment colors her voice.

"I want to get Marjorie settled in first." I picture Victoria again—pretty and popular, with a smile as sharp and as bright as a knife.

"Are you taking her to the Reachwood Festival?" Mother asks. The annual neighborhood celebration at the beginning of September, when the whole community journeys into the forest to hang lanterns like beacons from the boughs of the trees.

"I'm not sure. I heard another girl just disappeared," I say as the wind raises goosebumps on my skin. One child vanishes into the forest every decade or so. Just long enough for the neighborhood to start to forget. And then it happens again. "I don't want Marjorie to think it's safe to go in there alone."

"Well, I still think you should reach out to your friends soon." Mother stretches out a hand to study her manicured nails. Long and pointed enough to remind me of claws. "Before they come looking for you."

FIFTEEN YEARS EARLIER

CHAPTER 3

"Where are we going?" I asked as I followed my friends to the edge of Reachwood Forest. A few minutes earlier, the lunch bell had rung to signal the end of my first morning back in class and I had hurried outside to meet them, excited for our reunion. Now I trailed behind them as the trees rose before us.

We weren't supposed to go near the forest.

"We started hanging out here after you went away," Victoria Gallagher explained, glancing at me over her shoulder. Cyril Hart hesitated in front of us, waiting for Victoria to catch up with him. I said nothing—remembering the weeks I had spent at an out-of-state treatment center until I started eating again. I'd missed months of my senior year in high school, time I could have spent with my friends. Now there were only a few weeks of classes left until our graduation in early June.

"Yeah, nobody bothers us out here. We can do pretty much whatever we want," Nathalie Bellevue said and fished a bent cigarette out of her pocket. An honors student ever since I could remember, even though she spent pretty much all of her time getting high.

Green leaves sprouted from the boughs of the trees. The air smelled fresh and sweet as we walked along the border of the forest. Clouds clustered in the sky overhead, heavy with rain. As soon as the brick school building disappeared behind us, Nathalie lit the cigarette. A thin trail of smoke rose from its smoldering tip.

"Want to share?" She offered it to me.

"Sure. Thanks." I placed the cigarette between my lips and inhaled hot smoke before I passed it back to Nathalie. The small stones hidden in the grass grated beneath our sneakers. A hand touched my shoulder and I jumped.

"It's just me." Adam Albright laughed. A pack of half-familiar boys followed at his heels—the same boys who skipped class every day to hide away outside. They all grinned like they knew some kind of secret as they fell into step beside us.

"Don't scare me like that, it wasn't funny," I said, but I giggled anyway.

"Sorry." Adam's shoulders flexed beneath his jacket when he shrugged. Dressed from head to toe in expensive clothes—each piece probably cost more than my entire wardrobe. "How was your first day back?"

"Boring." I blushed as his eyes rested on my face. Nathalie passed him the cigarette and he drew a deep breath before he released it. Smoke billowed around his head.

We stopped walking when we reached several flat slabs of rock arranged in a semicircle at the edge of the trees. A barbed wire fence ran through the foliage, separating the forest from the schoolyard. Faded red-painted signs warned trespassers not to enter.

Victoria sat down on one of the smooth stones and Cyril settled beside her as she searched through her bag. When a few stray raindrops plummeted from the overcast sky, Victoria shivered and Cyril handed his varsity jacket to her. A quarterback, although he had never really excelled at the sport. A lot of other students whispered that his wealthy parents had bought him a place on the team, although nobody would ever dare say that to him directly.

"Did you bring these here?" I gestured at the semicircle of rocks.

"What? Oh—no, it was already like this when we found it." Victoria pulled a joint out of her bookbag, white paper rolled tight. The pungent smell filled the air when she lit it. Some of the boys tossed a pebble back and forth, watching the girls from the corners of their feral eyes.

"Want some?" Victoria waved the joint in my face.

"Not really," I said. Weed always made me feel too hungry.

"Suit yourself." Smoke coiled from her mouth as she spoke. Cyril accepted the joint when Victoria offered it to him and took a long drag before he exhaled.

Posters decorated the trunks of the trees. The weather had already worn the face and name printed across the tattered paper away to almost nothing. White ribbons adorned the branches, as if a search party had come through here recently.

"Did somebody go missing again?" I studied the posters. The faded face printed on the stained paper looked almost familiar. I had heard all about the disappearances here throughout the years, but the last child to go missing had vanished when I was only seven. Barely old enough to remember it.

"You didn't hear about Emily?" Adam dropped a spent cigarette onto the ground and crushed it beneath the sole of his shoe.

"I didn't see her in school today." I pictured her carefree smile and easy laugh. We sat next to each other in every class, passing notes back and forth whenever the teachers turned their backs to write on the blackboard. "I thought maybe she stayed home sick."

"She disappeared a few months ago."

"Nobody told me." A cold stone settled in the pit of my stomach. Emily had written letters to me while I was still getting better. Short notes about the latest drama at school, interspersed with hopes that I would return home soon. I hadn't thought much of it when I stopped receiving her messages. Just that she had probably been distracted with boys and homework.

I never thought she would venture into the forest.

"Yeah, they searched for weeks but never found a trace of her," Nathalie said. She coughed when she took a drag from the joint making its way around the circle. This time, I accepted it when she handed it to me. The heat chapped my lips as I inhaled the thick smoke into my lungs.

"Do you really think there's something in there?" Matthew Velasquez asked after we all fell quiet. Tall, dressed in the basketball jacket that marked him as one of our school's star players. He'd transferred here a few years ago, so he hadn't grown up with the stories like the rest of us.

Go down the path. Don't look back.

Everyone knew the phrase, passed down through generations of children like a dare or an invitation. The bravest ones among us used it to try to find the center of Reachwood Forest, where rumors promised that something would grant a wish in exchange for a gift. Something hungry, that occasionally claimed the children desperate enough to stray from the path and make the pilgrimage into the wilderness. I'd never thought to question it. Enough kids had disappeared here over the years to seem like evidence there was at least some truth to the urban legend.

"Don't tell me you really believe that?" Victoria laughed. The abrupt noise echoed through the trees and I realized all the other sounds had died around us. No tentative rustle of small animals searching for better hiding places to shelter from the rain. No trill of birds calling for each other in the forest canopy. Complete silence—as though the whole forest were holding its breath.

Or listening to us.

"Then why do you think so many people go missing?" Matthew persisted. "Your families have lived here forever. You really don't believe any of the rumors are true?"

Victoria, Cyril and Adam all cast quick glances at each other. The heirs to each of Reachwood's three wealthiest families—their names would always be tied to the first disappearance. Some people still whispered that it was suspicious how they'd struck gold so soon after it happened.

Almost as if they had made a pact with whatever lived here.

"Of course not. You'd have to be stupid to believe that." Cyril scoffed. I had known all three of them since childhood, but they always deflected any questions about the forest. Shut down the topic whenever someone tried to approach it. Students flocked around them at school, drawn to their power and wealth. But they chose to surround themselves with only a few close friends. I had been accepted into their circle when Victoria smiled at me on the first day of kindergarten.

I always felt lucky to be one of them.

"My parents are going away this weekend, after the vigil." Victoria changed the subject. "You all should come over afterward."

"What vigil?" I asked and picked up something long and white, shining against the dirt. A curved bone, maybe a rib from a rabbit or some other kind of animal. Or maybe a small bone from the bodies of one of the missing children. I flinched and dropped it back down on the ground, wiping my hand clean on the knee of my jeans.

"We're holding one for Emily," Victoria said as I covered the bone with leaves again. My skin prickled suddenly, like an animal was watching us from the trees. But nothing moved when I looked over my shoulder.

"Ava? Are you still there?" Adam touched my wrist.

"I'm fine. Weed makes me a little bit paranoid, sometimes," I said, but I twitched again when the undergrowth rustled behind me. "What do you think happened to her?"

"I heard she ran away. Walked into the forest after school one day." Cyril shrugged. I imagined her panic as she stumbled through the wilderness, searching for a familiar landmark to lead her back home. Her body decaying out there alone somewhere.

"Why would she do that?"

"Maybe she believed the stories and wanted to wish for something," Adam suggested as he drew a folding knife from his jacket pocket. An expensive blade, handle engraved with his initials. He flipped it open and shut, again and again until the sound formed a staccato rhythm. When he slashed at a tall patch of grass, the green blades scattered across the dirt.

We all groaned when the bell rang, the shrill sound carrying through the schoolyard. I rose to my feet and dusted dirt and debris from my jeans. Nathalie ground out the glowing tip of her cigarette against one of the flat rocks circling the clearing. Adam closed the knife, hiding it away in the pockets of his jacket.

"Do you think you can come over after the vigil?" Victoria fell into step beside me as we followed the border of the forest back to school.

"I hope so. I'll have to check with my parents though," I said, flattered by her attention. Above us, the sun broke through a gap in the clouds. Light shone down on our faces and illuminated Victoria's hair.

I had missed her the most while I was away. Before I went to the treatment center, I'd call her on the nights I was so hungry I couldn't fall asleep and we'd talk until the sunrise dyed the sky outside. Sometimes we'd hold hands on the walk back home after class, but only when we were alone. At the last party I went to before my parents sent me away, someone dared her to kiss me and she did—quick enough to make me doubt if it really happened.

Now I wondered what it would be like to kiss her again, but pushed the thought from my mind.

CHAPTER 4

"Why didn't you tell me about Emily?" I asked my parents at dinner. We sat in a semicircle around the kitchen table and I swung my feet back and forth beneath my seat. The metal blade of my knife grated against the porcelain as I dissected the meal into small pieces.

"What are you talking about?" Mother set her fork down on the tabletop. Irritation stiffened my spine as she poured water into her empty glass. She knew exactly what I was talking about. Of course she did. But she wouldn't admit it.

"That she went missing," I said. The rich smell of food filled the room. Oven-baked chicken glazed with honey and rosemary—probably packed with calories. My stomach growled, pinching beneath my ribs as my parents exchanged a guilty glance over my head.

"Who told you?" My father cleared his throat. Robert Montgomery, the star of every sports team at Reachwood High School. After he graduated, he faded into obscurity—marrying Mother and taking up a job at the Reachwood mines while she stayed home to raise me. Shoulders now slumped from another long day of work transporting ore from the mines to the processing plant at the outskirts of the suburb, where it would be ground down, separated with cyanide and refined into the precious metal that gave the Albrights, Harts and Gallaghers their fortunes. He always returned home tired, late at night. Barely able to keep his eyes open long enough to eat dinner and shower before he passed out on the couch in front of the television. Every morning, before I woke up, he rose and left to repeat it all again.

"My friends mentioned it today at school."

"We just didn't want to upset you," Mother said, eyes drifting to the untouched food on my plate. "We thought it was best to wait until you were feeling better."

"She was my friend," I protested. "You should have told me."

"You couldn't have done anything about it." Her voice tightened.

"I could have helped look for her." I pictured Emily lost in the forest. Hot anger rose inside my body. "I could have done something."

"It doesn't matter now. She's not coming back," Mother said. Tears blurred my vision. My father shifted in his seat as I blotted my eyes against the soft cotton sleeve of my sweater. Uncomfortable, although he would never speak a word against her.

"Don't say that."

"Well, it's true," Mother snapped as she stood to clear the remnants of our meal from the table. "And I don't want you going in there to look for her—she's been missing so long that she's gone by now. I don't want to lose you, too."

Her voice trembled. I picked at my food, remembering how Mother had always warned me to avoid the forest. She made no secret of the fact that she hated living in this house, so close to the border of the trees. Whenever I played in the backyard as a child, she watched me closely—fearful I would slip through the fence and vanish into the wilderness.

Never to be seen again.

"My friends said they're holding a vigil for her this weekend. I want to go." I changed the subject. My hands shook with helpless rage as I herded my peas across my plate. "And I was kind of hoping I could stay over at Victoria's place after."

"Why?" She frowned at me. The corners of her eyes creased.

"I missed her while I was away." I raised my fork to my mouth. When my parents looked at each other again, I set it back down untouched on the table.

"I think you should. It'll be good for you to get out of the house every once in awhile," my father said. Mother frowned at him as hope grew inside me. "Who else is going to be there?"

"Nobody—just her and me." I lied. Desperate to spend some time with my friends. To stay up late with Victoria long after the rest of them went to bed, whispering stories and secrets to each other until the sun rose again. To pretend I had never left.

And to forget about what happened to Emily.

"You can go, but only if you actually eat tonight," Mother said.

"I'm not hungry." I glanced down at the meal on my plate. Sliced into tiny pieces, meat and vegetables almost unrecognizable. A familiar ritual to hide that I hadn't actually eaten any of it. "I ate a lot at school today."

"Then you don't need to go to Emily's vigil. Or see Victoria either."

"Fine, I'll do it." I rolled my eyes before I took a small bite. My stomach clenched as it stuck against the roof of my mouth.

"You need to eat more than that," Mother prompted after I chewed and swallowed. My eyes watered. A tear trickled down my cheek when I blinked. It dribbled salty and sweet into the corner of my mouth as I took another bite. And another, until my plate was almost empty and my stomach heaved again.

"Stop it—that's enough," my father interrupted.

"She still has some left," Mother protested as he picked up my plate and carried it over to the sink. I seized my chance to escape and pushed my chair away from the table, wooden legs scraping against the stone tiles.

I retreated down the hall, their voices murmuring from the kitchen. After I closed the bathroom door, I knelt in front of the toilet to vomit until my stomach felt clean and empty. I rinsed my mouth with water from the sink before I returned to my bedroom. The sour taste still stung against my throat as I sat down on the sunflower-patterned covers of my bed and slid open the window.

The dark covered the yard outside. I pushed my hand into the narrow gap between my mattress and the headboard. My fingers grasped through the tight space until they closed around the box of cigarettes I smoked sometimes to suppress my appetite.

Flicking the wheel of the lighter until a flame burst to life, I lit the cigarette and stuck my head out the window to blow smoke into the night. Leaves rustled. Something stirred in the undergrowth as my eyes adjusted to the dim light.

"Hello?" I called, hoping maybe it was Emily—emerging like some kind of miracle from the forest outside, untouched and still alive.

I already missed her smile.

Nothing moved in the trees again. I placed the cigarette between my lips and inhaled, blowing a final gust of smoke out into the quiet night before I closed my window. The ashen aftertaste clung to my tongue.

I flushed the burnt remnants of the cigarette down the toilet before I brushed my teeth, spitting white foam into the sink and washing it down the drain. The thick pile carpet muffled my footsteps when I padded back down the hallway. The house was quiet, like my parents had already separated to spend their limited hours of free time away from each other.

"Good night," my father said when he opened my bedroom door later. "Try not to think too much about Emily, alright?"

"Why?" The question came out much sharper than I had intended.

"I've known people who disappeared in there, too." He hesitated in the doorway. "Some of them were my friends. It will be easier if you just forget it ever happened."

"Whatever." I sank back against my pillows and turned off the lamp on my nightstand. If he smelled the smoke still lingering in my room, trapped in my hair and sheets, he didn't say anything as he shut the door tight.

I turned away from the window, afraid of what I might glimpse if I stared too long at the forest outside.

TODAY

CHAPTER 5

"Mom, can you come here? I thought I heard something." Marjorie's voice carries down the hall in the middle of the night. I stop packing up my parents' belongings in the kitchen, stowing a tarnished set of silverware away inside the cardboard box marked for donation before I walk down the hallway to push open the door to my old room. Marjorie sits rigid in my childhood bed, shoulders tense as she stares wide-eyed at the window. Cautious, I crack open the blinds to reveal the empty yard outside.

"There's nothing there." I exhale the words, convincing myself as much as her.

"I saw a shadow through the curtain. It looked like a person," she insists. My muscles tighten as I picture someone stalking around the perimeter of our house at night. Hidden by the shadows as they search for a way inside.

"I'll go check," I say and turn to leave, fake bravery not quite hiding the quiver in my voice. It's probably nothing. Just a fragment of a dream as Marjorie drifted to sleep.

"Wait," Marjorie whispers.

"What?" I stop in the doorway.

"What if it's Dad—what if he's come here to hurt you again?" Her voice quavers. I walk back across the room to wrap her up in my arms. Her shoulders shake as she burrows her face into the crook of my neck.

"It's okay, we're going to be okay here," I repeat until Marjorie takes an unsteady breath and slips out of my embrace. But she digs her fingers deep into the sunflower-patterned sheets covering her bed when I stand up again, like maybe she doesn't really believe me. The same way she never believed my other lies. All the times I told her I was fine.

Marjorie has already filled the room with her belongings—posters of her favorite rappers, boy bands and animals plaster the lavender walls. Tubes of makeup scatter the surface of the desk in the corner.

Her closet door lies open to reveal the outfit she has chosen for her first day of school tomorrow. The same one she wore on her first day of eighth grade last year. A reminder I can no longer afford to buy her the designer clothes she loved to flaunt to her friends back at home. I always took pride in providing her with the very best, maybe to offset how young I was in comparison to the mothers of the other students in her class. But now I can't give her anything. Shame settles like a heavy weight upon me.

"How do you know, though?" she asks when I lean down to kiss her forehead.

"Your dad is scared of the forest. Always has been," I say and pull the covers back up to her chin as she settles into her pillows. "He thought he saw something there once, when we visited my parents. It scared him so badly he never came back here again."

"Really? What did he see?" Her eyes search mine for any hint of a lie.

"He never said." I remember how he'd stormed out of the house to calm down one night when Marjorie wouldn't stop crying. Irritable and impatient in the months after her birth, as if he hated all of the attention I paid to her. I chased him outside, desperate to apologize. But he ignored me and walked into the forest, only to return ashen-faced some time later. We made excuses to my parents in the morning and left before the sun rose above the horizon. "Of course, there's nothing out there—but we're lucky he thinks there is. Now go to sleep, alright? Good night."

"Night." Marjorie curls on her side as I close her bedroom door. The dim hallway stretches out in front of me, quiet except for the soft sound of the television playing in the living room. Nothing stirs in the master bedroom upstairs. Mother has probably already swallowed the pills she takes to knock herself unconscious every night.

When I push the back door open, I pause to brace myself before I step out onto the porch. My eyes dart around the deserted yard before they focus on the forest. The grass rustles, but no crickets sing hidden in the foliage. An old path waits just past the fence, covered in shadows. Half-overgrown, it leads deeper into the wilderness. I stare down it for a minute, straining to see anything in the darkness. Nothing stirs at all. I picture small wild animals standing still as they wait for a predator to move on through the undergrowth.

"Hello?" My shoulders stiffen as I wait for an answer. Half-expecting that my ex-husband will step out from the shadows, although it's over an hour's drive from Portland to reach this remote suburb nestled at the base of the mountains. A long journey through unlit roads that curve through Reachwood Forest before the neighborhood emerges.

Hopefully its presence will be enough to deter him from pursuing us here.

When no response—from my ex-husband or anything else—floats through the dark, I sigh and circle around through the garden. My car sits parked in the driveway. The headlights flash when I unlock it to bring our last few belongings inside the house.

Carrying the suitcases up the stairs, I stop to check the mailbox out of habit. A letter waits inside, sealed with a familiar golden crest. My name is written in delicate script across its paper surface. I freeze, eyes darting across the houses lining the street. It's been less than a week.

Who could have told them I'd returned home?

My wrist aches when I pick up the envelope. Sweat spreads across my palms. My hand slips against smooth metal as I twist the doorknob until the door finally swings open. I tread quietly down the hallway, passing my father sprawled across the couch in the living room. Awake late, retired for several years now. The muted light from the television plays across his worn face.

I set the suitcase down in my bedroom before I retrieve my prescription container and return to the kitchen, still clutching the envelope tight in my white-knuckled fist. After pouring a glass of water, I wash down a painkiller and wait for the pill to dull my senses as I turn the envelope over. The cursive script spelling out my name is unmistakably Victoria's handwriting. Even when we were children, she always had an uncanny way of knowing everything that happened in Reachwood.

"What's that?" my father asks from behind me. I flinch, spinning around quick.

"Nothing. Just a letter." I set the envelope down.

"From who? I thought you hadn't told anyone you were back home yet." Apprehension lowers his voice, as if he's remembering all of the anonymous calls and messages I received after Adam's body was found in the forest. He had defended me from the half-baked accusations and groundless suspicions until I couldn't take it anymore. Packed my bags and fled to Portland.

"I haven't read it." I pry at the edges of the gold crest stamped on the paper. Sealing whatever message might be waiting inside. My mouth grows dry.

"Did your mother talk to you about the Reachwood Festival?" he asks as he opens the fridge and rummages around inside for another can of beer.

"Yeah." I swallow.

"Are you going?" The can hisses when he pops the tab open. Froth spills over the metal rim and drips onto the spotless granite counter. He picks up the dishcloth hanging by the sink and wipes away the mess until the stone shines clean again. Spotless. Just how Mother wants it.

"I guess so." I remember the lanterns that hang on the trees each year, displayed as a part of the celebration. Pretty enough to look like a scene straight out of a dream or a movie. "Looks like everybody knows I'm here already. They won't leave me alone until they see me again."

"Don't you want to see them?" he asks, and I picture Victoria's face. Preserved in time, still seventeen years old in my mind. Beautiful and wild.

Her family closed in around her after Adam's murder. Forbade her to leave the house during the investigation, as if they were afraid she would be the next to disappear into the forest. I never got the chance to say goodbye before I left.

"I don't know." Uncertainty tinges my words as I pick up the envelope again, the crisp paper rough against my fingertips.

"Maybe you should give them a chance," he says before he leaves the kitchen, heading back toward the living room and the television.

I pack more of my family's old belongings away inside cardboard boxes while I wait for the painkiller to take effect. Not brave enough to read the contents of the letter without it. The envelope rests on the countertop as I organize a dented set of pots and pans inside the donation bin. The same ones my father taught me how to cook with, praising each creation no matter how burnt it was. I throw several sets of stained napkins into the garbage, along with other things my parents won't need to bring with them when they move to a new home in the city.

The medication finally hits me, softening the hard edges of the world around me. I carry the envelope into the guest room and sit down on my bed. Breaking the seal, I unfold the thick paper—decorated with more elegant handwriting. An invitation to the Reachwood Festival. My body grows cold when I read the note at the bottom of the page, penned in Victoria's neat script.

Welcome home, Ava.

CHAPTER 6

"Ava? Are you ready?" Mother knocks on the door.

"Almost." I model a floral-brocaded black dress in front of the mirror.

"Hurry up. We don't want the festival to start without us," she says and opens the door of the guest room to scrutinize my outfit. Clothed in black, a wide-brimmed hat perched atop her head. Body tense with nervous energy. She has always hated venturing into the forest, although she perseveres with the tradition every year. Another opportunity to present the perfect image of our family to the neighbors.

"I'll be ready in a minute." I swipe lipstick across my mouth, staining it soft pink.

"You should wear a jacket with that dress," she suggests, glancing pointedly at the scabbed incision on my wrist and the faint bruises still yellowing on my shoulders.

"I know." I roll my eyes. She always shied away from talking about my ex-husband. Never once attempted an intervention during the long years I spent with him. Probably just happy that at least we married before I had Marjorie, partially erasing the shame of my unexpected pregnancy. She had always been content to ignore the worst parts of my relationship, or pretend that it didn't happen.

Like some kind of stain on her own reputation.

After she closes the door again, I spin in a slow circle in front of the mirror. Elaborate fabric flares around my knees. Dressed in my best—if I have to meet Victoria and the rest of my wildly successful friends tonight, I want them all to be impressed.

"Marjorie, we're leaving," I call when I step into the hall.

"I'm not ready." Her faint voice travels through her closed bedroom door. I push it open and blink at the piles of clothes scattered across the carpet, stamped with popular brand-name logos. Marjorie stands in front of the long mirror propped up in the corner. Her forehead puckers as she studies her reflection.

"Hurry up." Mother appears behind me and I jump. "We're going to be late already."

"I don't have anything to wear." Marjorie brushes bubblegum pink lip gloss across her mouth. "These are all old—they were cool like a year ago."

"If you don't pick something soon, we're going to leave without you," Mother says. Marjorie sorts through the t-shirts still left hanging in her closet, searching for a new outfit as I wonder how her first day at school went. If she made any friends, or if she's upset because none of her classmates gravitated toward her the same way they had back at home. Drawn by her bright smile and flashy clothes.

"So what? I don't care." She sulks.

"Well, you should." Mother's tone hardens, as if she's preparing to scold Marjorie the same way she scolded me when I was a teenager. My back stiffens but Marjorie ignores her, completely unintimidated by the sharpness in her words. Much braver than I had been at her age.

"What's going on?" My father walks down the hallway toward us, drawn to the sound of our raised voices. He leans against the wall and pushes his glasses up the bridge of his nose. Dressed in black like the rest of us. The clothes look new, like he wanted to wear something nice in case he ran into some of his old friends tonight.

"She's taking too long," Mother says as his gaze travels between the three of us.

"Come wait with me in the car." He touches her hand. "We still have plenty of time. I'm sure Marjorie will find something soon, right?"

"Yeah, probably." Marjorie shrugs as Mother turns on her heel and disappears down the hallway after him, patent leather shoes tapping against the hardwood floorboards.

"She's right, you know," I say. Marjorie examines an oversized sweater in front of the mirror, turning to inspect her appearance from every angle. "We need to leave now or we're going to be late."

"Whatever." Marjorie drops the sweater onto the fast-rising pile of unwanted clothing at her feet and rummages through her dresser drawers for another pair of jeans.

"How did your first day at school go today, anyway?"

"It was okay," she says and picks up her phone from her desk to check her missed texts.

"Really?" I lean against the doorframe. "You don't sound very happy about something."

"Actually, it was pretty boring." Marjorie pulls a hoodie over her head, voice muffled for a moment underneath the thick fabric.

"Did you meet anyone interesting?"

"Not really." Her jaw twitches when she grinds her teeth together. The same way my ex-husband used to before another outburst, like a premonition of something vicious. "There's one boy I like. He seems nice."

"I know it's nothing like your old school, but I hope you at least try to behave."

Marjorie plants her fists on her hips. "What does that mean?"

"No picking fights with anybody."

"That other girl hit me first," Marjorie protests. On her last day of eighth grade, she returned home wearing blood-spattered clothes that wouldn't rinse clean no matter how many times I ran them through the laundry. I paid out most of my remaining inheritance in the settlement.

The other family's daughter would never be the same again.

"I mean it," I insist.

"I won't," Marjorie says and shoves her phone in her bag. "I just miss my friends back home."

"This is home now." My voice is harsher than I had intended. I smile to soften the words, saying, "At least for a little while, okay?"

Marjorie blinks, tears welling at the corners of her eyes. "Sure. Sorry, I—"

"You're going to do great at this school, too. Everyone here will love you," I say. She pushes past me without another word.

A dog barks again and again somewhere as my father backs the car out of the driveway. Marjorie scowls at the high-pitched sound, drumming her feet against the hard plastic floor mat as she asks, "Why are we doing this, anyway?"

"It's a community tradition," I explain. We follow the steady stream of vehicles down the street. The headlights cut through the dark night and shadows gather close at the edges of the road. "Lots of people get lost in the forest. This is how we remember them."

"The forest behind our house? Why do so many people get lost?" Marjorie sprawls in her seat. My father merges onto the main road, joining the procession of vehicles journeying toward the festival inside Reachwood Forest.

"Sometimes when you leave the path, it's hard to find your way back."

"How many people have disappeared there?" Marjorie checks a text message on her phone. The soft glow of the screen highlights her face—nose, mouth and cheekbones.

"I have no idea," I say and roll up my window.

Missing posters decorate the lamp posts as we drive down the street. A reminder that some things haven't changed since I went away—the posters look the same as the ones that blanketed Reachwood when Emily went missing. And again, after Adam disappeared later in the same year. Now the paper is printed with the face and name of the latest girl who vanished in the forest, too far away to read. Her photograph smiles at the seething traffic.

Or maybe she's not smiling. Maybe she's sneering.

We claim a parking spot at the border of the trees. My father flicks off the headlights before he pulls the keys from the ignition, cutting off the rumble of the engine. I open the door and step outside, inhaling the fresh night air.

My pulse quickens when we draw closer to the forest. Anxious at the thought of meeting my friends again as we walk toward the trailhead. We follow the lights floating through the dark and the trees close around us.

More posters adorn their trunks, plastered with the face and name of the girl who disappeared here a few short days ago. Kristen Zhang, fourteen years old. The posters list the date she disappeared along with her height, weight and the clothes she was wearing before she went missing. Gone long enough to be dead by now, body hidden somewhere in the undergrowth. A question is printed in bold letters underneath her photo.

HAVE YOU SEEN ME?

CHAPTER 7

Go down the path. Don't look back.

The phrase familiar to all the children of Reachwood repeats in my mind. Goosebumps break across my skin as we walk deeper into the forest, pushing through groups of parents and their children—screaming toddlers and sullen teenagers.

Their curious eyes follow me as we walk toward the table laden with lanterns at the edge of the path. The crowd parts to let us through, hiding their whispers behind their hands. I don't meet their prying stares, ignoring the voices that drift behind us. I should have expected this. Known my appearance would spur a storm of questions about Adam again.

Nobody would ever forget what happened to him.

"What's this?" Marjorie asks when I hand her a lantern. A small, solar-powered beacon, white light beaming through the dark night.

"It's for the festival," I say and pick up another lantern, grasping its handle tight. "We leave them here every year. It's like a way to pay our respects to the people who have disappeared."

"That's weird." Marjorie wrinkles her nose. Her gaze drifts across the lanterns hanging in the trees, leading the way into the forest. "It looks like a fairy tale or something."

"Yeah, I guess it kind of does." I shrug. Our shoes crackle against the gravel as I search for the faces of my old friends. Caught somewhere between anticipation and dread.

"Ava?" A familiar voice calls and I flinch before I can stop myself. When I turn around, Nathalie waves at me uncertainly. I recognize her face, although I haven't spoken to her since our high school graduation. She is still beautiful—hair braided, dark skin radiant.

"Hi, Nathalie." I wave back.

"I had no idea you were in town," she says and falls into step beside me. The child clinging to her side stares at me with round eyes.

"We only got here a few days ago." The incision on the inside of my wrist itches, hot and persistent. I resist the urge to pick at it.

"It's great to see you again." Nathalie wraps me in a warm embrace.

"Yeah, you too." I say, voice muffled against her shoulder.

"I love your dress. Have you got settled in yet?" She releases me and beams. Her face glows as bright as the lanterns surrounding us. "You should come around and visit."

"Not really." I kick a pebble. It skitters into the dense foliage as young children run in front of us on the path, shrieking with laughter. More lanterns dangle in the branches of the trees, lighting the way as we push deeper into the forest. "We're still unpacking everything."

"Mom?" Marjorie touches my shoulder. "I see someone from my class over there. Can I go hang out with him?"

"Okay," I say. Nathalie studies our faces.

"This is your daughter?" Nathalie asks. She smiles at Marjorie, but Marjorie doesn't smile back—eyes as wary as a wild animal.

"Yes. Marjorie." I picture Nathalie's mind grinding into overdrive, trying to calculate how young I had been when I had my child. Too young—not even nineteen when Marjorie was born on an overcast day in late February.

"She looks just like you," Nathalie says finally. "This is my son, Logan. He started preschool this year. I have a daughter, too—Sophie. She's in first grade."

"Hi, Logan." I smile at him. He stares up at my face, expression solemn. The remnants of a sugary snack stain his small basketball jacket. The edges of his mouth quiver like he might burst into tears at any given minute.

"Have you kept in touch with anyone?" Nathalie asks. Marjorie leaves my side, disappearing into the night.

"Not really. I've been too busy, I guess." I leave the rest unsaid. How our clique collapsed beneath a swirl of rumors after Adam's murder. Scattered apart after his funeral, unable to find something to hold us all together.

"I should have tried to reach out more. It was just hard after—"

"It's not your fault," I interrupt her apology and search for another subject. Anything to steer the conversation away from Adam. "Is Matthew here tonight, too?"

"Somewhere." Nathalie says and turns to scan the crowd for her husband. "You should go up and say hello to Victoria. I know she's missed you."

"How's she been?" I ask, giving in to my curiosity. The breeze blows my dress around my knees. Half-overgrown signs rise from the foliage around us, urging travelers not to stray from the path. Rusted strands of barbed wire snake through the trees. A weak attempt to discourage trespassers from journeying into the depths of Reachwood.

"She's been doing great. She's a goldsmith now—pretty famous in the art world," Nathalie says. I blink at the sharp edge of jealousy in her voice. "She has a son and a daughter. Twins. They're leading the procession tonight."

"I didn't know that." I try to picture Victoria's children. If they share her hair or eyes, the same way Marjorie shares mine. Or maybe they inherited all of Cyril's features instead.

"They were friends with Kristen, actually," Nathalie says as my gaze falls on a poster tacked to the rough trunk of a tree. "They were devastated when she went missing."

The procession stretches out in front of us. A long line of people dressed in the traditional black always worn at the festival. Teenagers cluster in large groups, heads pressed close together as they whisper their latest secrets.

Neighbors make small talk and zip their jackets against the wind. I catch a glimpse of Mother, deep in conversation with some other members of the Reachwood Community Association. My father walks a few steps behind her, laughing and joking with his friends.

Logan trips and falls on the path ahead of us. He cries, voice high and whining. Tears flow down his cheeks.

"Sorry, I'll talk to you more later." Nathalie hurries away. She scoops him into her arms and he rubs his snot-streaked face against her designer jacket. I hide a smile.

But my smile drops straight off my face as I catch a glimpse of Marjorie walking several feet in front of me, deep in conversation with a boy her age. His face reminds me of someone else—same fair hair, pale eyes and strong jawline.

Adam.

He leans in close to whisper something to Marjorie and she smiles up at him, practically basking in his attention. She says something back and he laughs. His teeth flash white in the light from their lanterns and for a moment it feels like Adam has stepped out of time.

Like he never died.

CHAPTER 8

Marjorie disappears into the crowd and I hurry after her, searching for the boy with Adam's face as I push through groups of people. Protests ripple in my wake. Anxiety clenches like a fist beneath my ribs by the time I reach the head of the procession.

No sign of them.

The three most powerful families in Reachwood lead the way into the forest, faces lit by the flickering lanterns held in their hands. Golden jewelry circles their necks and glitters on their fingers like a reminder of the fortune they struck here long ago. The Albrights, Harts and Gallaghers. Their children lead each festival—an unspoken acknowledgement of their connection to the forest and the wealth it blessed them with.

My eyes drift to the Albright family despite myself. I haven't seen them since Adam's funeral just over fifteen years ago, dressed in mourning clothes as they buried their oldest son in the earth. His parents have changed. Wrinkles crease their skin and their backs hunch over as though they've aged several decades while I've been away.

Their only surviving son walks beside them. Ambrose—younger than Adam by only a year, with the same handsome features. Maybe Adam would look just like him now, if he'd had the chance to grow older.

Ambrose turns as if he can sense my stare and our eyes meet. The curious expression on his face darkens. He opens his mouth as though he's going to say something and I look away before he can call out to me.

A thrill sparks through my body when my gaze settles on Victoria. She walks with the rest of the Gallagher family close to the head of the procession. I stare at her wide-eyed, as though I've just seen a ghost. Beautiful and dressed in expensive clothes, the rising breeze blowing her long auburn hair around her head.

Victoria smiles when she catches sight of me. She says something to her family before she leaves their side, walking toward me through the night. We fall into step as dread and excitement wrestle inside my body. For a moment, I forget all about the Albright family and the boy with Marjorie as we stride together into the darkness, following the lights through the forest.

"You managed to make it—I wasn't sure if you got my invitation," Victoria says. My heart startles at hearing her voice again. Stars emerge in quick glimpses beyond the leafy canopy, shining like distant beacons. The moon climbs toward the center of the sky, illuminating the long parade of people winding through the trees.

"You surprised me." The gravel grinds beneath the soles of my shoes as we walk down the path. "I didn't realize anybody knew I was here. Who told you I'd come back home?"

"I heard rumors," Victoria says as the surgical incision on my wrist itches again. My fingers twitch. I curl them into fists before I can scratch at the still-healing skin.

"So, how have you been?" Victoria asks.

"I've been okay," I say, hoping she won't push any further.

"I'm glad to hear that—I've been doing well, too." Her voice is still as self-assured as when we were teenagers. For a breathless moment, it feels like no time has passed between us.

She walks close enough that our shoulders almost brush together. I struggle against the urge to reach out and touch her wrist, to make sure she is real and not some kind of dream or memory. A smile curves the corners of her mouth, as if she guesses what I'm thinking about.

I never realized how much I'd missed her until now.

"That's great," I say and wonder if she is also lying. The years since I left here have been anything but wonderful, between dropping out of college to become a too-young mother and placating the ever-shorter temper of my ex-husband.

We move toward the front of the procession, where two figures lead the parade down the path, bodies small against the darkness. Still children, dressed in black with leaves and white flowers woven through their hair. Faces so alike they look like reflections in a mirror. They both hold lanterns in their hands, casting light onto the path ahead. The only two lanterns to be lit by actual candles, the flames flicker in the night as I ask, "Are they your children?"

"Yes—Virgil and Catherine." Victoria smiles at them.

"How old are they?"

"Fourteen," she says, and I blink at the thought of Victoria Gallagher knocked up before her nineteenth birthday. Her parents must not have been happy with the stain the teenage pregnancy brought to their family name.

"I have a daughter the same age. Her name is Marjorie." I search for Marjorie's face in the crowd but she has still disappeared somewhere. So has the boy with Adam's smile.

"Maybe they'll have some classes together."

"That would be nice," I say, not quite lying as we follow the parade of lanterns through the trees. Silence falls between us, filled with unspoken questions. Not for the first time, I wonder what the years have been like for her after Adam died. If she had been isolated by the rumors about what happened to him, driven to live alone with her family at the crest of the hill. Or maybe the whispers dissolved in the face of her parents' wealth and influence.

Faded away into nothing.

"You should come over to our place after the festival." Victoria touches the back of my hand and heat rushes through my body. "I invited most of the neighborhood over for a celebration."

"Maybe," I say, twisting a bracelet around my wrist. The same one Marjorie saved up her allowance to buy me for my last birthday. I hate the thought of being apart from her, even only for a few hours. But raw hunger chews at my stomach. "I drove here with my family."

"I'm sure everyone else would love to catch up with you, too."

"Why did you really invite me out here tonight?" I ask. There must be a reason. Some unseen motive for sending me that invitation.

"I missed you," Victoria says instead, like a confession.

"I missed you, too." The words fall from my tongue before I can stop them.

"Get your family to drop you off at my place. I'll drive you home later," Victoria offers. I trace the old scar across the center of my palm. Healed skin rough against my fingertips.

I never could say no to her. Never just turn and walk away.

"Okay." I give in, and the same smile that occasionally surfaces in my dreams illuminates her face again. When we reach the center of the forest, Victoria's children blow out their lanterns and plunge the path ahead back into darkness.

Before we leave, we hang our lanterns in the trees.

CHAPTER 9

The neighborhood changes after we drive through the tree-filled ravine that divides the newer suburbs from the founding town. Identical houses replaced by spacious estates, secured behind high iron gates that remind me of ornate cages. Each mansion a marvel of architecture, built over a century ago from the fortune discovered in the Reachwood mines. Their gabled windows peer sightlessly into the night. I lean back in my seat as the manors pass by outside and wonder what happens within their walls.

Behind their perfect façades.

The house where Victoria lives with Cyril rests on the crest of the hill, as vast as a castle. Probably the first new building constructed in the historic neighborhood in several decades, it looms large over the car when my father steers through the open gate and parks in the driveway. Turrets stretch from its roof to impale the harvest moon as it travels through the star-spattered sky. Light glows through the stained glass windows decorating the second floor. A brilliant kaleidoscope of color.

"Do you know when you'll be home?" my father asks as the engine idles. The same question he used to ask every time he dropped me off at one of Victoria's parties when we were still teenagers. He used to stay up late, waiting for me to slip in through the front door. Anxious that I might vanish without a trace—the next child to be drawn into the forest.

"Sometime later tonight." I crack open the door of the car.

"Don't do anything stupid." Mother doesn't turn around to watch me leave. She uncaps a tube of lipstick and brushes the coral color across her mouth. Marjorie kicks the back of her seat.

"I'll see you later." I pull Marjorie into a hug before I step outside into the night. The car drives away as I hurry up the front steps. I glance over my shoulder to catch a last glimpse of Marjorie, forehead pressed against the window before the vehicle disappears around the corner. A pang shoots through my chest as I ring the bell.

"It's not locked—come in," several unfamiliar voices call from inside the house. I push the door open and follow the sound of drunken chatter and raucous laughter through the hallways. People gather together in the living room, sipping drinks as they raise their voices above each other. They all pause when I walk through the doorway. I flinch underneath the sudden weight of the many gazes fixed on my face.

Not this again.

"Ava! I'm glad you could make it." Victoria waves at me from across the room. An old scar crosses the palm of her hand like a promise.

"Hey." I wave back and push through the crowd until I reach her side. The half-forgotten faces of old acquaintances follow my progress across the room, voices dropping to whispers as I pass by, like nothing has changed since high school. Since Adam's death and the subsequent investigation, pitting everybody against one another as rumors swirled through Reachwood.

Now their stares never waver and sweat gathers on the back of my neck. I smooth the brocaded fabric of my dress. Maybe I should have worn something less eye-catching.

"Grab a drink and meet us outside," Victoria says and points to a table laden with food and beverages before she disappears out the door. I squeeze through tight groups of people. Snippets of conversation drift past me as I pour a glass of wine from one of the many bottles lined up like offerings on the marble countertop.

I take a sip and the sweet taste fills my mouth as the crowd seethes around me. I recognize many of the people here from high school, even if I can't remember their names. Everyone looks the same, unchanged by time.

Except for their eyes—their eyes look tired.

○━━╋━○

The night breeze blows around me when I venture outside into the quiet, eager to escape the loud celebration inside the house. A garden cascades in careful terraces down to a brick courtyard. A bonfire flickers there and I follow the stone-cobbled path down toward it, inhaling the smoke-sweetened air.

My closest friends from high school huddle together around the fire. Nathalie pours another glass of wine and whispers something to Victoria, cupping her words behind her hands. They both glance at me. Cyril and Matthew lounge on stone benches as a mixture of shadows and light play across their faces. I clutch my wineglass tight and join the circle.

"Hey, Ava." Matthew waves at me and smiles. Still tall and thin, with the long limbs that catapulted him into international basketball stardom. I'd caught glimpses of his games on television sometimes. Startled at the sight of his face as he scored or dribbled the ball back and forth across the court. Like a ghost had stepped from the distant past.

"Hey—nice to see you again." My voice sounds small.

"I didn't think you'd ever come back here," Cyril says. Still handsome, with thick dark hair and the same green eyes all the girls liked in high school. Victoria sits beside him, far away enough that their skin never touches. Golden wedding bands glimmer on their fingers. For a brief moment, I wonder what their life is like together. If they really love each other, or if it was a marriage of convenience when Victoria got pregnant. She never liked him in high school—never even looked at him twice.

But something must have changed her mind.

"I didn't think so either, actually." I force a smile as I remember the warm summer day I left this place, running away barely over a week after Adam's funeral. Desperate to escape the shadow his death had cast across Reachwood.

Hesitant, I take a seat on one of the stone benches lined up by the fire pit. Smoke blows into my face as the wind changes. I cough and sip more wine to wash away the ashen taste.

"Why did you?" Matthew asks. Victoria frowns at him from across the fire and he adds, "I mean, we're all happy to see you. Just curious, I guess."

"I won't be here for long. My parents just need someone to help them move out of the house." I repeat the same lie I've rehearsed ever since I arrived back in the suburb. Not eager to explain the divorce, or how I'd been forced to hide here by my ex-husband's ferocious temper.

"What happened while I was away?" I change the subject.

"Nothing, really." Matthew swigs from the beer bottle sweating in his hand. "I guess you've already heard another kid's gone missing."

"Yeah, I saw the posters," I say, and all of their eyes rest on my face again. My hand shakes when I pour more wine. Liquid splashes over the crystal rim of my glass. It stains the stone table with splotches of red dark enough to remind me of blood. "Is she the first one to vanish since . . . Adam?"

"Yeah, she is," Nathalie says as the autumn breeze rises.

"What do you think happened to her?" My teeth chatter. Bone clicks against bone.

"The same thing that happens to everyone who leaves the path," Cyril says. The lanterns glow in the forest below. "She got lost and couldn't find her way back."

We all fall quiet. I cast quick glances at their faces, still surprised to find myself here among my high school friends. Almost as if the night we left Adam in the forest never happened. Maybe they feel the same way.

They probably never expected to see me again.

"Did you hear Adam's family wants to build some kind of monument for him?" Nathalie asks, breaking the uncomfortable silence. "In the forest this year."

"No, I didn't." I clasp the stem of my wineglass tight. "Are they here tonight?"

"They weren't invited." Victoria shakes her head. "We kind of stopped talking after what happened to him. They still have their shares in the company, of course. But we don't see each other very much anymore."

"I saw my daughter talking to someone at the festival earlier," I say. A chill runs through my body and I move closer to the fire. "A boy her age. He looked like Adam."

"That's Aidan." Victoria pours more wine. "Ambrose's son."

"How's he doing, anyway?" I ask. Ambrose used to show up at every party in high school and sold every kind of drug he could lay his hands on. Rumors circulated through the school that he'd give some girls the pills and weed for free if they were pretty enough.

If they were willing to fuck him.

"He went kind of wild after Adam died. Got into a lot of fights," Victoria says as she waves smoke away from her face. "You should stay away from him."

"Why?" I ask, although I remember the way Ambrose's expression darkened when he caught sight of me tonight.

"He won't let go of what happened to Adam." Victoria's mouth tightens. "He wouldn't leave us alone for years. I think the monument was probably his idea—a way to renew interest in the case again."

"Well, they can't build anything until we vote to approve it." Cyril tosses another log into the fire and it flares for a split second. Flames rise against the settling night.

"Are you going to let them?" I ask. The Albrights, Harts and Gallaghers share ownership of Reachwood Forest. For as long as I can remember, they have protected it—blocking any logging or construction projects. Now that the Gallagher and Hart family empires have been united through Cyril and Victoria's marriage, it would be easy for them to overrule any proposal from the Albright family. Exert complete control over the forest and the mining company.

"No." Victoria folds her arms across her chest like she feels cold. The bonfire quivers in another gust of wind. Smoke blows thick enough to cover our faces as she says, "They shouldn't put up a monument when people won't even leave his grave alone."

"What are you talking about?" I cough. My eyes water.

"Someone keeps vandalizing it. His family actually had to move his body to a tomb," Victoria explains. I sip wine until the buzz from the alcohol numbs my face and hands. "It's like somebody won't let us forget about him."

Between the frantic news coverage and the ensuing neighborhood panic, it seems unlikely anyone ever will forget what happened to Adam. I've spent years trying to forget, but I still remember.

"Did you ever hear about what they found during the autopsy?" Nathalie asks. She taps her manicured nails against the stone bench as the fire spits sparks into the dark.

"No. What was it?" The reluctant question slides from my tongue.

Nathalie's mouth curves into something that almost looks like a smile. Her voice drops to a whisper as she says, "His heart was missing."

CHAPTER 10

"What?" I almost choke on the words as I remember the way Adam's clouded eyes stared at the sky. The open hole in his chest, coated with blood. I never looked close enough to notice his heart was missing.

Stolen away by something.

"No one told you?" Nathalie asks and leans forward in her seat. The light from the bonfire accentuates the contours of her face.

"No." I drink down the last dregs of wine fast. "I didn't know."

"They never found it," Matthew says and sets his empty beer bottle down. I reach for the wine bottle and tilt it until the last few mouthfuls of liquid swirl into my glass.

"Let's stop talking about it." Victoria sighs like they have all speculated about this a million times. She glances at me and says, "Some things are best forgotten."

"I've always wondered—who told them Adam was in the grove?" Cyril asks. His gaze travels around the circle before it rests on me. I stare down at the ground, pushing away the memory of Adam's body lying in the forest.

"Some kids probably went in there on a dare and found him." Matthew cracks open another bottle of beer and I startle at the loud sound. Distant lightning flickers, followed by the slow rumble of thunder. Clouds gather close in the night sky that stretches out above our heads.

"That's not possible. Nobody else knows where to find it," Cyril argues. His eyes meet mine when I raise my glass to swallow more wine. Dark with suspicion.

"I don't know," I say and glance away. Not sure what I'm afraid of—I never said anything. Never told anyone what we found in the grove. "Maybe someone just didn't think his body should stay out there alone."

"Are you sure you really don't know?" His mouth narrows. "Because I noticed you left pretty quickly afterward."

"What's that supposed to mean?" I bristle at the unspoken accusation. Matthew and Nathalie cast a panicked look at each other as another brief glimpse of lightning ripples through the sky. Cyril leans forward in his seat and opens his mouth to say something else.

"I said, let's stop talking about it." Victoria interrupts our confrontation. "Adam deserved everything that happened to him."

"Fine." Cyril drops the subject. He stretches in his seat to sling a possessive arm around Victoria's shoulders but she slips out of his grasp, leaning forward to pick up the wine bottle from the table. Something like frustration flashes across his face before it vanishes again.

○─✦─○

I relax when the conversation turns back to more mundane topics like careers and children. The wine bottles empty as the moon rises in the sky.

The forested ravine runs deep through the neighborhood beneath us, three miles of wilderness separating the suburbs from the wealthy estates that climb up the side of the hill. My home lies down there, across the other side of the divide somewhere—indistinguishable from all the other four-bedroom houses in the neighborhood. The lanterns still glow from the boughs of the trees below, blowing back and forth in the rising storm. The rippling lights make the forest look almost alive.

"I should go—it's getting late and Marjorie is probably waiting for me to come back home." Guilt pulls at me when I think of how I left Marjorie alone, with only my parents for company. I stand and sway when the breeze buffets my body.

"I'll drive you back," Victoria says and sets her wineglass on the table beside an empty bottle. Its crystalline surface sparkles in the dim moonlight.

"Are you sure you should do that?" Cyril asks as Victoria rises to her feet.

"What?"

"Drive. You've had a lot to drink tonight." He slurs the words. Maybe he also drank too much while we talked around the fire.

"I'm fine." Her eyes narrow.

"You know what will happen if you get pulled over again," Cyril says, and a faint blush spreads across Victoria's face. Matthew and Nathalie dart another uneasy look at each other as Victoria glares at Cyril.

"We should leave, too." Matthew limps when he stands up. Gait stiff, a sharp contrast to the fluid way he used to move across the court. He leans on Nathalie's shoulder for support as they turn toward the house.

"You can take Ava with you," Cyril suggests. The breeze strengthens again, whirling strands of my hair around my head. The solar lanterns in the forest begin to wink out one by one as they lose their charge from the sun.

"I said I'm fine to drive. Ava's place is out of their way, anyway." Victoria's voice rises slightly, like she is preparing for a fight. She takes a step forward as Matthew and Nathalie retreat toward the house.

"No, you're not." Cyril grabs her forearm. The same way my ex-husband did when he broke my wrist. My body tenses.

"Let go of me." She twists free. His fingers leave a white imprint against her skin. He opens his mouth and then closes it again, as if he's trying to think of something else to say to convince her to stay. He never liked how much time we spent together. How we had secrets we only shared with each other.

"Ava should decide." Victoria's mouth tightens into a stubborn line. Lightning flashes across the sky overhead as they both turn and stare at me. Victoria's expression is hopeful.

I haven't been alone with her since I left fifteen years ago.

"I don't mind if you drive me back home," I say and smooth my dress as it whirls around my knees. Not ready to leave her just yet. To wake up in the guest room the next morning and wonder if this was only a dream.

A triumphant smile teases at the edges of Victoria's mouth before Cyril leans in and kisses her. Grips her shoulders hard, like a reminder she belongs to him now. It lasts long enough to make me blush and glance up at the storm above us.

"Come back right away, okay?" he says after she pulls away, words almost swallowed by the roar of thunder above our heads. The ground shudders beneath my feet. I lean against the table as sparks from the bonfire whirl in the breeze.

We return to the house as the first drops of rain fall from the sky. I say my goodbyes to Nathalie and Matthew before I follow Victoria into the garage and climb into a vehicle so clean and immaculate that it must be a new purchase.

The last light winks out in the forest below as we drive outside.

CHAPTER 11

"What did you think?" Victoria steers the car down the curve of the driveway. I buckle my seatbelt as she turns onto the street so quickly that the car drifts into the other lane before she corrects its course. The road twists down the hill toward the forested ravine. I settle into the passenger seat as the wine buzzes inside me, numbing my hands and feet.

"Of what?"

"Of everybody—what was it like to see them all again?" she asks. Her eyes never stray from the black asphalt that curls like a dark ribbon in front of us. Historic estates pass by outside. Turrets stretch high enough to pierce the sky.

"It was okay, I guess," I say and tap my nails against the armrest. "It's kind of strange to see how everyone has pretty much stayed exactly the same as I remember them."

"A lot has changed since you went away." Victoria brakes hard for a red light. My seatbelt cuts into my neck. Rain taps against the roof of the car as we wait for the light to turn green again. The road stretches out before us. Empty except for the wink of two distant headlights.

"It was still nice to catch up with everyone tonight." I fidget with my seatbelt. Snap the buckle open and shut again. "It sounds like we've all done well for ourselves."

"Not really—Nathalie's company is going to declare bankruptcy. And Matthew tore a tendon in his knee. He might never play again if surgery doesn't work," Victoria says. She presses down on the accelerator when the light changes, and the vehicle speeds fast through the intersection. "They had to sell their house. They're moving out soon."

"I'm sorry. I had no idea."

"It's kind of a secret, so don't tell anybody." She drums her fingers against the wheel as she drives the car through the rising storm. Silence stretches between us as I search for something else to talk about.

"Why did you really want to see me again?" I ask when we cross the ravine. There must be a reason why she was so eager to drive me home. To speak to me alone, away from the presence of our friends and the mistrustful eyes of her husband.

"I was curious, I guess. You moved away without saying anything," Victoria says. She never turns in her seat to look at me as the forest swells against the edges of the street. We pass underneath a street lamp and the light illuminates the delicate contours of her face.

She still looks the same—long auburn hair and eyes dark enough to swallow the light. Longing hits me quick enough to steal my breath, like nothing has really changed in the many years I spent away from this place. I still can't stay away from her.

Not even over a decade later.

The houses become new and identical when we emerge from the ravine. Picket fences stake each small parcel of property like territory. Victoria parks in front of my house. The rain drums hard against the roof of the car. It runs in thick rivulets down the windows and obscures the street outside, like we could be the only two people in the world left alive.

"Are you mad at me?" My voice is soft in the quiet. I should never have expected things to stay the same between us. Not after I fled as soon as the police cleared me to leave in the aftermath of Adam's death. Investigation stalled by a lack of evidence. I left her here alone to face the rumors and suspicions while I started a new life somewhere else.

"I just thought I'd never see you again."

"Did you really want to? After everything that happened?" I ask. My shuttered house waits in front of us. No light glows behind the curtains drawn across the windows.

"Of course I did. I told you—I missed you." Her voice shakes. I lean across my seat to wrap her in a tight embrace. When I pull away, we both hesitate.

Panic flutters inside my stomach.

"It's late. I should let you go back home." I crack open the car door. Victoria says nothing as I lean down to scoop my bag up from where it rests on the floor.

I climb out of the car, but pause in the open doorway. I have to ask. "When did you and Cyril get together?"

"Just after you left," she says. Maybe I only imagine a hint of resentment in her voice.

"Do you ever wish things had turned out differently?"

"Every day. Nothing was the same after you went away." Victoria never turns to look at me, as though she's afraid to show the emotions on her face. I should know what to say—it should be easy. I told Victoria everything when we were teenagers. But now we're alone again and I don't know how to apologize. To explain I couldn't have stayed.

I had been so afraid.

Mute, I close the door as thick ribbons of water drain into the gutters. I stand on the curb to watch her drive down the street. Retreat back to her beautiful house and the life she has made with her husband and children while I stayed far away.

A respectable life—I wonder what that must be like.

I fumble with the door, struggling to fit the key into the lock. It finally swings open and I stumble inside, almost toppling over as I kneel down to unlace my shoes on the mat. Fingers numb and clumsy.

Walking softly through the quiet house, I retrieve my pajamas from the guest room. In the bathroom across the hall, I brush my teeth and spit the foamy liquid into the sink before I swallow another pill from the medicine cabinet. An early dose, but close enough to the time I'm supposed to take it in the morning.

I exit the bathroom and pause. The empty hall yawns out in front of me. A thin ribbon of light glows beneath Marjorie's door. She must have stayed awake late, waiting for me to return home safe. I crack open the door to peek into her room. Marjorie lies sprawled across her bed, fast asleep. She breathes slow and steady as I pull the covers over her body. I turn out her light before I return to my own room and climb into bed.

My phone vibrates a few hours later. I sit up and blink, still a little bit dizzy from all of the wine I drank at the party. My head spins as I rummage through the books and papers on my nightstand. The phone buzzes again and again. My hand closes around it and I squint at the unknown number flashing across the too-bright screen.

"Hello?" I answer the call, voice still thick with sleep. No response. I press my phone against my ear but still hear nothing on the other end of the line.

Nothing but the slow and steady sound of someone breathing.

CHAPTER 12

wake to red horror in the morning. Blood from the surgical incision on my wrist stains the sheets. I must have picked at it sometime during the night, ripping the still-healing wound open while I slept. I raise my hand and turn it over to study my forearm. The edges of the scalpel-straight laceration on the inside of my wrist are red, like some kind of infection might already be burrowing inside my body.

Hurrying into the bathroom, I scrub my hands clean in the sink. Rust-red water swirls down the drain as I open the medicine cabinet, rummaging through it for a bottle of antiseptic. I pour the pungent liquid onto a soft cotton pad and shove it against the wound, grimacing as it stings against my exposed flesh.

After I wrap a bandage tight across my wrist to hide the fresh injury from sight, I shake a powder-white pill onto my palm and swallow, although I already took my morning dose when I got home a few hours ago. It plunges down my throat. The remaining painkillers sit at the bottom of the bottle and I frown at the small pile.

I thought I had more left.

"Ava? Are you awake?" Mother calls, voice muffled by the bathroom door. "Breakfast is on the table."

"I'll be there in a minute." I raise my voice and wipe my hands clean on the towel hanging from the rack. My fingers leave red smears across the white cotton.

I check my phone in the bedroom, scrolling through its record of recent calls. The unknown number sits at the top of the list. Sweat beads in the creases of my palms. Not a dream. Someone really did call me last night. I shudder at the memory of the steady breathing on the other end of the line.

Maybe my ex-husband violated his restraining order after he drank too much at one of the bars he frequents. He's done it before when I tried to leave. Contacted me constantly until I broke down and agreed to give him another chance.

Or it could have been Ambrose or someone else from the Albright family, furious at my return to Reachwood, although years have passed since Adam's murder. Determined to drive me out again, the same way the rumors about his death did when I was still a teenager.

Maybe I never should have returned here.

Reachwood Forest waits at the edges of our yard outside when I open the blinds. The leaves ripple in the autumn breeze, illuminated by the early sunlight. This is the only place my ex-husband was ever afraid of.

The only place that will keep us safe.

<hr />

"You slept late," Mother says. Her hair shines underneath the ceiling light. It falls in stiff waves around her face, like maybe she had applied a fresh coat of bleach last night. "I had to drop Marjorie off at school this morning."

"You should have woken me up. I forgot to set my alarm."

"I just hope you didn't make a fool of yourself last night." She slams a cup of coffee down in front of me. I jump at the sudden movement. Hot liquid spills over its ceramic brim and steams dark against the stone countertop.

"What's that supposed to mean?" I ask and take a sip. It burns my tongue.

"You know what you were like before." She sets down a plate laden with food. Bacon and eggs, toast and oatmeal. My throat tightens against the thick smell of grease.

"Don't worry about it. I didn't even drink that much."

"I hope not," Mother says. Her eyes study me as closely, as though she's searching for the traces of a hangover on my face.

"I don't understand why you're upset with me." I swallow more coffee and push the food around on my plate. The bitter brew puckers in my stomach. "You told me to visit everybody."

"I know." Her forehead crinkles when she frowns at me.

"So what, then?" I ask as I slice my bacon into careful pieces. My knife grates against the wildflower-patterned plate.

"I don't think you should spend so much time with Victoria. Not as much as you did before, anyway." Mother rinses the dishes. The pans clatter against each other in the sink. Outside the window, the forest looms at the border of our yard. Brambles stretch toward the trimmed hedges. Trees cast long shadows across the clean-cut lawn.

"Why not?" I nibble on a piece of toast. The crust scratches against the roof of my mouth.

"I guess you haven't been here long enough to hear the rumors," Mother says as she lines the pots and pans up on the drying rack. "She's still as wild as she was when she was a child."

"What does that even mean?" I ask, although I shouldn't be surprised Mother would seize the first opportunity to smear Victoria. She always blamed her for everything. Jealous of the vast wealth of her family, despite reveling in the popularity Victoria's friendship brought me. She always resented that we would never be as respected by the community. That my father rose early each morning to transport the ore that gave them their fortune while Victoria's parents sat in their mansion and basked in the riches it afforded them.

"Nothing—just that the two of you used to be so close. Sometimes I think it wasn't really healthy," she says. I stand to scrape the uneaten food on my plate into the garbage can my parents keep hidden beneath the sink. Cold water numbs my hands as I rinse my plate clean and place it in the dishwasher.

I head to the living room after breakfast to pack away more of my parents' belongings. Things they want to bring with them to the city—the illustrated collection of history books that my father used to read to me at bedtime each night. A battered set of romance novels that Mother never let me open, although I skimmed through the pages sometimes when she wasn't looking. Dust drifts up from their covers as I organize them inside cardboard boxes.

The song on the radio drifts in from the kitchen. I hum along until the music ends and the announcers start to speak again, somber voices providing an update on the search for Kristen. Still missing, lost out there in the wilderness somewhere. The forest has probably swallowed her body whole by now.

Just like all the other children.

"I'm going out today," I call, seizing my chance to escape. To avoid spending the day alone in the house, packing old memories into cardboard boxes with nobody but Mother for company. "I want to help the search party look for that girl in the forest."

"Have some lunch before you leave—you barely ate anything this morning." She almost sounds worried.

"I'm not hungry." I throw the words over my shoulder as I pass the kitchen.

"Do you need me to pick up Marjorie after school, too?"

"No, she texted me earlier," I say as I walk away down the hallway. "She's working on a project with Victoria's daughter. I'll pick her up after the search is over."

Mother doesn't say anything as I return to my bedroom. She doesn't need to. I can sense her disapproval. The door creaks when I close it tight behind me. My duvet lies crumpled at the foot of the bed. Clothes spread out all over the floor. I search for a clean outfit to wear—a loose sweater to hide how thin I've become this summer. A pair of jeans, wrinkled slightly.

I pull on the clothes and cross the hall into the bathroom. My hand wraps around the prescription bottle and I hesitate as the pills rattle around inside. I don't have another refill left—when I run out, I'm done. I don't really need it. Probably shouldn't take it with me.

But it will drive away the anxiety still prickling inside me.

I shove the clear orange container into my purse before I shrug into my jacket at the front door. Cars rush by on the street. The sun peaks at the center of the sky as I step outside and blink in the afternoon light.

CHAPTER 13

The search party gathers at the border of the forest. The busy chatter of volunteers and the crackle of police radios interrupts the silence as I walk toward the sign-in station. More volunteers comb through the area in disciplined rows, tying ribbons onto the branches of the trees to mark the places they have already been. The thin pieces of fabric shiver like memories, stark white against the leaves.

The same way they did fifteen years ago after Adam went missing.

I lean against a tree as a wave of dizziness hits me. The landscape whirls, a kaleidoscope of sharp-bristled thickets, stones and brambles. I blink hard. My eyes water. I squeeze them shut and when I open them again, the world snaps back into focus.

"Are you okay?" A police officer asks as I take an unsteady step forward.

"I'm fine." I force a stiff smile. More police officers surround the volunteer tables and mill around the search site. Maybe some of the same ones who helmed the investigation after Adam died. Several watch me closely as I move toward the sign-in station. I avoid their curious stares, wondering if they still recognize me years later.

After scribbling my name on the sign-in sheet, I cross the border of the forest. Volunteers spread out in a grid formation as they search through the undergrowth. Some of them still look hopeful. Others look like they already suspect they'll never see the missing girl again.

At least not alive and well.

I take a surprised step backward when my eyes settle on Ambrose. He knots another ribbon on the low-hanging branches of a nearby tree before he turns and his eyes rest on me. The last person I expected to see here—I thought he'd never want to return to this place again. Not after what happened to Adam.

"Ava?" Ambrose asks. A shadow crosses his face as he splits away from the search party to walk toward me. Victoria's warning repeats through my memory. *Stay away from him.* But it's too late to flee as he falls into step beside me.

"Hey," I say and quicken my pace. Maybe he'll leave me alone once I catch up with the rest of the volunteers grouped through the forest.

"I saw you at the festival last night." He matches my speed as we push through the undergrowth—struggling through tall grass, saplings and tangled weeds. I fight the urge to bolt away through the foliage as he says, "I tried to get your attention."

"I didn't notice," I lie, wondering again if he called me last night in another attempt to catch my attention and drive me out of Reachwood. The past years must have been difficult for him, living so close to the place where Adam died. Mother said he never moved out of the ancestral home where he was raised with his older brother. Everywhere he goes must hold memories from when Adam was still alive.

No wonder he can't leave the cold case alone.

"What are you doing here?" Ambrose asks as I weave through the trees. Eager to get away from him as the forest canopy spreads out above our heads. Leaves dense enough to block out the sun above us.

"I heard a girl went missing," I explain as I hurry after the rest of the search party. They comb through the forest ahead of us, searching for a sign—for anything Kristen might have left behind when she vanished from the path. "I wanted to do something."

"That's not what I meant." His voice flattens. "Why did you come back here again?"

"I'm helping my parents move. They're looking for a new place soon," I say. Nervous energy churns through my veins when I glance up at his face.

He still looks like the same boy I knew back in high school—the one who found excuses to talk to me between each class. Who used to show up at all the same parties and sell me weed, powders and pills. The same kind of painkillers I need now. Maybe he could use his connections to get me more, if the pain still lingers after I finish my prescription. But the warmth in his eyes has been replaced by a coldness I don't recognize.

"I haven't heard anything about you since you moved. You pretty much disappeared after Adam's funeral," he says like an accusation.

The memory of Adam's body emerges in my mind. Buried three days after they discovered him in the forest, face tranquil as he lay inside his casket. Everyone in Reachwood attended the service, cramming close together in the narrow pews. Ambrose sat with his parents in the first row, close to his brother's coffin. Eyes rimmed red as he struggled against his grief.

Maybe he blames me.

"Well, I didn't have any reason to stay here." My voice hardens as I remember the rumors that swirled around me and my friends after Adam's death. "Not after the investigation cleared me to leave."

"I guess. I just hope something like that hasn't happened again," Ambrose says. The expression on his face never indicates if he believes me or thinks I'm guilty as we pass more white ribbons twisted against the boughs of the trees.

"I should go." My stomach twists when the other volunteers disappear over a ridge ahead of us, leaving me alone with him. I hurry to catch up with them, but Ambrose says something behind me. Voice too low to make out the words.

"What?" I turn to face him again.

"You knew he was there. For three days, and you never said anything," Ambrose repeats and I freeze. We stare at each other for several seconds as I wonder how he knows. If he noticed the offering I left in the grove when the police showed him the photos of the crime scene.

Someone shouts. The sound interrupts our confrontation and we both flinch away from one another as the voice echoes through the trees. Crows shriek in the forest canopy, bursting into flight as police officers and volunteers rush toward the source of the noise. I follow them as dread grips my throat like cold fingers.

People circle around something, pointing and whispering. A woman hunches over like someone punched her in the stomach. Her face crumples. Tears drip from her nose and chin. A man turns away to cover his eyes as someone else starts to scream. I hurry toward the crowd and catch a glimpse of something crumpled on the ground.

Red fabric. Maybe a jacket.

Kristen's body lies curled beneath the fallen leaves. Only fourteen years old when she went missing. The same age as Marjorie—face so still and peaceful that, for a moment, it looks like she might only be sleeping.

CHAPTER 14

After they carry Kristen out of the forest, I drive to Victoria's house. I caught another glimpse of Kristen's body as I made my statement to the police. Draped beneath a white sheet. The same way they covered Adam's body when they discovered him in the grove years ago.

Lifeless and cold.

My hands shake against the wheel. I grit my teeth as the trees gather against the edges of the street. Kristen's face flickers through my memory again and again, despite my attempts to push it away. Sunlight flares against my windshield as I follow the road leading up to the estate Victoria shares with Cyril at the crest of the hill.

I brake in front of the closed gate, roll down my window and press the button to state my name into the intercom. The gate swings open a moment later and I drive through to park my car in the shadow of Victoria's elaborate house. Footsteps hurry down the corridor toward the front door as I walk up the stairs of the porch.

"Hey," Victoria says when she opens the door. Her smile is radiant enough to chase Kristen from my thoughts.

"Hi." My voice is soft and shy.

"Come inside. I think the kids are still working on their project upstairs." She steps aside to let me into the house. I cross the threshold and walk through the long hallway into the living room. Filled with expensive furniture, so clean it feels almost empty. As if there had been no celebration here yesterday.

The extravagant space reminds me of the home I left behind in the city, bought with some of the money I received from my inheritance—spacious rooms filled with beautiful things. Located in a wealthy and safe neighborhood, it had been the perfect place to raise Marjorie until my ex-husband's temper forced us both to flee and leave everything behind.

Maybe he's already smashed it all just to spite me.

"Catherine, Marjorie's mother is here to pick her up." Victoria raises her voice but no response carries back to us. I study the mural that decorates the vaulted ceiling, abstract colors swirling above our heads. A vase rests on the coffee table, gilded with golden leaves. It gleams in the sunlight.

"That's beautiful—did you make it?" I admire the intricate pattern. Many of the heirs to the Reachwood Mining Company learn to some extent how to work the precious metal that gives them their fortune. But Victoria had always possessed the most talent.

"Yes." Victoria fidgets with the rings decorating her fingers. No trace of the resentment she displayed last night remains in her voice now. Maybe she's forgiven me. Or maybe she just keeps her feelings well-hidden.

"Didn't you go to school to study art? I think my mother mentioned it once," I say as the breeze blows through the open door that leads to the backyard. We both sit down on the sofa and my body sinks into the pliable leather.

"I studied goldsmithing, but only for a year. I dropped out when I had Catherine and Virgil," Victoria explains. Something like shame flits across her face before it vanishes again. "It was too difficult to go to school with the two of them."

"I dropped out too, after I had Marjorie. I wanted to keep studying, but it was so hard with a new baby," I say before silence settles between us again. Heavy with the weight of the years we spent apart.

"You should show me the rest of your home—it's beautiful." I clear my throat.

"Sure," Victoria says. She stands and leads me through immaculate rooms, probably kept clean by a legion of housekeepers. Ceilings soar high above our heads as I wonder if Victoria plays the same games her parents did—if she hosts events in this house for wealthy investors, or holds fundraisers for Reachwood High School to cement her family's influence on the board of directors. The Albrights, Harts and Gallaghers control almost every organization in the neighborhood and have poured money into the community for as long as I can remember. Although they have more than enough wealth to move elsewhere and send their children to prestigious academies, they choose to stay here instead, year after year.

Refuse to leave the forest where they struck their fortune.

"What's that?" I ask when we pass a circular door, crafted from heavy metal, on our way toward the staircase. A wheel rests at its center.

"Our vault. I store most of my work in there before I send it out," Victoria says. We climb the stairs, and I follow her down the hallway. Animal skulls decorate the walls—proud horns gilded in gold.

"Did you make those, too?"

"Yes. Cyril likes to go hunting in the forest, sometimes. He keeps those as trophies." Victoria never glances at them as we walk past. Their blind eye sockets watch as we move through the long corridor. Somewhere, my daughter's voice giggles behind a closed door.

⚬—✦—⚬

When I step into the room at the end of the hall, I have to catch my breath. I stare at the jewelry lining the tables of Victoria's workshop—delicate necklaces and bracelets, ornamented with precious stones. Machines and tools I have no clue how to use rest on polished countertops. The wax copy of a ring hardens inside a clear mold beneath the stained glass windows facing out toward Reachwood Forest.

The house rests so high on the crest of the hill that I can see the forest spread out against the edges of the suburb. Trees stretch to the base of the mountains in the distance. The sunlight falls through the multicolored window panes to pattern the floor in bright mosaic colors.

"These are lovely," I say, turning in a circle to admire the artwork on the walls.

"Thanks." Victoria crosses the room to stand by the window. "It keeps me busy."

"Do you sell them?" I ask as my eyes rest on the bed pushed against the corner. Its flower-carved headboard rises tall above linen sheets. Maybe Victoria prefers to sleep here when she works late. Or maybe she would rather fall asleep alone than in the bed she shares with Cyril. My heartbeat quickens.

"I do, actually. I have space at a few galleries across the country."

A dried corsage of roses hangs framed on the wall. I point at the preserved petals and ask, "Are those the same ones I gave you—for the dance at the end of high school?"

"Yes. I kept them so I'd have something to remember you by."

A hole opens in the bottom of my stomach. "I'm sorry."

"No—I'm sorry about what I said before." Victoria wraps me in an embrace. Her breath brushes against the hollow of my neck. "I was just so upset when you left."

"I should have told you."

"I'm just glad you came back," Victoria says. She smiles when she pulls away and I immediately miss the warmth of her body against mine. "Do you think you'll stay?"

"I haven't decided yet." The half-scabbed incision on my wrist stings underneath the bandage. I wrap my hand around it as I remember my journey through the forest this morning. "I helped look for the missing girl today. I was there when they found her."

"I heard about that. I'd been hoping they'd find her alive."

"Me too. It reminded me of Adam." My voice trembles as I remember what Ambrose told me. "Ever since I moved back, it's like I can't stop thinking about him."

"Why did you really come back here?" Victoria asks, and I blink at the sudden question. Not really surprised that she saw through the stories I told everybody at the party—she'd always had an unsettling way of knowing when I was lying. Of pushing and pulling until she teased the real answer from me.

"I'm getting divorced, actually." I cross my arms tight across my chest. "I don't want my husband to find me. This is probably the only place he won't come after me or Marjorie."

"Are you afraid of him?" she asks, and I remember the sound my wrist made when it snapped. The visits to the hospital and the lies I told the doctors.

"Yes." I blurt the words like we are still teenagers and I can tell Victoria anything. "I think he's looking for me again—I got a call last night from a number I didn't recognize. I could hear somebody breathing on the other end of the line."

"Did he—" she hesitates. I guess what she wants to ask next.

Did he hurt you?

"Yeah. That's actually part of why I came to see you today," I say. The pill I'd swallowed in the morning numbs my body as I work up the courage to speak the next words. To see how much things have really changed between us. "You know everything that happens in Reachwood. I thought maybe you could help me. Tell me if you hear of anybody looking around for me."

"Of course I'll help you. I always do." She smiles, and for a moment it feels like we have both stepped outside of time. Like the long years we spent apart meant nothing at all. "I'll let you know if I hear anything."

The sun plunges beneath the horizon. The fading light stains the sky with shades of purple and blue like a bruise. Victoria turns away from the window, standing close enough to kiss me. But she wraps me in another embrace instead, and I bury my face against her shoulder. She smells as sweet and as clean as the air before a summer storm.

I close my eyes and pretend we are both still seventeen and not afraid of anything.

FIFTEEN YEARS EARLIER

CHAPTER 15

The neighborhood congregated at dusk for Emily's vigil. Victoria led the procession into Reachwood Forest, where we left lanterns swaying in the breeze. A line of lights to guide the way through the wilderness.

I stayed quiet on the drive to the Gallagher house. The forest followed us, trees climbing up the steep hill to crowd against the end of each street. Brief glimpses of their leaves flickered between the buildings as my father steered through the wealthy enclave. He didn't say anything, occasionally switching between the channels on the radio. Face lined and tired from another long day of working at the mines.

"See you tomorrow," I said after he parked in front of Victoria's house. I leaned down to scoop up my overnight bag from the floor of the vehicle.

"Stay safe." He waved when I stepped outside. I rolled my eyes and slammed the car door shut without another word. The soles of my shoes scraped against the concrete as I hurried up the flower-lined driveway to ring the bell on the porch.

"Hey." Victoria opened the door a moment later. Still dressed in the same black gown she'd worn at the vigil. A crown of budding leaves and white flowers decorated her hair.

"Where is everybody?" I asked after I stepped inside. The house was quiet. Devoid of the chatter of my friends or the soft murmurs of the staff who catered to the Gallagher family's every whim.

"You're the first one here." Victoria led me through vast rooms decorated with expensive furniture. Family portraits that looked like they were taken a long time ago hung framed on the walls. Even in black and white, they shared the same dark eyes as Victoria. Their solemn faces watched as we walked past.

"I'm sorry—maybe I should have waited," I said as we climbed the staircase leading to the second floor of the house.

"Don't be." Victoria waved a dismissive hand. "I'm glad you're here. It gets creepy at night, especially when I'm the only one home."

"Creepy how?" I asked as we strode through the doorway into Victoria's bedroom. Easily five times the size of my own room back home. Hand-painted roses patterned the wallpaper. More flowers embroidered the covers of her bedspread, gold-threaded petals decorating the sheets.

"I hear things outside sometimes." Victoria removed the crown of leaves and flowers from her head and set it down on her nightstand. "It's probably nothing. Just an animal or something."

"Yeah, I guess so." My skin prickled. The nocturnal sounds of the forest drifted into my bedroom at night, too. Shrieks and howls that my parents always told me not to worry about. I crossed the room to peer out the window at the ravine cutting through the neighborhood beneath us. A swath of dark amid the lights of the houses. "You looked really nice at the vigil tonight."

"Thanks. I'm glad it's over, though—I felt so bad for Emily's family." Victoria fidgeted with the clasp on the back of her dress as I remembered the grief-stricken faces of Emily's parents. Her mother looked gaunt and withdrawn, as if a part of her had disappeared with her daughter. "Can you help me with this?"

"Sure," I said and she turned away from me. I fiddled with the stuck zipper until it came undone, exposing the smooth curve of her shoulders.

"Thanks." A slight smile curled at the corners of her mouth. As she undressed, heat crept up my face.

"Yeah, no problem." I glanced away. Victoria walked over to the closet and rummaged through it to find a new outfit, tossing different options across the sheets of her bed. She tried on clothes in front of the mirror and spun in a circle to study her reflection.

"What do you think?" Victoria asked finally. Dressed in a skirt short enough to show her thighs, cropped top clinging to the curve of her ribcage.

"You look great." I blushed. Victoria picked up the dress and opened the rose-carved hope chest at the foot of her bed. She folded it away inside and placed the woven crown of leaves and flowers on top of the garment. Then she leaned forward to search through the contents of the chest until she pulled out a clear plastic bag. The colorful ecstasy pills inside rattled together as she waved it at me and smiled.

"Where did you get all those?" I asked, impressed.

"From Ambrose," she said as she unsealed the bag and shook a few pills onto the palm of her hand. "Which one do you want?"

"You choose."

Victoria plucked two green pills from the colorful pile and rolled them between her slender fingers before she swallowed one down dry and passed the other to me. I choked for one breathless moment when it stuck in the back of my throat.

"You're going to feel so good in a few minutes." Victoria sat down on the floor. She leaned back against the intricate bedspread, tilting her face up toward the vaulted ceiling. "Like nothing bad could ever happen."

"That sounds great." I sat down beside her and wrapped my arms around my knees.

"I'm glad you're back. It was so boring at school after you got sent to the hospital."

"Me too." I remembered the sterile rooms and white gowns that covered the thin bodies of the girls who moved like ghosts through the hallways.

A lonely place, despite the daily therapy sessions and mandatory group activities.

"I hated not being able to see you," Victoria said and rested her head against my shoulder. My skin tingled at her touch.

"I missed you, too." I settled against her and closed my eyes for a moment. Her hair smelled sweet. Like cherries.

"Do you like Adam?"

"What?" I opened my eyes again.

"I've noticed the way he looks at you—I guess I was wondering if you felt that way, too." Victoria pulled away to study my face.

"I haven't really thought about it. It still feels like I just got back from the hospital."

"Be careful around him." Victoria stood to hide the bag of pills inside her hope chest. Pupils already wide enough to nearly eclipse her irises, as if she had tried out a few of the pills before I arrived.

"Why?" I asked. Victoria paused, searching for the right words.

"He was the last person to see Emily before she went missing. They were kind of dating." Victoria sat back down beside me and clasped her hands together in her lap. When she bit down on her lower lip, my eyes followed the movement. For a brief second, I wondered again what it would be like to kiss her, for real this time. Then I shoved the thought from my mind.

"He never told me," I said and rose to my feet. Victoria's eyes followed me as I crossed the room to rummage through my overnight bag. Searching for the box of cigarettes and the lighter I had hidden beneath my clothes. "Why didn't he lead the procession for her tonight?"

"He wasn't chosen." Victoria hesitated. I selected a bent cigarette from the cardboard package. "His family has had some trouble recently. My parents haven't really explained it to me, but I think they don't want him to represent us publicly right now. Until it all dies down."

"So what, you think he did something to her?" I struggled with my lighter. Sparks flew until a flame finally burst to life.

"I don't know. I just think you should be careful."

I lit the tip of the cigarette. A thin stream of smoke trickled up toward the ceiling. Gold rings sparkled on the table beside the window and I picked one up to admire the floral pattern engraved into its surface. "Did you make this?"

"Yeah, I did," Victoria said. She climbed to her feet and I passed her the cigarette.

"It's beautiful." I turned the ring over and over again in my hands.

"It isn't perfect." Victoria shook her head. "I'm still learning how to cast them—you can have it, if you want it."

"Really?" I slipped the ring onto my finger, metal smooth against my skin. "I mean, isn't it valuable?"

"No. My parents don't let me practice on anything close to pure gold." Victoria shrugged. "And besides, I want you to have it."

"Are you sure?" I hesitated, although I wanted nothing more than to keep it.

"Yeah, I mean it." Victoria moved closer to hand the cigarette back to me. Her fingertips brushed my wrist when I took it. She didn't step away and we stood face to face—if I leaned in only a few inches, I'd be able to kiss her. My heartbeat hurried as she smiled at me, like we were both standing on the brink of something.

The doorbell rang. We flinched away as the sound echoed through the house.

"That's probably Nathalie." Victoria extinguished the spent cigarette on the windowsill and tossed it into the yard below. Before we left the bedroom, she said, "I meant what I told you about Adam. Promise me you'll be careful around him."

"I will be. Don't worry." I pictured Adam's face as I followed her downstairs. He'd always been reckless, but I never thought he could hurt somebody. Especially not Emily.

Did he really leave her in the forest?

CHAPTER 16

"Let's play a game," Adam said later. After we had gathered downstairs to raid the liquor cabinet, take some mushrooms and share our favorite memories of Emily. The way she laughed loud enough to disrupt the entire class. How much she loved animals, texting us cute pictures of dogs and kittens from the veterinarian clinic where she volunteered every weekend. She could make each one of us smile, even on our worst days.

She always knew the right words to say.

"Like what?" Cyril asked. He sprawled on the floor, voice already slurred by the whiskey he had been drinking all evening. Nathalie almost tripped over his long limbs when she stepped over him to light a joint beside the open window.

"Spin the bottle?" Matthew pointed to an empty beer can and laughed.

"No way." Nathalie made a face. "Pick another game."

"Okay, what about truth or dare?" Adam suggested. He had changed out of the somber clothes he had worn to Emily's vigil, now dressed in casual sportswear that fit his lean body perfectly. He grinned at us.

The last person to see Emily before she went missing.

"That's lame, too." I shook my head. Not eager for a repeat of the last time we had played the game—Matthew had stolen a bench from the neighbor's garden and almost sprained his shoulder trying to hoist it over the fence.

"Can you think of anything better to do?" Cyril demanded.

"Not really," I admitted. I took a sip of rum and Coke. The sweet mixture bubbled against the roof of my mouth.

"Fine, whatever. Who goes first?" Nathalie said and rolled her eyes. Victoria swallowed a pill and waved another at me playfully. When I opened my mouth, she placed it on the tip of my tongue.

"I will," Adam volunteered. "Ava, truth or dare?"

"Dare," I said as Victoria rose to her feet to turn down the music. She swayed when she sat down beside me and I placed a hand on her shoulder. Cyril's eyes narrowed when he noticed the ring on my finger. The one she had given me earlier.

"I dare you to eat the rest of that." Adam gestured at an open box of pizza lying on the floor between us. Three slices still sat inside it. Grease congealed on the cardboard.

"Can I pick something else?" I asked. My stomach twisted beneath my ribs.

"Come on, what's the problem?" Cyril leaned forward. Expression intent, like he sensed an opportunity to get back at me for stealing Victoria's attention all evening. "Unless you're not really better yet."

"I am." My voice cracked and betrayed the lie.

"Do it, then." Adam grinned. My gaze swept around the circle. Rested on each of my friends, searching for an ally or something—anything—to get out of this. But Nathalie looked away and plucked at a loose thread on her sweater. Matthew gulped down another mouthful of beer. Concern furrowed both of their faces, but neither said anything. No one ever did.

Not against the members of the three most powerful families in Reachwood.

Victoria's eyes met mine, clouded with anxiety. She had been so worried when I stopped eating. Wrote me letters while I stayed at the treatment center. Encouraged me to get better so I could return home again.

"Okay." I gave in and pulled the cardboard box toward me. Grease coated the inside of my mouth as I chewed the first bite. I almost gagged when it slid down my throat. I blinked back tears before I took another bite. Then another. Until the hunger that accompanied me everywhere disappeared.

"I can't do it." I pushed the box away. Half a slice remained.

"You only have a few bites left."

"That's not fair, you know you're going to make her sick," Victoria protested as I picked it up again, resisting the urge to tally how many calories I had eaten. Already too many—stomach so full it felt almost like it could explode at any second.

"There. Happy now?" I said after I chewed and swallowed the last bite.

"I knew you could do it." Adam smiled, exposing bleach-white teeth. So perfect they must have cost a fortune, although his parents could afford it. A breeze blew into the room. It carried the smell of the forest with it—wet dirt and leaves growing up from the earth.

"Or not." Cyril laughed as I covered my mouth and stood up.

"I'll be right back." I hurried to the bathroom. After I slammed the door, I knelt on the floor to vomit chunks of undigested food into the toilet. Sour acid stung my tongue as I flushed it away. My stomach lurched again and I clutched it, spitting up a thin stream of bile. It dripped from the corners of my lips until I wiped it clean with my hand.

I flinched when Victoria pushed the door open. She sat down beside me without a word and I leaned against her as loud voices drifted from the living room. A blush spread fever-hot across my skin and I turned away, embarrassed she had witnessed a moment so private.

"I'm sorry," I said. The words rasped in the back of my raw throat. "I know how much you wanted me to get better."

"You are better." She steadied me as I climbed to my feet. My legs trembled and I leaned against the counter. "It's Adam's fault—he shouldn't have asked you to do it. He's just pissed he didn't get to lead Emily's vigil and took it out on you."

"You should go." I twisted the taps of the sink and waited for the water to run cold. Still not able to look at her, I said, "I need to be alone for a few minutes."

"Are you sure?"

"I really don't want you to see me like this." I forced the words out.

"Okay." Victoria cast one last glance at me over her shoulder before the door clicked shut behind her. I took a sip of water and swished it around my mouth to wash the bitter taste out.

<hr />

"My turn next," Victoria said when I sat down beside her again. Throat still sore as I drew my knees up to my chest and avoided looking at my friends. "Adam, truth or dare?"

"Dare." Adam produced a rolled joint from the pockets of his hoodie and lit it. Smoke drifted up to gather in a strong-smelling cloud beneath the ceiling.

"Okay, I dare you to hurt yourself."

"What?" The grin fell from Adam's face.

"Just enough to draw some blood." Victoria smiled.

"Fine—I'll do it, but only if you do, too." Adam pulled the folding knife from his pocket, flipped it open and pricked his finger. A bead of blood bubbled up from the cut.

"That's not good enough." Victoria shook her head. "Are you scared or something?"

"Of course not," Adam said although his face paled when he pressed the sharp edge of the knife against the palm of his hand. He drew it across the thin skin and blood gushed from the newly opened wound, dripping red onto the carpet.

"Your turn." He offered the knife to Victoria. But she waved it away and bit down hard on the soft cushion of flesh beneath her thumb until her teeth drew blood.

"Gross." Nathalie wrinkled her nose. Pungent smoke stung my eyes when I took a drag from the joint making its way around the circle. I coughed as I handed it over to Victoria.

"My turn." Cyril set down an empty bottle of whiskey. "Ava, truth or dare?"

"I just went. Pick someone else," I protested.

"Everyone else went while you were throwing up," Cyril said, and I glared at him. Reluctant to risk another dare. But not eager to tell the truth either.

"Dare." I blinked as the patterned wallpaper shifted. The wooden grain of the floorboards writhed beneath us as the mushrooms I had taken earlier finally hit me.

"Okay. I dare you to steal one of the gifts at Emily's memorial." Cyril grinned. A chill rippled through my body at the thought of walking down the hill to the border of the forest, where Emily's memorial waited at the edge of the wealthy neighborhood. It felt disrespectful to take something from Emily. But if she was still here, she would probably think it was funny.

"You know it's not safe to go out there at night," Victoria objected. Nathalie and Matthew both murmured in agreement. Cyril and Adam remained silent. They were never close friends, although they had grown up together. But tonight, it felt like they had formed some kind of unspoken alliance to torment me.

"I'll do it." I stood up and the circle quieted. "It's not far from here."

Worry shadowed Victoria's eyes but she didn't say anything as I turned and walked down the hallway, buttoning up my jacket by the front door. My breath fogged out in front of my face when I stepped outside alone into the dark night.

CHAPTER 17

The forest followed me as I hurried down the street toward Emily's memorial. Trees cut through the stately neighborhood, growing tall behind the walls of immense houses. Boughs tangled against high iron fences. Flowers breathed on the branches. Maybe it was the mushrooms I had taken earlier, but the bark-covered limbs reminded me of prying fingers.

Trying to find a way inside.

An animal screamed somewhere in the distance when I left the neighborhood behind. The moon floated through the sky. Stars swirled above my head and the wind bit at my skin again and again as I strode through the dark.

I hesitated when I reached the border of Reachwood Forest. Stood still for a moment to listen to the silence—to reassure myself nothing waited for me just out of sight, hidden by the night. Nothing moved as I walked toward the makeshift memorial at the head of the path. A haphazard cluster of pictures and handwritten letters, stuffed animals and wilted flowers. Still tended by the community, although the wind would soon blow pieces of it away and people would forget to visit. Eventually it would disappear, just like all the other monuments to the children who vanished.

As if they'd never existed.

Emily's familiar face stared back at me when I reached the memorial. Caught in a snapshot taken sometime during school last year, a flare of sunlight circled her head like a halo. Frozen in time, she laughed like she wasn't afraid of anything—not even of going missing.

I looked away as I knelt down on the ground to sift through the gifts left at the edge of the forest. It still felt wrong to take something from Emily. Like spitting on her memory. But some small part of me almost hoped it would make her angry enough to inspire her ghost to return and haunt me. At least then I would get to see her again.

My hands trembled, but I plucked a stuffed rabbit from its resting place against the dirt. Debris and wet earth stuck to its cotton fur. Its glassy eyes stared up at me as I wondered what it had seen out here at night.

If something hungry really did live inside the forest.

A dark shape stirred in the trees. I froze like startled prey as I rose to my feet, peering into the undergrowth. Still half-expectant that Emily would step from the shadows and flash her radiant smile. Explain that this was all just a game, a prank she had played on me for leaving.

"Hello?" My voice shook as the stars whirled like a hurricane in the sky above my head. The foliage rustled again but no response drifted back to me. I turned away, eager to return to the safety of the party.

Something burst from the tree line. It rushed toward me and I screamed, covering my face with my hands. Laughter followed a moment later. The abrupt sound echoed through the night as I peeked between my fingers.

Adam stood in the middle of the path, breathless with glee. The trees rippled around us as he walked toward me and said, "It's okay—it's just me."

"What the fuck? That wasn't funny." I shoved him away when he reached out to touch me. Anger coursed hot through my body.

"Sorry. I didn't think I'd actually scare you like that," Adam said and fell into step beside me. Still smiling, as though his apology meant nothing.

"Whatever." I scowled as I followed the path that led back up to the crest of the hill. Walked quick, shoes slipping against loose gravel.

"Are you mad at me?" Adam asked and nudged my shoulder. Face still playful, but concern clouded his eyes like he thought maybe I actually was angry at him.

"Not really." I sighed. My breath blew like smoke through the cold air. "How did you get here so fast, anyway?"

"I took a shortcut through the forest."

"You're not scared of it?" I blinked at him, surprised.

"No. My family owns it." His dismissive laugh carried down the street. "We've lived here for a long time and none of us have ever gone missing."

"Really?"

"Yeah—my grandparents told me once that we made a deal with something in there. It can't touch us." He grinned like maybe he was joking again, but I remembered the other stories about the forest. About a place inside it that could grant a wish in exchange for a gift.

Maybe it really existed.

"I'm actually having a party there next week. On Friday." His voice interrupted my thoughts. "Want to come with me?"

Curiosity rose inside me. "What kind of party?"

"It's a kind of celebration. We go into the forest and get high," he said and touched the back of my hand, fingertips rough against my skin. "I only invite the people I like."

"Then why were you so mean to me tonight?" I swallowed down the sour taste in my mouth. The only evidence of the food I threw up after I accepted his stupid dare.

"I didn't mean it." He smiled, flirtatious. "I didn't think you'd actually do it."

"You're really not scared to go in there?" I studied his expression, searching for any trace of a lie. "Even after Emily disappeared?"

"Yeah. Don't worry, you'll be safe with me." A shadow crossed his face at the sound of Emily's name, and I wondered again why she ran away into the forest. She had everything she could have wanted—perfect grades, a supportive family and a popular boyfriend.

What wish was so important that she would risk anything for it?

"Is Victoria going, too?" I asked. The streetlamps cast our shadows out in front of us as I remembered her earlier warning. Her suspicions about Adam's involvement in Emily's disappearance.

"Did she give that ring to you?" He never answered my question. I glanced down at the ring on my finger. It glittered gold in the dim moonlight, etched with the same roses that decorated most of Victoria's artwork.

"Yeah, she said I could have it."

"She never gives her work away to anybody." His eyes lingered on the piece of jewelry. Uncomfortable, I curled my fingers into a fist to hide it from his curious stare. "She must really like you."

"I mean, she *is* my best friend," I said. A blush heated my face as I wondered if he was implying something else.

"I don't know if she's going to the party yet. She's probably busy with Cyril again," Adam changed the subject, voice flat with contempt. Although they presented a united front to the outside world, Victoria and Adam had turned from once-close friends into fierce rivals as they had grown older. Locked in a struggle to cement their position as the favored child of all three of their powerful families—to prove their worth to inherit control of the Reachwood Mining Company. Her accusations against him might be baseless.

Just another attempt to smear his reputation.

"What's going on with them?" I asked as something sank in my stomach. Victoria and Cyril would have spent a lot of time with each other while I was away. Maybe her feelings for him had changed.

"Nothing—I mean, they haven't told me anything yet. Not officially. So, will you come with me?" Adam slung an arm around my shoulders when the wind rose. One of the most popular boys in school, with a handsome face and powerful family. I should have felt elated he was paying attention to me. But I felt nothing like the electricity that shivered through my body whenever Victoria smiled at me.

Maybe those feelings would disappear if I left a gift in the forest.

"Okay. Sounds like it could be fun."

"Great." Adam's face lit up as the Gallagher house appeared at the end of the street.

We slipped through the open gate to follow the winding path through the garden, night air sweet with the scent of flowers. The moon shone down from the sky. It washed the petals with silver light as we hurried inside.

TODAY

CHAPTER 18

"Marjorie? It's time to go home." I knock on Catherine's bedroom door. The voices behind it fall silent.

"You both can work on your project tomorrow," Victoria says as she pushes the door open. Her children look up from their phones, schoolwork spread around them. Dressed in high-end designer clothes, they look just like their mother—same pale skin, auburn hair and delicate features. Like Cyril had contributed nothing to either of them.

Except for their eyes, green and wild.

"Marjorie left. She had a headache so she went out to get some fresh air." Catherine taps her pencil against her textbook. Virgil picks up his phone again to type out a message. No trace of Marjorie remains in the room—no familiar jacket, backpack or sticker-decorated tablet left behind to mark her presence.

I turn and head downstairs without a word. My feet drum against the floor as I walk quickly toward the front door, pushing away the memory of Kristen's face when we found her body in the forest. Marjorie won't disappear in the few moments she spent alone.

"I'm sorry. They should have told me she was leaving," Victoria apologizes. Eyes clouded with unease, like she's thinking about Kristen, too.

Or any one of the other children who went missing as we grew up here. Maybe Emily.

Or Adam.

"It's fine. She's probably waiting by the car, playing on her phone." I open the door and the empty driveway stretches out in front of me. My locked car sits parked on the concrete.

No sign of Marjorie.

"It was really nice to see you," Victoria says and hesitates like she's working up the courage to say something else. To reach across the space that grew between us in the years I spent away from this place. "Will you visit again sometime?"

"Of course. I'll talk to you soon." A rush of heat warms my body when she smiles at me, despite my worries about Marjorie. I turn and hurry down the driveway. The door clicks shut behind me.

◦━┼━◦

"Marjorie?" I raise my voice. The sound echoes down the empty street. "Where are you?"

Nothing answers me. The silent neighborhood spreads out before me, quiet and patient, as if it were waiting for something.

"Marjorie?" My tongue sticks to the roof of my mouth. Reachwood Forest lurks like a dark beast at the end of the street, and I take one reluctant step toward it. Then another.

A faint trail leads into the trees at the border of the forest, gravel covered beneath a patchwork of fallen leaves. Signs litter the undergrowth, advising hikers not to stray from the path. Strands of barbed wire thread between the trunks of the trees to discourage curious trespassers.

But this place has always drawn children to it like a magnet. Maybe it called to Marjorie the same way it called to me years ago. It's so easy to ignore the warnings. To slip beneath the fence and into the wilderness.

"Marjorie!" My voice cracks when my eyes rest on my daughter. She stands silent at the edge of the forest, expression intent as she stares into the darkness. Like she is fascinated by it.

"What are you doing?" I hurry down the street until I reach her side.

"Nothing—I just thought I heard something."

"Come back to the car with me," I say. Goosebumps cluster on my skin. Marjorie follows me down the sidewalk, sneakers shuffling against the concrete, as though she doesn't really want to leave. Little pieces of gravel scatter into the thickets that crowd against the edges of the road. Stray drops of rain sting my face as a storm gathers in the sky overhead.

"Haven't you been listening to a single thing I've said? Children disappear out here," I reprimand, remembering the missing posters stapled to the trunks of the trees, asking passersby if they have seen the faces of the children printed on the faded paper. It always seems to be children who vanish without a single trace in the forest. I picture their small, white bones hidden in the trees—covered by thick foliage growing close around their bodies.

"I didn't go in there, so whatever." Marjorie shrugs. The thin fabric of her jacket crinkles.

"I mean it." My voice hardens. "I was there when they found the body of that missing girl this morning. And two of my friends disappeared here when I was in high school. They only found one of them."

"I heard my friends talk about him. His name was Adam, right?" Marjorie asks. Her eyes brighten. I almost shudder when she pronounces his name, recoiling from the interest that sharpens her voice. "Is it true what they say—that something in there grants wishes and eats children?"

My body stiffens at the mention of the familiar urban legend. "Who told you that?"

"Somebody at school," Marjorie says and pulls the hood of her jacket over her head to protect her carefully styled hair from the downpour. "I don't remember who."

"Was it Aidan?" I ask, remembering the night I followed Adam into the forest. Aidan's face looks just like his. Maybe the resemblance runs even deeper.

"How did you know about him?" Marjorie glances up to study my expression. Tone so guarded that I can't guess what she's thinking about.

"I saw you two talking at the festival. You should stay away from him." The muscles in my wrists twitch. I fold my fingers into fists, hard enough that my nails bite my skin. "He doesn't come from a good family."

"That's not true—his family is as rich as Catherine and Virgil's," she protests, and I realize I've made a mistake. Maybe my words will push her closer to him, instead of warn her away and keep her safe.

"There isn't anything in the forest. Those are just stories," I snap. We walk through the rain, to where my car still sits parked at the end of Victoria's long driveway. "And I want you to promise me you won't go in there."

Marjorie opens her door and slides into her seat. I twist the keys in the ignition before I turn on the headlights, crank up the heat and back out onto the street. Marjorie stays silent, eyes fixed on her phone as she texts the friends she left behind in her old school. Or maybe Virgil and Catherine.

Or Aidan.

"I mean it." My hands clench against the steering wheel. I can't lose her. Not after I moved here to protect her. "I don't want you to go missing, too."

"Okay—I promise." She rolls her eyes. I hold my breath when we cross the ravine and the forest grows deep at the edges of the street.

Marjorie presses her forehead against the window and stares out at the trees.

CHAPTER 19

A silver knife rests beside the back door the next morning. The sharp blade glitters as I pick it up and turn it over and over again in my hands. Spots of rust speckle the metal, as dark as splotches of blood. The familiar initials carved into the handle chafe against my skin. My pulse skips as I picture someone creeping up to the house at night to leave the weapon behind like a message.

Or an accusation.

Reachwood Forest swells against the fence. Branches grasp toward the house. No early birds sing or flit through the leafy canopy, and I shudder in the perfect silence. Draw my thin sweater close to my body as the knife rests heavy in the palm of my hand.

Who could have left it here? Maybe somebody stumbled across it in the forest after it was lost. Recognized the initials and left it here to taunt me, the same way strangers called in the wake of Adam's death to rant baseless suspicions and threats. Or maybe Ambrose discovered it—after all, he figured out I knew about Adam's body in the grove somehow. He probably blames me for his brother's death.

Or maybe something else.

Something from the forest.

"Ava?" My father calls, loud enough to carry down the hall. "Are you awake?"

"Yeah." I raise my voice, lingering in the doorway.

The sun is rising later as the autumn draws nearer to winter. It is still dark outside, although the first rays of light spread hesitantly across the sky. Nothing stirs inside the forest as I stare into its depths. So tranquil it looks almost peaceful.

"You slept late—your mother took Marjorie to school again." His heavy footsteps travel toward me. I fold the knife quickly, clasping my hands behind my back.

"Is something wrong?" he asks when he appears around the corner.

"No. I mean—" I stutter over my words.

"Did you hear anything from your lawyer about the divorce?" He peers at me through his round glasses.

"No," I say, hoping my panic doesn't show on my face. "I haven't heard anything yet."

"Have you thought about what you're going to do when the divorce is finalized?"

"Not really. Why?" I ask. Once I win my assets back, I'll probably auction everything off. Buy a new house somewhere far away from here—a home not haunted by memories of my marriage. A place where I can start over again.

"I think you should go back to school. You were doing so well before you had Marjorie—wouldn't you like to go back and finish your degree?" he asks. I remember the pride on my father's face when my acceptance letter came in the mail. He had never bothered to apply for college, staying in the same place he was raised to take up a job at the Reachwood Mining Company as soon as he graduated from high school.

"We'll see," I say. Before Marjorie was born, I spent months studying architecture in college. Loved to learn about the construction of different kinds of buildings until suddenly I didn't have the time anymore. "Can I ask you something?"

"Of course." He pushes his glasses up the bridge of his nose.

"Do you ever hear anything strange outside?" I catch the handle of the knife when it almost slides between my fingers.

"I don't think so. Why?"

"Marjorie thought she heard something in the forest a few times," I say and tighten my grasp. His eyes drift to the trees bordering our yard, resting on the faint path waiting just past the fence.

"It's probably her imagination." He dismisses it the same way he used to dismiss my fears when I was still a child, afraid of the sounds I heard outside in the forest late at night. The cries and screams that carried from the trees. "Once she settles in, she'll forget about it."

"I hope so." The knife almost slips between my sweat-slick palms again. The initials carved into its hilt dig into my skin. "She probably heard some stories about it at school."

"Probably. Everybody's still talking about Kristen." He clears his throat. "It's too bad, what happened to her—I'd hoped everything would stop with Adam."

"Me too." I flinch at the sound of Adam's name. He retreats upstairs to the master bedroom, and I hurry to the guest room, hiding the knife away inside the drawers of my nightstand.

While I wait for my father to leave the house, I begin to pack up my parents' belongings in the study. Framed photos of our family on the few vacations we had taken to the coast when I was a teenager. A portrait of Marjorie at the hospital just after she was born. Face red, she squints up at the camera in confusion. Taken over fourteen years ago, although it doesn't feel like that much time has passed at all.

Finally, the front door opens. It slams shut again a moment later, signaling that my father has left for the run he still goes on each morning. I wait a few minutes before I retrieve the knife from its hiding place in the guest room. My hands shake as I button up my jacket in the foyer and unfold the knife—blade still as sharp as the day it was lost.

When I touch it, the point pricks my fingertip hard enough to draw a bead of blood.

○━◆━○

Go down the path. Don't look back.

The familiar phrase whispers through my mind as I journey into Reachwood Forest. I take one tentative step and then another down the path, until the suburb disappears behind me—swallowed by the trees. Shivers ripple through my body. My fingers curl around the knife folded inside my jacket pocket.

I pause when I reach the first landmark—a pile of flat stones stacked like some kind of waypoint at the edge of the path. Small enough that I would have missed it, if I didn't know what to look for. Hesitant, I toe the line where the path ends and the wilderness begins. A beetle scurries through the dirt, hard shell shining iridescent in the early sunlight. Birds burst from a thicket, shrieking as they soar away into the sky.

Brambles tear at my hair and scratch at my face when I step off the path. Signs warn me to stay out of the forest as I head toward the barbed wire fence. I duck underneath it and one of the metal spikes snags my jacket. Undeterred, I plunge through the undergrowth to follow the piles of rocks through the foliage.

Sometime later, the forest fades away into a clearing. I pause before I enter, wrapping my sleeve tight against my injured wrist like something here might recognize the scent of my blood on the wind.

In the middle of the clearing, a grove of hawthorn trees stretches up from the dirt. Offerings nestle between their gnarled roots. Gold coins and rusted jewelry. Old, like nobody has made the pilgrimage here in many years to leave a gift in exchange for a wish.

The tree where Adam's body lay for three days presides over the center of the clearing. Its boughs fan out wide enough to hide the sky. A crack splits its trunk to form a dark crevice. Offerings crunch beneath the soles of my feet as I stride toward it and I wonder if the police left everything here after they processed the crime scene. Maybe even they were afraid to take anything out of this place.

My legs shake when I kneel between the roots of the cracked tree and retrieve the knife from my jacket pocket. Pebbles dig into my knees hard enough to leave a mark. The blade sparkles in the sunlight as I dig a hole in the dirt and bury the weapon as deep as a secret, returning it to its rightful place among the other offerings. Nothing moves when I rise back to my feet. I stand in the perfect silence as the grove rests quietly all around me. Like it's waiting for me to wish for something.

But all gifts from the forest conceal some kind of poison.

The sun sits high in the center of the sky by the time I follow the stacks of stones back home. I never look back, trying to shake the uncomfortable feeling that something is stalking through the trees close behind me.

FIFTEEN YEARS EARLIER

CHAPTER 20

climbed into Adam's car, dressed in my best clothes for the party inside the forest that night. Tight jeans and a loose tank top. Bare shoulders covered by my favorite jacket.

"You look great." Adam smiled.

"Thanks. You do, too," I said and blushed when his eyes met mine. I'd spent an hour in front of the mirror before he arrived, trying to get my makeup just right. Now I hoped it would hide the nervous excitement on my face as he drove toward Reachwood Forest.

Maybe tonight I would find out the truth behind the stories.

The engine of the car rumbled as we sped through half-deserted suburban streets. My phone buzzed in my pocket and I flipped it open to check my texts.

I'm bored. Are you doing anything tonight? The message from Victoria flashed across the screen.

Going to Adam's party. Are you coming? I typed my reply and hit the send button.

Adam parked the car at the border of the trees, turning off the headlights. The dark settled in around us. I fidgeted with the keychain on my phone as Adam reached down beneath his seat to search for something. Loose change and a spare set of keys scattered across the floor. Tarnished metal gleamed in the dim light.

"Want some?" He grinned, pulling a half-empty bottle of whiskey from the debris.

"Sure." I smiled back, eager for something to dull my nerves before we ventured into the forest. Not sure if he invited me to this party as just a friend, or if he expected something more. I'd dated boys throughout high school, but I'd never slept with one before. I still felt nothing when I looked at Adam. Not the same giddy rush of attraction I felt toward Victoria.

But maybe I could change that tonight.

"Here." Adam uncapped the bottle and passed it to me.

"Thanks," I said and took a sip. The liquor burned against my tongue and throat when I swallowed it.

"I brought some of these, too." He shuffled through the mess strewn across the dashboard until he produced a bag of dried mushrooms from the haphazard pile. I smiled when he waved them in my face. After we swallowed them, my phone buzzed in my pocket again.

What are you talking about? Victoria asked.

"Why didn't you tell Victoria about the party?" I said with a frown, opening the car door. Stars spattered the night sky above our heads.

"What?" Adam asked as he slammed his door shut. The sound echoed through the trees clustered against the edge of the road.

"I asked her if she was coming here later. She had no idea what I was talking about."

"I didn't invite her." His broad shoulders shifted in the dark as he shrugged. "Maybe you didn't notice, but we haven't exactly been great friends lately."

"What's the deal between you two, anyway?" I hurried to catch up with him as he moved toward the border of the forest. The suburban lights vanished behind us. The night closed in like an impenetrable blanket.

"She's been acting all high and mighty ever since my dad checked in to the hospital." Adam's voice tightened. "He made some bad decisions, but he left to get better. Her family and Cyril's are helping us out until he comes back. But now it's like she thinks she owns us."

"I'm sorry." I touched his forearm. "I didn't know."

"What's it like—in the hospital?"

"It's fine." I searched for the right words to reassure him. "I got better, didn't I?"

"I guess so," Adam said as he stepped off the path. I paused when my eyes fell on the signs in the undergrowth. Printed with warnings not to leave the trail through the forest. He halted when he realized I wasn't following along behind him and asked, "What's wrong?"

"Are you sure we won't get lost?"

"Don't worry. It's easy if you know where you're going." He laughed. "But I can take you home if you're scared or something."

"I'm not scared." The skin on the back of my neck itched as an animal rustled unseen through the leaves. I held my breath until the sound faded away.

"Then I dare you to follow me," he said, like it was some kind of game. A continuation of the same one we had played last week at Victoria's place. I took one cautious step off the path, then another—not wanting him to tell everyone at school I was so scared of the dark that I missed the party. Or to believe I was some kind of coward, afraid of stories about monsters in the forest.

The trees breathed as we pushed forward. The night sky rippled like a vast ocean above our heads. We struggled through the lush foliage until we reached a pile of stones stacked against the earth.

"What are those?" I pointed at the monument, almost small enough to miss in the thick vegetation.

"Landmarks." Adam veered to the right.

"Why are they here?" I asked when we passed another stack of stones that rose from the dirt, guiding our way through the wilderness. "Who made them?"

"They've been here for as long as I can remember. Maybe someone from my family put them here a long time ago," he said as we waded through a thick copse of trees. A branch snapped back and hit me. Struck hard enough to leave a mark across my cheek.

"Fuck." I clutched my face.

"Are you okay?" Adam turned. His eyes rested on the raised welt on my skin.

"It's nothing," I said, blinking back surprised tears.

"Are you sure?" His expression softened with concern.

"Yeah—let's keep going. How much farther is it?"

"Not much longer now." He grasped my hand, skin warm as he led me through more dense foliage. I held it tight and tried to feel something—the same kind of heat that flickered inside my body when Victoria's eyes met mine, sometimes. But I felt nothing.

Maybe something was wrong with me.

⊶

A clearing waited for us deep inside the forest. I drew in my breath when we entered it. Hawthorn trees reached up from the earth. White-flowered boughs stretched toward the night sky. Rusted coins and jewelry piled high between their roots like offerings.

This must be the place that inspired all the stories.

"What do you think?" Adam asked and let go of my hand.

"How many people know this is here?" I turned in a slow circle. Twigs crackled beneath my sneakers.

"Not very many. This place is important to my family," he said, and I wondered if he had told Emily about this place, or shown it to her—if maybe she got lost when she tried to return here to leave an offering in the grove. Her body might rest close by, hidden in the undergrowth.

"Why's it so important?"

"I told you already. We made a deal with something here." Adam gripped my hand again and led me through the clearing. My skin prickled with the rise of the wind and I wondered what he would say if I told him I wanted to go home. If he would lead me back through the forest or leave me to make the journey alone.

"Where is everybody?" I asked as I brushed against a pile of coins. They scattered across the ground, hard metal edges clinking together. Some of them looked old—so old that they could have been left here a century ago.

I slid a ring off my finger as we moved through the grove. The same ring Victoria had given to me before the party the previous weekend. I had wanted to offer it to the forest to make my feelings for her disappear. But now that I was finally here, I hesitated—not really sure if I wanted those feelings to go away.

To never feel that warmth again.

"The party starts later." Adam strode toward the tallest tree in the clearing. It towered high above our heads, boughs laden with flowers. A fissure split its trunk, leading down into the earth. A gold bracelet dangled from a low-hanging branch. Adam unclasped the piece of jewelry and handed it to me.

"What's this?" I twisted it between my fingers.

"I want you to have it," Adam said and fastened the delicate chain around my wrist before he leaned in slowly and kissed me.

I closed my eyes as Victoria's face flickered through my mind. His lips felt hard and rough—not as sweet as the girls I had kissed before at parties. When he pulled away, he ran his thumb across the raised mark on my cheek.

We undressed beneath the shadow of the cracked tree and Adam climbed on top of me, fumbling with the condom. It scraped uncomfortably inside of me, gold coins and jewelry pressing hard against my back as Adam's body bore down against mine. He shivered when he finished, and we dressed in silence as I wondered if Victoria had done this with Cyril yet. If she liked it.

A twig snapped at the edge of the forest.

"Did you hear that?" I flinched. The words fell slow and slurred from my tongue as the alcohol buzzed inside my body. My head spun when I turned around to face Adam.

But the grove lay empty. Wide-eyed, I glanced around the clearing.

Something moved through the trees behind me.

CHAPTER 21

woke sprawled out across the floor. A white sheet covered my body like a shroud. The room whirled when I sat up and squinted against the light seeping in through the curtains. Still dizzy as I tried to piece together the previous night.

Drinking, following Adam through the forest and then—nothing.

Delicate, hand-painted flowers patterned walls that rose up to a vaulted ceiling. A bed rested below the window, linen sheets rumpled and unmade. A hope chest carved with roses sat at its base. Victoria's room. My pulse quickened.

How the fuck did I get here?

My legs shook when I climbed to my feet. A mirror on the vanity reflected my pale face back at me. Clothes torn to reveal the bruises mottling my chest. Dried blood crusted at the base of my neck, thick enough to hide the wound beneath it.

The door swung open and I jumped, balling my hands into fists. Victoria froze as she entered the room. We stared at each other for one long moment before I relaxed.

"Sorry. I didn't mean to scare you." She cradled a glass of water in her hands.

"What happened?" My voice rasped. She passed the glass of water to me and I drank it down fast. The sound of distant conversation carried up the stairs. Victoria's parents.

"You don't remember anything?" Victoria asked and sat down on the unmade sheets of her bed. I settled in beside her, setting my now-empty glass of water down on her nightstand. The white rabbit I had stolen from Emily's memorial lay on the small table.

"No. How did I even get here?" I picked up the stuffed animal.

"You rang the bell in the middle of the night." Victoria studied my face like she was seeing me for the first time. Like I was somebody she didn't recognize. "I let you inside."

"Did I say anything?" I asked and ran my fingers through the rabbit's soft cotton fur, stained with dirt.

"No." Victoria paused. "At least, not really. You just said something had chased you through the forest."

"Something like what?" Fragments from the previous night drifted through my memory. How we had passed the flask of whiskey back and forth in Adam's car before he led me into Reachwood Forest. The warmth of his hands. Sharp pain when a branch slapped across my face. Fucking beneath the shadow of the split tree as gold coins and jewelry pressed against my back hard enough to leave a mark and still—nothing. No frantic chase through the undergrowth. No blurry recollection of anything pursuing me through the dark.

"I don't know—you were pretty hysterical. You just kept repeating something was following you, over and over again," Victoria said. "I brought you upstairs and put you to bed. I was hoping you could tell me more in the morning."

"I can't remember anything." A headache throbbed at my temples. It grew stronger every time I pried at the blank spaces in my memory. Frustration prickled inside me as I fidgeted with the gold bracelet still fastened around my wrist. The thin chain bit into my skin.

"Why did you go in there with him, anyway? I told you about Emily." Victoria's eyes never wavered from my face. Hot shame flooded through me when I remembered the wish I had wanted to make in the forest. To take away my feelings for Victoria.

"He invited me to a party." My tongue scraped against the roof of my mouth. "I thought he liked me."

"Who else was there?" Victoria asked as she lay back against her sheets. If she guessed I had only told her half of the reason why I followed Adam into the forest, her expression never betrayed her suspicions. "Do you remember?"

"No—he said they were coming later. For some kind of celebration," I said and curled up beside her. My skin tingled when she combed her fingers through my hair, teasing the knots and tangles loose. Touch soft and soothing, like maybe she felt something for me, too. "We went to some kind of grove in there. We drank and took mushrooms and after that I don't remember."

"Could he have drugged you?" Victoria frowned like she knew I wasn't telling her everything. The memory of how Adam's heavy body had pressed against mine last night surfaced in my mind. Victoria might look at me differently if I told her what happened.

If she found out I slept with Adam.

"I don't know." I searched through my hazy memories. "I mean, I don't think so."

"My family has stories about the place he took you." Victoria stretched. Body patterned by the warm sunlight falling across her bed. "We're not supposed to show it to anybody."

"Why not?" I prodded at the blood crusted thick across the hollow of my neck. The wound hidden beneath it stung as I wondered again if the rumors held some small shred of truth.

"Because it's easy to get lost if you go that deep into the forest." She brushed off my question.

"But that's the place, isn't it? The one everybody talks about." I shivered, remembering the gold, coins and jewelry littered all over the clearing. "Adam told me something lives there. He said his family made a deal with it."

"That's what the stories say, anyway." Victoria laughed like she thought it was completely ridiculous. "Adam and Cyril both believe it. So do our parents. But I think someone probably just made it up to keep people out of there. The trees are so thick—it's easy to lose your way if you stray too far from the path."

When I crawled out of her bed, Victoria sat up and said, "Where are you going?"

"Can I take a shower? I want to feel clean again." I crossed my arms tight across my chest. Our eyes met and we both hesitated—each waiting for the other to speak.

"You can borrow some of my clothes. Yours are all ruined," she offered finally. I glanced down at my dirt-smudged sweater.

"Thanks." I chose an oversized hoodie and a fresh pair of jeans from her closet before I locked the bathroom door tight behind me.

I twisted the knobs on the shower and waited until the steam fogged the mirror before I undressed, leaving my torn clothes heaped in a crumpled pile on the floor. When I stepped underneath the water and the hot liquid touched my sore skin, I winced.

Leaves, pine needles and debris fell from my hair and disappeared down the drain. Shallow cuts lined my fingers and bruises marked my body—wrists, ribs and hips. I grimaced as I scrubbed the crusted blood from my neck to reveal the wound below. A bite mark from sharp teeth. Sunk deep into the hollow space between my neck and my collarbone.

What the fuck happened last night?

The ragged cut ached as I ran my fingers across the broken skin. Bright red, as though it were infected. Too swollen to tell if it had been made by a person or some kind of animal.

Did Adam bite me—or did something else?

CHAPTER 22

"I should probably go home," I said when I returned to Victoria's bedroom. Dressed in her clothes, hoodie pulled up to hide the fresh laceration on my neck. "Before my parents notice I'm missing."

"Before you go, there's something else you need to know." Victoria lay sprawled across the covers of her bed, typing a message on her phone.

"What?" I asked, sitting down beside her. Dread clutched at my stomach.

"Adam sent me a photo of you last night." Victoria tilted the screen of her phone toward me. Heat flared across my face at the sight of my naked body in the grove.

Fat had gathered on my hips since I came back from the clinic, although my ribs still showed like some kind of emaciated animal. Skin slick with sweat. Adam must have surreptitiously taken the photo while I was getting dressed. After we had sex.

"How many people do you think he sent it to?" I asked. My breath caught, revolted at the thought of other people seeing my body.

"I don't know." She flipped her phone closed.

"I should go." I repeated the words and retreated to the doorway. Eager to return home and fall asleep. Maybe when I woke up, this whole thing would turn out to be a bad dream.

"I'll walk back with you," Victoria said and climbed out of her bed. "We'll have to sneak out. My parents don't know you're here."

"Thanks, but I kind of want to be alone right now." I forced the words out. Not sure how I would ever be able to look Victoria in the eye again after what happened last night. Not after Adam sent her the photo and showed her all of my imperfections.

"I don't think you should be by yourself right now." Concern shadowed her face.

"I'm fine," I insisted. My mouth tightened into a stubborn line.

"No, you're not," Victoria said and touched the back of my hand. Expression worried, like maybe she still really cared about me in spite of everything. "Just let me walk with you."

"Okay." I gave in. We crept downstairs together and slipped out the front door unnoticed, the voices of her parents drifting from the kitchen. The breeze hit my face as we walked away down the street. The fresh welt across my cheekbone stung against its cold touch.

⚬━━⚬

"Wait." I stopped on the sidewalk. We had followed the road along the border of Reachwood Forest until we reached the street that led through the ravine. Leaves opened on the trees. Flowers spread toward the sun overhead as sweat itched between my shoulder blades.

"What? Why?" Victoria paused midstep and looked back at me.

"That's his car." I pointed at the sports car parked in the ditch across the street. Flecks of silver paint peeled from its metal body. A dent bent the rear door inward like a crater. Expensive, although Adam treated it like garbage. If he ever wrecked it, his parents would just buy him another one.

"Do you think he stayed out there all night?"

"Maybe," I said as I moved toward the vehicle. The path where Adam had led me into the forest last night lay beyond the car. A faint passage, foliage worn down by the traffic of countless shoes.

Why did he spend all night outside in the dark?

I crossed the street and climbed into the ditch.

"What are you doing?" Victoria asked. I ignored her, fragile twigs snapping as I pushed forward. Insects hummed through the undergrowth. I slapped at a mosquito when it landed on my wrist, squashing it before it could draw blood. Victoria waited for a car to drive past before she darted across the road and hurried to catch up.

"Nothing." I peered through the dust-covered windows. Empty cans littered the floor of the vehicle. Spent cigarettes rose in a pile from the ash tray. "Just looking."

"At what?" Victoria said when she caught up with me. "He isn't here— let's go."

I tried the car door. It swung open and I glanced around the deserted street before I climbed inside. Hopefully the tall grass would hide me from the sight of anyone passing by. Goosebumps crawled across my skin when I pictured Adam watching me from somewhere beyond the tree line. But anger pushed all the apprehensions from my mind.

"What are you doing?" Victoria repeated. I rummaged beneath the seat until I retrieved some loose change and the empty bottle of whiskey I had drank with Adam before we walked into the forest. The glass bottle sparkled in the light.

"I saw a spare key in here somewhere," I said as the sour taste of vomit bubbled up my throat. I swallowed and blinked hard, shuddering as I remembered Adam's rough mouth against mine last night. How the grove had stretched out before me after he left me there alone with whatever had chased me through the trees.

My fingers closed around the key. I hesitated before I shoved it into the ignition. This was probably a bad idea. Adam would be furious if he returned from the forest and found out his car had vanished. But the urge to hurt him overpowered my misgivings. It would be worth it if I could bruise his pride even a little bit.

To hurt him the same way he hurt me.

I cranked the key and the engine sputtered to life. Victoria slid into the passenger seat and I backed the car out of the ditch, engulfed in a cloud of exhaust smoke. She laughed as I gunned the engine and raced the car down the open road.

"Where do you want to go?" She rolled down the window.

"I just don't want to go home." My stomach lurched. Had my parents found out about the photo yet? Knuckles white, I chose every turn that led away from Reachwood. We drove farther and farther, until we left the neighborhood behind.

But the forest followed us even after we exited the suburb. Trees stretched out toward distant mountains, tall peaks wreathed by white snow. The wind whistled through the open window, tearing at our hair and clothes. My cheeks flushed red from the cold.

"Why did you fuck Adam?" Victoria asked when the song changed on the radio. "I didn't think you liked him."

"I don't—not really. I guess I just wanted to know what it was like." A blush heated my face as I remembered the weight of Adam's body bearing down against mine. How I had waited to feel something, anything, but still felt nothing the whole time.

"So, how was it?" Victoria asked. I couldn't read her expression.

"It hurt a lot. I think maybe he got the condom on wrong."

"Oh." Victoria said and turned away from me. My phone vibrated in my pocket and I jumped. Probably my parents, asking why I hadn't returned home yet. It vibrated again and again but I ignored it. Not ready to speak to them. To find out how much they knew about what happened last night.

"What's going on between you and Cyril?" I changed the subject as static crackled through the speakers. "Are you dating now?"

"No," Victoria said. Relief lightened the weight I had carried on my shoulders ever since I woke up in her bedroom. "I know he likes me, and it would make our parents happy. But I don't like him. Not like that, anyway."

"Do you like someone else?" I blurted. Immediately, I wished I could take the words back. I still didn't have a chance. Not really. Even though she kissed other girls at parties sometimes, she would never date one. The whole school would turn on us in a moment.

"Yes—I just haven't said anything yet."

"Why?" I blinked, surprised by her admission of shyness. Victoria had never flinched away from anything. Always faced everything head on, even if it scared her.

"Now isn't a good time," Victoria said finally. "Something bad just happened and I don't want to cause any more problems."

"You should say something. It might make them happy—I know I would be." My hands almost slipped against the steering wheel as I wondered if she could possibly be talking about me. Victoria said nothing. Just smiled and leaned back in her seat.

⚬━┼━⚬

After the sun disappeared below the thin line of the horizon, I turned the vehicle back toward the suburb again. Colorful rays of fading light scattered across the cracked windshield as I followed the familiar road home. Although I wished we could drive forever. People never glanced twice at us when we stopped for gas and snacks.

Outside of Reachwood, nobody recognized my face or knew my name.

"Where are you going?" Victoria asked after we entered the neighborhood again. Houses replaced the mountains that had surrounded us all afternoon. Instead of returning home, I pressed my foot down on the gas pedal and steered toward the forest. Parking the car in an empty lot, I unbuckled my seatbelt and pushed open the door.

The night closed in around me. I climbed onto the hood of the vehicle, sat down and tilted my face up toward the distant stars. After a moment, Victoria joined me. She settled down beside me and pulled her jacket close to her body. Expression patient as she waited for me to say something.

"I still don't want to go home." I swallowed. "What if he sent the photo to everyone? My parents will kill me if someone tells them."

"You can stay over at my place." Victoria's voice echoed through the quiet. "We can figure everything out in the morning."

"I guess so." I slid off the hood of the vehicle and pulled the car door open again. The trunk unlocked when I pushed the button beneath the driver's seat.

I rummaged through the dirty clothes, empty boxes and sweaty sports gear inside until I unearthed a baseball bat hidden at the bottom of the mess. My hands trembled as I picked up the weapon.

I couldn't hurt Adam, but I could hurt something that belonged to him.

"Ava—" Victoria said when I swung the bat against the windshield. Cracks spread across the glass. I brought the bat down again and again, throwing my whole weight behind the blows. Splinters grew like spider webs. Victoria laughed when the windshield collapsed. Fragments of glass sprayed across the dashboard.

I handed Victoria the bat and she smashed the rear window. Blood hummed like electricity through my body as we attacked the vehicle. Dented the metal. Scraped the paint. Broke every window, slivers of glass scattering across the pavement.

Exhausted, I dropped the bat. We both laughed—high-pitched and breathless. Victoria slipped a piece of broken glass into her jacket pocket like a trophy, still giggling as she leaned against the dented side of the vehicle.

Eventually we both fell silent, staring at the damage. Shattered windows gaped blindly into the night. Battered metal rose and fell like craters across the body of the vehicle. Something wet ran down my cheeks and I reached up to wipe it away from my face. Tears left slick tracks against my skin. They dripped from my chin and plummeted down onto the ground. Maybe I had been crying this entire time.

"What's wrong?" Victoria asked and touched my shoulder.

"I just wish I never let him kiss me." My voice shook. Shards of glass shimmered beneath my feet and Victoria moved closer. We hesitated when our eyes met, as though we both knew we had approached the edge of something irrevocable.

When she leaned forward and kissed me, it felt as soft and as sweet as a daydream.

CHAPTER 23

During our walk back home, I tossed the bat into the overgrown grass at the side of the road. It rolled into the ditch until the undergrowth hid it from sight, covering up the evidence of our crime. The ruined car sat abandoned somewhere behind us. How long would it take Adam to find it?

He would be furious once he discovered the wreckage.

"Are your parents going to be mad you left without telling them?" I asked, pushing the thought of Adam away. Happiness still glowed inside me, in spite of everything, whenever I remembered the way Victoria had kissed me earlier.

"I don't think so—it's not like I ever really tell them anything," Victoria said with a shrug. Her parents never seemed to notice or care where their daughter went, as long as she met their expectations and never damaged their reputation. I always envied her freedom. A sharp contrast to the careful watch my parents kept over me.

"My mom's going to be so angry. I told her I'd be home this morning." I bent my head down to hide my face as vehicles rushed by on the street.

"You don't have to go back, you know." Victoria touched my hand. "I could hide you at my place. My parents probably won't even notice you're there."

"That's okay," I said, although I wanted nothing more than to stay with Victoria for a little while longer. "I don't want them to think I've gone missing. If I don't show up soon, they'll probably call the police or something."

"Are you going to tell them about Adam?" Victoria asked. Panic fluttered in my chest at the thought of confessing to my parents what had happened in the forest. My father would be upset—maybe enough to confront the Albright family and lose his job at the mining company. And my mother would be so ashamed of me. She'd probably blame me for everything.

"Fuck no—they'd never let me out of the house if they knew." I scuffed at a tall tuft of grass with the toe of my sneaker. "Anyway, I don't care if they're angry. The worst they can do is ground me."

"Are you sure?" Concern quirked at the corners of her mouth.

"Yeah," I said, raising my hand to shield my eyes from the headlights of another vehicle. "If I tell them what he did, we'll probably move away and then I'd never get to see you again."

"I'd really hate that," Victoria said, and I laughed despite myself as we darted through the park, following a well-known shortcut. A headache still pulsed inside my skull, dull and painful. Bruises throbbed like old wounds. My nerves twisted in knots beneath my skin when I wondered how to explain the cuts and scrapes to my parents. If only I could somehow hide all of it, the same way I hid how thin my body became after I stopped eating.

"Thanks for letting me in last night," I said after we emerged back onto the sidewalk. Lights shone from the shuttered windows of the houses like muffled beacons in the night. Silhouettes flickered sometimes behind the drawn curtains.

"Don't worry about it." Victoria shrugged, uncomfortable.

"No, really. I mean it," I insisted and she glanced away. The entire neighborhood was quiet around us—empty yards, shiny new cars parked in every driveway.

"I'm sorry." Her voice was so soft that I had to step closer to hear the words.

"What? Why?"

"I should have done something after you texted me about the party," she said and crossed her arms tight across her body. "Maybe I could have stopped it all from happening."

"It's not your fault," I said, but Victoria's expression never changed. As if she still blamed herself for everything.

We paused when we arrived at the intersection where we usually parted ways. The street twisted like a serpent up to the crest of the hill, where the historic neighborhood rose above the forest. Immense mansions reduced to dim outlines in the darkness. Adam might be up there right now, safe and untouchable inside his family's house.

"I guess I'll see you on Monday." I wondered if I should kiss her again. The idea sent ripples of warmth through my skin. But doubt still clawed at the back of my mind—maybe she would push me away this time. Maybe she only did it in the heat of the moment, or to make me feel better. It would be easier for her to pretend it never happened.

"I'll walk you home," Victoria offered.

"You don't have to." I shook my head, although I didn't want her to leave yet. It would take her over an hour to walk home from my place, and I'd imposed enough on her already. Stolen her entire day.

"But I want to stay with you a little bit longer," Victoria said.

"Okay." I gave in. We took the familiar shortcuts back home in silence. Dashed across small parks and unlit backyards. I grasped for Victoria's hand in the dark and when her fingers clasped mine, I smiled.

The driveway in front of my house lay empty. Nothing moved as we walked toward the front door, like maybe my parents had already left to look for me. I pictured them searching through the neighborhood—probably frantic with worry that I had vanished into the forest. Just like Emily, or the friends who had disappeared while they were growing up here.

I turned the doorknob and the lock held firm. "Fuck."

"What?" Victoria studied my face.

"I left my key in the forest. It was in my jacket," I said and pictured the piece of clothing lying crumpled on the ground. Maybe Adam had noticed it and searched through its pockets. Found a way inside my house.

Maybe he was waiting in there for me right now.

I shoved the unpleasant thought from my mind as Victoria asked, "Are you locked out?"

"No, there's a spare under the mat by the other door." I retreated back down the steps and opened the gate that led into the backyard. The red-rusted hinges groaned when we slipped inside. Shadows hid us from any curious eyes.

"What's that?" Victoria frowned at something drawn across the door as we climbed the porch stairs. Sentences, scribbled across the laminated wood.

slut!

The word was written clearly among more obscene graffiti. Paint still wet enough to leave a smudge against my palm when I touched it. Embarrassment warmed my face. I turned away when Victoria looked at me, too ashamed to meet her gaze.

"Who do you think did it?" I asked. My heart pounded beneath my skin, so hard that for a moment I thought it might stop completely.

"I have no idea. Probably somebody who saw the photo," Victoria speculated as she examined the words scrawled across the side of my house. Expression cold and impassive, as though she were already planning a way to get back at whomever left the message. "Or Adam. He probably figured out we stole his car by now."

"I can't let my parents see this. I have to get rid of it." I unlocked the door and headed into the kitchen to retrieve some spare rags from underneath the sink.

We didn't speak as we scrubbed at the words until they disappeared.

"Why do you think he did it?" I asked after we cleaned the last smudges of paint away.

"What?" Victoria climbed to her feet.

"Why did he leave me in the forest—what do you think he was trying to do?" The porch lamp cast a soft pool of light around us. It caught Victoria's eyes when she studied my face. This time, I didn't turn away.

"He probably thought he could leave you as an offering." Victoria chose each word carefully, as though she were trying to decide how much to tell me about the legends passed down by her family. "That something in there would grant his wish if he left you as a gift."

"You really don't believe any of the stories about the forest?"

"No. But Adam does." Victoria glanced at the trees crowded against the edges of the yard.

"What do you think he wished for?" My skin prickled as I pictured the empty grove of hawthorn trees. How something had moved unseen at the edges of the clearing. Paced, actually—like it was ravenous.

"I don't know. Maybe he wanted his dad to come home," Victoria suggested, and I said nothing, remembering the catch in Adam's voice when he asked me what it was like at the hospital. How worry clouded his face whenever he talked about his father.

Victoria pressed a quick kiss against my mouth before she left. The gate slammed shut as she walked down the driveway and disappeared into the dark. I paused when I opened the door of my house, standing still to listen to the silence.

Nothing moved for several long minutes. Floorboards creaked beneath my light footsteps as I crept down the hallway to my bedroom. I closed the curtains to block out the sight of Reachwood Forest waiting outside before I turned off the light.

TODAY

CHAPTER 24

Who left adam in the forest?

The question is scrawled across the door when I venture outside in the morning. Etched in fresh paint, the words rest like a threat against the doorway's wooden surface. My breath catches, so unexpected I almost choke.

Who left the message?

My eyes glance around the houses on the street. Across vacant driveways, shuttered windows and closely mown yards. Probably the same person who called me earlier. Maybe a neighbor who remembered the rumors leveled against me after Adam's body was found in the forest. Or somebody from the Albright family—Ambrose?—determined to let me know Adam's death hadn't been forgotten. Or maybe my ex-husband followed me here and left the words to frighten me back to the city.

But that's impossible—I never told him about Adam.

The faint hum of the television drifts from the kitchen while Mother cooks breakfast. My stomach lurches at the heavy smell of food as I hurry to the bathroom, skirting around the half-packed boxes stacked in the hall. Careful not to make a sound and alert her that something is wrong.

I lock the door behind me and lean back against the wall. My heart beats fast. I gasp for breath as a panic attack sends a sudden surge of adrenaline trembling through my body. My eyes rest on the medicine cabinet and I yank the door open, scrabbling for my medication.

I rummage through vials of moisturizer and packages of bandages until my fingers close around the prescription bottle. Pushing down on the cap, I twist until it springs open and shake a painkiller into my hand. It rests white against the red scar that crosses the center of my palm.

I place the pill on the tip of my tongue and wash it down with a sip of water. Before I replace the plastic container in the cabinet, I count out the capsules at the bottom of the bottle.

Fewer than I remember.

"What's wrong?" Mother looks up from the stove when I walk into the kitchen. Worry wrinkles the skin on her forehead as her eyes travel across my face. I turn away and kneel to search through the clutter of cleaning supplies beneath the sink for something to scrub away the mess outside. Marjorie's bedroom door opens, and her footsteps travel down the hallway. The shower sputters to life in the bathroom a few moments later. Water rattles through the pipes.

"What's wrong?" Mother repeats as she follows me back down the hallway. Her face drains of color when I open the door to reveal the message scrawled across it.

"How long has that been there?" she asks. Her eyes dart back and forth across the empty street, as though her first concern is that one of the neighbors will notice it and start to gossip.

"How should I know? Probably since sometime last night," I say. My voice quivers. Mother grabs my wrist and drags me back inside the house like I'm still a child. She closes the door tight and I twist free of her grasp, folding my arms across my chest.

"Did you do something?" she demands.

"What?" I bristle.

"Did you do something to make anyone angry?" She peeks through the blinds. The sun has started to rise, coloring the clouded sky with pastel pink and orange shades of light.

"No, I've barely talked to anyone since I got here," I protest. Of course she would find a way to make this my fault. Although I've only been here for just over a month now—hardly long enough to make somebody this angry.

Not unless we share some of the same troubled history.

"Are you sure you didn't do something?" Mother asks. I turn back toward the kitchen but she grabs my arm and yanks me to a halt. "Where are you going?"

"To call the police." I shake her hand from my elbow and hurry into the kitchen. Charred bacon still sizzles on the stove. I turn off the burner as black smoke spirals toward the ceiling. "We need to report this."

"Are you sure that's a good idea—what if they start asking questions about him again?"

"I don't care." I retrieve my phone from the countertop, hesitating as my fingers hover above the smooth screen. She's right. This might ignite enough interest in Adam's death to reopen the cold investigation. I'd have to sit through another interrogation. Answer the same questions they asked me fifteen years ago. And maybe this time they would dig a little deeper.

Discover my secrets.

"You should just clean it off. Before the whole neighborhood starts to talk." Mother snatches at my phone. I pull it away before her fingers can close around its smooth plastic case.

"They're not going to stop. Even if we cover it up," I say, but I pause after I unlock my phone to type the emergency number onto the keypad. Still reluctant to involve the police and draw any more attention back to Adam's case. Mother lunges for my phone again before I can press the call button. It falls onto the stone tiles and the screen shatters. Shards of glass scatter across the floor.

"What's going on?" Marjorie appears in the doorway, towel wrapped around her head to cover her damp hair. Her sleepy eyes travel across our faces.

"Nothing." Mother brushes off the question. I crouch down to sweep the pieces of glass into a neat pile. The sharp edges glimmer. One of the jagged fragments catches my skin and opens a ragged cut across my thumb.

"Don't come in here," I warn Marjorie. "There's glass everywhere."

"What happened to your phone?" Marjorie asks. She stares at its smashed screen when I set it down on the table. Although it will be expensive to replace, some small part of me feels almost relieved. At least I won't receive any more calls from unknown numbers. No more breathing on the other end of the line, like somebody wants me to know they're watching me.

"I dropped it." My voice never changes when I lie. A reflex left over from my marriage. Suspicion shadows Marjorie's face as she glances between us.

"I'll buy you a new one," Mother offers as I pour a bowl of cereal for Marjorie. The expression on her face almost looks guilty.

"Take this to your room. Get ready for school." I pass the bowl to Marjorie. She smiles at me before she disappears back down the hallway toward her bedroom.

"I'm sorry," Mother says after the bedroom door clicks shut. She folds her hands together. "I didn't mean to—it was an accident."

"I know." I search through the pantry for the broom, sweeping the rest of the glass into the dust pan. The fragile edges chime together as I empty it into the garbage.

"Anyway, don't worry about it." Mother dismisses my concerns. "It's probably nothing. Some kids probably left it as a prank or something."

"Whatever." I retrieve a bottle of cleaning fluid and some gloves from underneath the sink. Mother retreats from the kitchen as I pull them on, smooth latex sliding over my skin. The question rests like an omen against the front door when I return to the porch.

We can't stay here any longer.

Faint splotches of paint still stain the front door when Marjorie follows me outside later. Dressed and ready for school, bubblegum-pink backpack slung over her shoulders. If she notices the last traces of the message, she doesn't say anything as we climb inside the vehicle. I drive away fast, foot pushed hard against the gas pedal. The house vanishes behind us.

"Did something bad happen?" Marjorie asks. I don't turn to look at her as I navigate through the early morning traffic that streams through the streets of Reachwood.

"Don't worry about it," I say. My eyes dart to the rearview mirror to check the next lane before I merge, swerving into the empty space.

"But what were you arguing about before?" Marjorie persists.

"Nothing important." My fingers tighten against the wheel as the car idles at a red light.

"Are you sure?" Marjorie studies me like she knows I'm lying. Her eyes examine the new cut on my thumb. "It looked like she hurt you."

"Someone vandalized the house last night," I say when the light turns green again.

"What? Why?" Marjorie changes the playlist on her phone as I wait for a gap in the oncoming traffic to turn left. She shuffles between several songs from her favorite boy band before she decides on one she likes and settles into her seat.

"It doesn't matter." I turn the car onto the busy road that leads to the school. "I should never have come back. We're leaving this weekend."

"I don't want to go." Her lip juts out in a stubborn pout. "You said we'd be safe if we stayed here."

"I was wrong." I park the car in front of Reachwood High School. Marjorie sinks into her seat and crosses her arms across her chest. The muffled noise of the schoolyard drifts through the window as children chatter and laugh before the start of class.

"Who doesn't want us to be here?" She digs the toes of her sneakers hard against the plastic floor mats. Something flashes in her eyes for a moment—a trace of the same anger I saw only once before, when she had hurt that other girl back at her old school. It darkens her face before it vanishes again. Quick enough to make me wonder if I had only imagined it.

"I have no idea," I say, but I picture my old classmates and childhood friends. None of them would benefit from unearthing our long-kept secrets or from forcing the police to ask more questions about Adam's death.

None of them except Ambrose.

"You can't keep running away from everything forever." Marjorie unbuckles her seatbelt and scoops her backpack up from the floor. I open my mouth to protest that I'm not running away. I'm just trying to keep her safe. But she slams the door shut before I can say anything. When someone waves at her, she disappears into a pack of teenagers.

She never looks back.

CHAPTER 25

"Ava, what are you doing here?" Victoria asks. I shuffle my feet on the mat and run my wounded thumb along the ragged scar that interrupts the skin of my palm. The friction makes the fresh laceration tingle as I search for the words to explain why I've shown up unannounced this early in the morning. I can't admit the real reason: I always flee to her at the first sign of trouble.

"I'm sorry I didn't text you before I drove over," I apologize finally. "My phone is broken. I was hoping—can I talk to you for a moment?"

"Of course," Victoria says and steps back to let me inside. "Are you alright?"

"Yeah. Why?" The house sits as quiet as a tomb. We walk through its spacious rooms, clean and empty enough to make me wonder if maybe Cyril and Victoria store most of their personal belongings in separate spaces. Hidden away from each other.

"You're bleeding."

"Oh—this is nothing." I turn my hand to cover the fresh injury from view. "I cut myself while I was picking up some glass."

"I'll get you a bandage."

Blood oozes from my thumb as we climb the long staircase. Victoria pushes open the door to her workshop to reveal the stained glass windows facing out toward Reachwood Forest. Sunlight tumbles through the glass. It casts multicolored patterns across the floor while she rummages through her desk.

More bracelets and brooches gleam on the tabletop. Several wax rings rest inside rubber molds, waiting to be cut free and encased in plaster before Victoria melts them away to replicate the design in gold later. The horned skulls of trophy animals rest on a bench near the window, smooth bones swirled with the precious metal.

"Did Cyril kill these, too?" I ask.

"Yeah, he did." Victoria glances at the skulls before she hands me a bandage.

"They're beautiful." I fumble to pull it open.

"I've never really liked them." Victoria studies the gilded bones. Maybe they hit too close to home. Remind Victoria too much of her own life, displayed at Cyril's side like a trophy wife. "Do you want something to drink?"

"Sure," I say, and she picks up the half-empty wine bottle resting on her desk. I wrap the gauze around the cut on my thumb as she pours the red liquid into two glasses. It's too early to start drinking—just past nine in the morning. But I need something to dampen the panic that's been welling inside me ever since I discovered the question written across my front door.

I don't want to think about Adam or the forest.

"So, what did you want to talk about?" Victoria asks after she passes a glass to me. I take a quick sip as my eyes drift to the framed pictures on the wall behind her. Photos showing how much Catherine and Virgil have grown over the years. Their faces laugh, trapped behind clear glass.

No photos display Cyril and Victoria together, except for the one taken on their wedding day. Victoria looks young and sullen, dressed in bridal white. She glances somewhere off to the side as Cyril smiles at the camera. I wonder again what had happened to make her marry him. If she grew closer to him after Adam's death.

After I left.

"Ava?" Victoria stares at me.

"What?" I blink, shaken from my thoughts.

"You said you wanted to talk—is everything okay? Did your husband follow you here after all?" Concern crosses her face as I picture the question scrawled across the front door this morning.

Could he have left it?

The idea is ridiculous. But maybe he talked to someone in Reachwood and found out about what happened to Adam in the forest. Wrote those words to frighten me away from the safety of my childhood neighborhood.

"I haven't heard from him since we moved here. At least, not for sure," I say, remembering the strange call I received after the Reachwood Festival. My hands shake as I raise my wineglass to take another sip of the sweet liquid. "But I found a knife on my doorstep."

"Was it—?"

"It was Adam's." The taste clings to the inside of my mouth. "I got rid of it. But someone left a message on my door this morning. Asking who left him in the forest."

"Did you see who did it?"

"No, I have no idea." I shake my head. "But somebody's not happy I moved back here."

"Probably. You left so suddenly after they found Adam's body," Victoria says and turns toward the window. The forest stretches out below, deep and unknowable. "Everybody talked about it, you know—I couldn't walk two steps without hearing some kind of new gossip."

"What did they say?" I ask. The wine turns sour against my tongue.

"Nothing important. I told them to stop it."

"I ran into Ambrose during the search for Kristen. Do you think he'd do something like this?" My words come out slow and hesitant. I don't want to believe Ambrose is behind all this. Not when we used to be friends.

But I can't forget the cold way he spoke to me. If he really believes I'm responsible for his brother's murder, he might have left the question to spur another investigation.

Before I escape again.

"Maybe. He caused all kinds of problems after Adam died." Victoria's expression grows thoughtful. "He even showed up here once or twice to accuse us of having something to do with it. We actually had to take out a restraining order against him."

"He knows I saw Adam's body in the grove," I say and take another sip of wine. Desperate to stifle the anxiety fluttering inside of me. "And that I never told anybody about it."

"How did he know that?" She frowns.

"I'm still not sure—maybe he recognized the gift I left there or something," I say, and she remains quiet. Probably considering what else he might know. If he had also noticed the offerings she left in the grove.

"So what? Plenty of kids left gifts there over the years. I wouldn't worry too much about it." Victoria laughs after a moment. Words flippant, as if she's trying to convince herself as well. "He's been trying to open the case for years and hasn't succeeded yet."

"I guess so," I say. Maybe Ambrose would back down if I threatened him with another restraining order. Confronted him now, when he's least expecting it. I don't want to receive any more threats before I leave this weekend.

No more questions about Adam's death.

"It was a bad idea to come back here," I say after several seconds pass in silence. Nothing has changed—Reachwood still remains divided, even though Adam's death happened a long time ago. His murder festers like an untreated wound below the neighborhood's picturesque surface.

I'll never escape the rumors for as long as I stay here.

"Are you leaving again?" Victoria asks, and the weight of our history settles between us. Filled with the things I should have said before I left and the secrets we shared. For a moment, I wonder what would have happened if we had just kept driving after we stole Adam's car fifteen years ago. If we would have stayed together and been happy, or if the pressure from our families would have torn us apart eventually.

"Yeah. This weekend," I say, draining the last remnants of my drink. The empty glass clicks when I set it down on the table.

"I'm glad you decided to say goodbye this time." Victoria taps her manicured fingernails against the crystal edges of her glass. Guilt presses against my chest. "Do you know where you're going to go?"

"Not yet. Somewhere in the city, I guess," I say, although I have no idea how I'm going to afford it. At least not until I receive everything back from the divorce settlement.

"Does Marjorie want to leave, too?"

"Not really. I'm worried about her, actually." I bite down on my lip.

"Why?"

"She's been drawn to the forest from the very first moment she saw it. I think someone's been telling her stories about it—she asked me if it's true that something in there grants wishes." My mouth grows dry as I remember the keen interest painted across Marjorie's face when she asked the question. How her eyes focus sometimes on the forest outside her bedroom window.

"She's friends with Aidan, right?" Victoria asks.

"Yeah." I picture the way Aidan follows Marjorie outside every day after school.

"If you let her spend time with him alone, who knows what he's told her."

"Can I ask you something else?" I change the subject.

"Of course." Victoria says. She leans closer, and emotions I had tried so hard to bury stir inside me. For a brief second, I wonder if Victoria feels the same way—but she's changed so much since I left.

The girl I knew before might as well be dead.

"Have Catherine and Virgil said anything about Marjorie?" I ask.

"I don't think so. Why?"

"I was wondering how she's doing in school. If maybe the other kids are bullying her or something." I force the nervous words out. My lungs constrict, tight enough that I struggle to breathe. "One of them could have left that message as a prank this morning."

"They've never mentioned anything. But I'll ask when they come back from school."

"Thanks." Unexpected tears well at the corners of my eyes. I blink them away.

"Don't worry about it." Victoria touches my shoulder. "If she's anything like you, I'm sure all the kids love her at school."

"Thanks, but—Marjorie has her father's temper."

"What do you mean?"

"People get hurt when she gets angry," I say, remembering the quick kind of viciousness Marjorie sometimes displays when things don't go her way. How she went straight for that other girl's face, like she knew it would hurt her the most. "I was thinking maybe she got into a fight with somebody, or something."

"If anything like that happened, I'm sure you'd know about it."

"I hope so." I give her a shaky smile before I turn toward the door. "I should get going, though. I still need to buy a new phone."

We don't speak as we walk downstairs. The driveway outside sits wide and empty, bordered on both sides by manicured hedges that rise like walls from the earth. Victoria searches through the closet for my jacket.

"Will this be the last time I see you?" Victoria asks when I open the door. The wind blows into the house, pulling at our hair and clothes. I fold my arms against my chest to protect my body from the cold.

"I don't know yet—I'd like to see you again, before I go." I pause in the doorway. Dead leaves whirl across the lawn outside like a bright hurricane. "Have you ever thought about leaving, too?"

"Not really," Victoria says. She takes another sip of wine as clouds cover the sun in the sky. "You can't leave behind your history. My family, this place—I'll always carry it with me."

Before I leave, she embraces me—holding me close enough to make me wonder if she knows I don't want her to let me go.

CHAPTER 26

A slow ache grows in my wrist as I drive to the Albright house late in the afternoon, before Marjorie returns home from school. I stop by the mall first to purchase a new phone, reluctant to confront Ambrose alone. The machine takes a few moments to process the charge after I swipe my card. I exhale after the purchase is approved.

Hopefully Mother will transfer the money for the replacement soon.

The Albright family still lives in the middle of the wealthy enclave, in the same home their family has inhabited for over a century. Its walls rise above me when I brake in front of its iron gates. My voice shakes when I press the bell and state my name into the intercom. Victoria warned me to stay away from Ambrose. Maybe this isn't the best decision.

But maybe the threats will stop if I talk to him.

The gates swing open a few moments later. My wrist twinges again when I park the car in front of the house, and my fingers curl inward. The gabled windows of the mansion watch like vacant eyes as I rummage through my purse, and I picture Ambrose staring out at me, hidden somewhere inside just out of sight. My hand closes around my bottle of painkillers and I hesitate. It's too soon to take another one.

But I hate the way the pain reminds me of my ex-husband.

I swallow the pill down dry before I count the capsules at the bottom of the container. None have disappeared since the last time I checked this morning. But it's still not enough. It won't even last the rest of the month.

Ambrose waits in the doorway when I climb out of the car. Eyes wary, he studies my face as I walk up the steps toward the house, searching for the right words to say. Still not sure if this will work or if I'm making a mistake.

Would he even believe me if I explained everything?

"What are you doing here?" Ambrose asks. He never moves from the door, blocking the entrance with his body.

"You need to stop," I say and wait for a reaction. Any kind of indication that he left the message on my front door this morning. But I don't see anything.

"What are you talking about?" Ambrose frowns.

"Someone's trying to scare me out of here." I examine his expression again. Still looking for any hint of guilt or recognition. Any sign that he might be behind the call after the celebration at Victoria's house, or the knife left on my porch. "I just wanted to let you know you succeeded. We're leaving this weekend."

"I still don't know what you're talking about," Ambrose says. Tone hard and flat, just like when he asked me why I really moved back here. Vehicles rush by on the street outside. Tires grind against the asphalt as he says, "I didn't do anything. Really."

"You expect me to believe that?" Frustration roughens my voice. "Who else would write a message asking who left Adam in the forest?"

"Who knows?" Ambrose leans against the doorframe. His eyes narrow as he says, "Most people still remember what happened between you two before he died."

"It didn't just happen—he started it," I snap, remembering the grainy picture on the screen of Victoria's phone. My naked body in the grove, sent to everyone at school. "He didn't have to take that photo. Or show it to everybody."

"I know," Ambrose says, and the hard edges of his face soften. Something like regret flickers through his eyes, so quick I almost miss it. "We fought about it a lot before he died. I told him it was a shitty thing to do to you."

"I can't convince you I didn't hurt him," I say as the breeze buffets my body. It carries a chill with it, like a signal that autumn is drawing closer to winter. "But I didn't. So please just—"

"If you really didn't hurt him, why didn't you say anything?" Ambrose cuts off my words. "I know you saw his body."

"You can't prove that," I say as Adam's dead eyes flash through my mind, stiff lips frozen in a rigid smile. Leaves and flowers decorated his brow like a crown, petals stark white against the blood-soaked ground beneath his body. Who left them in his hair? We all visited his body in the days leading up to its discovery. Left gifts there like apologies for what happened to him. It could have been any one of us. But maybe it was something else.

Something from the forest itself.

"I found him, you know." Ambrose's voice lowers. "When he didn't show up for a few days, I checked the grove. I saw your ring there—the one Victoria gave you."

"I left it there as a gift," I protest. "That doesn't mean I killed him."

"I tried to show it to the police. But when I went back again, I couldn't find it," he says and my mind flits to the piles of offerings nestled between the roots of the trees. Even if the police combed through the entire grove, the ring was small enough to escape notice. The wind could have buried it beneath dirt and dead leaves, or small animals could have carried it away. It would be easy to miss it.

Or maybe something else took it.

"I *did* see his body out there," I admit finally. "But I never said anything because I was scared. I'm sorry."

"I'm sorry, too." Ambrose sighs. He looks tired as he steps back from the door to let me inside the house. "It's just—it's been so many years and I still have no idea what really happened to him."

I linger on the threshold. Not sure if he's telling the truth or lying to my face. He could just be playing dumb to make me feel safe before he strikes again. The same way an animal sometimes plays with its prey. But my wrist stings as I stand in the doorway, pain intense and unexpected enough to make me lose my breath.

I still don't trust him. Not really.

But maybe Ambrose can help me.

"My whole life fell apart after he died. I guess yours did, too." Ambrose closes the door tight after I step inside the house. For a moment, I let myself imagine what life would be like if Adam had never died inside the forest. I would never have lived beneath a cloud of suspicion. Never fled Reachwood or met my ex-husband.

My life would be so different.

"You could say that." I fake a smile as I follow him through the rooms of the home. It looks the same as it did when we were children—tall walls rise above our heads, ceilings high enough to make me feel small in comparison. The wheelchairs, lifts and medical equipment are new, however. Evidence of his now-frail parents.

"I just wish there was something I could do to fix everything. For both of us," Ambrose says as we enter the kitchen. The house is quiet enough to seem completely vacant. Maybe his parents have left for a doctor's appointment, or to visit their friends. My wrist throbs again.

Now is my chance.

"You actually might be able to help me with something." My fingers fumble against the prescription container as I pull it from my purse. "Do you still sell these?"

"You'll be in deep shit if you get caught with these without a prescription." His eyes flick back and forth across the label. "Why do you need them?"

"My ex-husband broke my wrist. Badly," I say. Not eager to talk about what happened before I returned to Reachwood. But I need those pills.

If Ambrose feels sorry for me, he might be convinced to help me. "I had surgery to fix it, but it still hurts a lot."

"I didn't know." Ambrose shrugs, uncomfortable.

"I never told anybody." I fold my arms across my chest. "Anyway, I'm on my last refill and I don't have a new doctor—at least not yet. I was hoping you could help fix that."

"Maybe. I have a buddy who skims pills from the clinic he works at." Ambrose shifts his weight from foot to foot. "I could ask him to get some for you. But if you want them, you're going to have to do something for me, too."

"Like what?" My voice tightens.

"I saw you talking to Victoria at the festival. How is she?"

"She's fine. Why?" I ask, surprised.

"I haven't talked to her or Cyril since I lost my position in the company. Did she say anything about me?" he asks, and his voice hardens. So that's what he expects in exchange for the pills. Information about Victoria, Cyril and the business he was forced out of after his brother's death.

"Not really," I lie as I remember what Victoria had told me earlier. How Ambrose hurled so many accusations at her that she had to take out a restraining order. I can't betray her. Not even for more medication. "I don't know anything."

"Then I'm afraid I can't help you." Ambrose shakes his head.

"Please. I need them." My voice wavers.

"There's something else you could do," he says after a moment. Something ravenous surfaces in his eyes. "I always liked you. Maybe I could be persuaded to help if you gave me something else."

He leans in to kiss me, but I turn my head and his lips press against the edge of my mouth instead. I haven't touched anyone since I left my ex-husband. Can't even bring myself to imagine it. Not yet, with the consequences of my last relationship still fresh in my memory.

Except when I look at Victoria.

"I can't." I step back.

"I guess you're out of luck then." He still doesn't move, looming tall in front of me just like my ex-husband. My breath quickens as panic shivers across my skin.

We both jump when the front door swings open. Ambrose steps away fast as voices fill the hallway, traveling closer until two children burst into the kitchen. Aidan and Marjorie grin as they shrug out of their backpacks. Their cheeks flush pink from the long walk outside.

"Mom? What are you doing here?" Marjorie stares at me.

"Why are you here?" I counter her question. "I thought you were studying with Catherine and Virgil today."

"They weren't feeling good, so they went home after class. I thought I'd study with Aidan instead. He's in our project group, too," Marjorie says, and Aidan smiles at me. The heat leaves my body.

"I was about to go." I turn toward the front door. "You can come home with me."

"I don't want to." Marjorie plants her feet firm on the floor. "I want to spend more time with Aidan before we move."

"I'm sure Ambrose wasn't expecting to have to entertain you after school."

"She can stay. It's no problem." Ambrose leans against the wall. My stomach drops at the thought of leaving her alone with him. Of all the things he could tell her. Stories about my past, best left forgotten. Or the real reason why I came to see him today. Marjorie and Aidan stay silent, and I study their faces for a moment, searching for—something.

"You can study at home." Resolve sharpens my voice. Marjorie opens her mouth like she wants to argue more before she closes it again. She sulks as she follows me outside. I blink in the sunlight.

"Let me know if you change your mind," Ambrose says. Marjorie's curious eyes dart between our faces.

"I will." I bite down on the inside of my cheek and repeat to myself that I don't really need the pills. No matter how much my body shakes whenever I take one late.

"Guess I'll see you soon." He closes the door, and I take a breath of fresh air.

It smells dry and cold, like the first warning of snow.

CHAPTER 27

don't change my mind about the pills before we leave, although the pain
from my injured wrist keeps breaking through more and more quickly
after each dose. A persistent ache grows in my forearm as we carry our
belongings to the car. My fingers stiffen when I load the heavy suitcases
inside the trunk. Not quite through my supply yet, but I'll finish it soon.

After that, I don't know what I'll do.

Marjorie pouts as she drags her bags out of the house, scuffing her
sneakers against the concrete while the suburb wakes up around us. Lights
turn on one by one in every bedroom. Garage doors grate open to release
minivans onto the street.

"Here—let me take that." My father reaches for Marjorie's suitcase. She
hands it to him and he stacks it on top of the others already piled in the
back seat. Mother sips coffee on the porch. She doesn't say anything as we
move back and forth, packing the last bags inside the car.

"Thanks for letting us stay here while I was getting everything together,"
I say after my father takes the last suitcase from me. Sweat slides down the
straight line of my spine as he slams the trunk shut. "I'll call you when we
reach Portland."

"Do you have somewhere to stay?" Concern furrows his face as he
embraces me.

"Yeah—I've booked a hotel for a few days. Until we find a place to rent." I still don't know how I'm going to afford it. Maybe I'll pawn off a few of the expensive items I managed to bring with me when we fled the city. Or find a place to work until I finally get the money from the divorce settlement.

"Bye. I'll miss you." Marjorie hugs him after I pull away.

"I'll miss you, too." He holds her close and an unexpected pang runs through my chest. I'll miss him, too—despite everything, it's been nice to see him again. If he had ever been disappointed by any of my choices, he had never shown it.

Not like Mother had.

"We'll come back and visit." Marjorie glances at me as she steps back. "Won't we?"

"Of course," I say and regret it immediately when her gaze strays to the trees behind the house. A small smile lifts the edges of her mouth.

"Stay safe." Mother waves at us from the porch. My eyes drift over her shoulder to the faint traces of paint that still stain the front door. The last remnants of the question someone scrawled against its wooden surface.

"I will. Don't worry," I say and hope I'm not making a mistake. Not falling straight into some deranged plot my ex-husband made up to drive me away from Reachwood. To frighten me back to the city, where he still waits for me.

"You can always call us if you need anything," my father says as I open the car door. Marjorie sits in the passenger seat, eyes focused on the forest outside like she's trying to memorize it. Unease shifts inside me at the intensity on her face.

She remains quiet as I back out of the driveway and turn onto the street that leads through the neighborhood. If I drive fast, it will take us just over an hour to reach the city. Relief lightens my body.

I press down on the gas pedal, eager to leave Reachwood behind me.

Marjorie doesn't say anything for several long minutes, uncharacteristically silent as suburban houses pass by outside.

"How are you feeling?" I finally ask.

"How do you think I'm feeling?" She throws the question back at me. We turn toward the forest and I catch a glimpse of the mansions on the crest of the hill. Barely visible from this distance. Victoria is still up there somewhere—maybe asleep, or working on a piece of jewelry. Something heavy settles against my chest as I remember the expression on her face when she said she could never leave this place.

"I'm sorry," I say as the steering wheel vibrates beneath my fingers. The engine rumbles hard enough to shake the car. "I know I told you we'd be safe here, but I think we're better off in the city."

"You don't know that." Marjorie's eyes flash. "We shouldn't leave just because someone doesn't want you back here. You always run away from anything that scares you."

"That's not true." My voice never changes, although her accusation hits a little too close for comfort. "And anyway, we're not safe here either."

"But at least Dad won't come after us." Marjorie sinks down in her seat. I brake for a red light and search for the words to convince her we'll be safer in the city. Far away from the forest and the rumors about Adam's death. We have to leave.

Somebody here still hasn't forgiven me.

The light turns green again. I press down on the gas pedal and the engine whirrs as the vehicle struggles to speed up. I stamp my foot down harder against the accelerator as another car honks behind me. Marjorie twists in her seat to glare at them through the rear window.

The vehicle finally rolls through the intersection, and I sigh. But my relief is short-lived: it speeds up but then shudders as I steer through the ravine.

All of the lights wink to life on the dashboard, blinking like warning signs. The car jolts again and slows on the open road.

The engine grinds to a halt in the middle of the next intersection. I flash my hazard lights as more vehicles honk behind me. Exhaust spews from the tailpipe, engulfing the car in smoke. Cars swerve around us, and drivers glower at me through their windshields.

"What happened?" Marjorie asks and leans forward in her seat.

"I don't know. It stopped working," I say, twisting the key again and again, like maybe that will be enough to restart the engine. But it never roars back to life.

"Fuck." I groan and rest my head against the steering wheel as more cars rush past on the street outside. I was so close. So fucking close to escaping this place forever.

After several more attempts to revive the dead engine, I pull my new phone out of my purse to call a tow truck. Marjorie plays a game on her phone in the passenger seat as I give them directions to our location. Her fingers flash rapidly across the smooth screen.

"What are you going to do now?" she asks when I end the call. My chest rises and falls with each shallow breath. I clench my hands tight in my lap.

"Nothing. We'll have to wait until they take it to the shop," I say and open my door to step out of the car, eager to escape the enclosed space. Marjorie climbs out of the vehicle and follows me to the edge of the street.

"So, we're going to stay here a little longer?" Hope fills her voice.

"I guess." My shoulders slump. "But only until they figure out what's wrong with it."

"I don't want to leave. I really like it here." Her face glows with triumph.

"Well, it looks like we're stuck here now." I sigh, running a hand through my hair as the tow truck pulls up. I give them my contact information while they load my car onto the back of their vehicle.

After the tow truck drives away, I unlock my phone again to call my parents. But I pause before I type their number onto the screen. Not ready to admit my defeat to anybody.

"Let's walk home," I say. It's not far, after all. Barely a twenty-minute hike back to where we started.

"Maybe this is a sign that we're not supposed to go." Marjorie practically skips down the side of the road on the way back home.

"I don't think so." My throat tightens. Marjorie smiles when we emerge from the ravine and the familiar neighborhood stretches out before us. Her eyes linger on the forest for one long moment. The trees overflow from the steep valley to spread out behind the suburb like some kind of disease. Branches grasp upward, attempting to pluck the sun from the sky. An unwelcome thought crosses my mind.

Maybe something inside Reachwood Forest doesn't want us to leave.

CHAPTER 28

stay awake all night—huddled on my side, eyes wide open. The moon rises and falls in the sky, reduced to a dim outline by the curtains I drew across the windows before I climbed into bed. Nocturnal animals call to each other in the forest. My breath catches each time something stirs outside the house. Trapped here like prey while I wait for the malevolent presence that has haunted me ever since I returned home to reveal its face. Maybe Marjorie's right.

I can't just keep running away.

"Can I borrow the car this morning?" I ask when I venture into the kitchen, dressed in some of my best clothes. Bright-eyed despite my fitful sleep, hair styled in an intricate braid. Breakfast steams on the counter. My stomach churns at the smell.

"Why?" Mother raises an overplucked eyebrow. She sits at the head of the table and spreads strawberry jam across a piece of toast. Red enough to remind me of blood.

"I thought I'd visit the cemetery," I say as I take a seat. Maybe if I visit the place where Adam's body is buried, I might be able to get over it. Find some kind of closure.

"Why do you want to go there?" Mother's mouth puckers into a frown. Marjorie stands beside my father as he cooks an omelet, frying pan simmering on the stovetop. She hands him ingredients and he tosses them into the mixture. Shadows darken the soft skin beneath her eyes, like maybe she had crept outside to visit her friends last night.

"It's been a long time since I left flowers for grandma and grandpa."

"You never cared before," Mother observes. It's true—even as a teenager, I never accompanied my parents on their annual journey to the cemetery. The long rows of weatherworn gravestones always repulsed me. A morbid reminder that everyone dies eventually. "What made you change your mind?"

"Nothing," I say as I rise to my feet. "I just thought it would be a nice thing to do."

"It's fine." My father passes Marjorie the frying pan. She flips over the omelet as he says, "Just bring the car back before tonight."

"Thanks." I retreat to the doorway.

"Have you heard anything back from the shop yet—will they be able to fix your engine soon?" he asks, and Marjorie finally glances away from the stove. Her brow furrows.

"They still don't know what's wrong with it," I say. Unease pinches beneath my ribs. Still no explanation for why the car stopped working. Almost as though I've been cursed to remain in Reachwood forever.

To never escape.

"Don't forget you need to help us move out if you want to live in this house," Mother says, as if I haven't spent the last few weeks packing away their belongings. Her bleached teeth gleam as she speaks. "We found a place we like yesterday. Hopefully we'll close on it soon."

"I didn't forget. I'll work on it some more later—maybe in the evening." I pluck the keys from the counter and hesitate before I say, "Thanks again for letting us stay here a little longer. I know it's been inconvenient."

"Don't worry about it. Stay as long as you want," my father says. A frown pulls Mother's eyebrows downward like she disagrees with him. The first pinpricks of annoyance dart down my spine and my body stiffens.

"I've been misplacing things ever since you moved back," Mother pushes her plate away and changes the subject. "Like my glasses—have you seen them?"

"No, I haven't." I swallow down my temper. "Maybe you forgot where you left them."

"Yeah, old people forget everything." Marjorie brings her breakfast to the table and sits down. Triumph shines on her face when Mother glares at her, like she knows she's hit Mother where it hurts the most. I stifle a smile and turn toward the front door.

"See you later," Marjorie says, loud enough to carry down the hallway.

"Have a good day." I slip into my jacket and button it up to my throat. The woolen fabric scratches my skin as I leave the house.

<hr />

I drive the borrowed car until the cemetery appears on my right. Shiny new tombstones rise in straight lines as I steer through its open gates. The wheels bump across rough ground as I follow the narrow dirt road that twists through the graveyard.

The headstones grow older as I draw closer to the plots where members of the three most powerful families in Reachwood lie buried. Crooked rows poke up from the frozen earth, stone faces cracked and mottled with age. Moss-covered marble angels cover their eyes. Withered flowers litter the ground.

I park the car underneath a tall tree in the oldest section of the cemetery and struggle to catch my breath. Adam lies within the Albright family's plot somewhere nearby, body entombed inside one of the intricate stone mausoleums that rise like shrines from the dirt. Too close for any semblance of comfort.

I search through the contents of my purse until my grip closes around my prescription bottle. After I swallow another painkiller, I roll down my window and close my eyes, waiting for the drug to slow my breathing and calm my rapid heartbeat. I should have rationed the pills more carefully—I'll run out any day now. If I want more, I'll have to contact Ambrose and let him know I've changed my mind. Trade information or sex in exchange for the medication. But I'm not that desperate.

At least not yet.

The cemetery stretches out before me, silent and empty. Nothing stirs as the sun climbs toward the center of the sky. Feeble rays of light illuminate the names inscribed on the graves.

Maybe paying a visit to Adam's tomb will bring me some kind of closure—a reassurance this is really over. Or maybe it won't bring me anything, and his ghost will follow me through my dreams whenever I fall asleep. I drum my fingers against the arm rest as I wait for the opiates to hit my system. Impatient to feel nothing again.

The drugs still haven't done anything by the time I work up the courage to leave the vehicle. I long for the comforting numbness as I walk slowly through the rows of tombs and gravestones, reading the surnames etched onto their weathered faces. Reachwood Forest borders the edges of the cemetery. Trees tangle against the wire fence. Weeds sprout from the grass that grows wild across untended plots. Some areas cave inward, as if the lid of a coffin has collapsed below the surface of the earth.

Nausea surges up my throat when I reach the Albright family's plot of land. The scar on my palm aches as I read the name carved over the awning of the first tomb. But it's not Adam's final resting place—just the grave of a distant relative who died at the start of the last century and who shared the same name.

I continue down the row of mausoleums and elaborate headstones, gnawing on the inside of my cheek. My knees wobble as I take one unsteady step after another, reading names under my breath. All members of the Albright family, interred in this corner of the cemetery for over a century. I've seen several of the names before, written across buildings donated to the community. They all lived lives of luxury, and even in death their bodies rest beneath expensive tombs. As though each member of the family were touched by luck from the day they were born.

Maybe they really did make a deal with something in the forest.

The tomb where they moved Adam's body sits alone at the end of the row, the stone dappled golden in the growing light. Its roof rises into a pointed steeple. Marble columns border the decorative door. It yawns as wide as an open wound underneath the sunrise-spattered sky, revealing the small room inside.

I hesitate in the entryway and glance at the broken lock someone has tossed on the ground. The interior smells dry and stale. I wrinkle my nose as I step farther into the mausoleum. Adam's stone tomb rises at the center of the room.

Its broken marble lid lies askew to offer a glimpse inside. The stale scent of decay hits my senses again. Discolored bones lie scattered across the stained fabric of the coffin—ribs, vertebrae and femurs. Yellowed with age, they shine in the dim light. The warmth rushes from my body as I lean closer and realize something.

His skull is missing.

FIFTEEN YEARS EARLIER

CHAPTER 29

*W*hore.

The word marred the surface of my locker when I returned to school on Monday, letters scratched into the chipped paint. Carved with something sharp. The exposed metal shone underneath the fluorescent lights. Bitter stomach acid crept up my throat. I swallowed and stepped closer to block the word from view.

The other students stared at me as they walked past, moving in packs through the long corridor. Their eyes glinted like animals catching the first scent of blood on the wind. My blood. Easy prey—wounded and separated from the rest of the group. How many of them had Adam shown the photo to?

Maybe the whole school knew.

I fiddled with the lock. Fingers clumsy, I had to twist the combination several times before it finally sprang open. After I hung my backpack on the hook inside, I pulled my stash of weed from beneath the pile of clothes crumpled at the bottom of my locker and shoved it into my jacket pocket. Curious whispers followed my retreat down the hallway.

I pushed open the school doors and blinked in the early sunlight. The wind teased at my hair as I followed the trampled path through the grass around the side of the building. Rolling a joint between my fingers, I lit it and placed it between my lips. Smoke drifted around my face as I took one drag, then another, until my head spun.

Ambrose appeared around the corner and I jumped. He stopped at the sight of me, and we stared at each other for a few uncertain seconds until he asked, "Are you skipping today?"

"No. I just needed to get out of there for a few minutes," I said. Clammy sweat condensed on the palms of my hands. "I hate the way everyone's looking at me."

"What happened, anyway? I've only heard rumors." Ambrose lit a cigarette. Inside the school, the bell rang to signal the beginning of homeroom. Neither of us moved.

"You don't know?" I coughed as hot smoke filled my lungs. Only a little bit left—the charred tip of the joint almost touched my fingertips.

"No." He scuffed his new shoes against the cracked tarmac.

"I thought maybe Adam would have told you. Sent you the photo."

"He never tells me anything," Ambrose said, shaking his head. I dropped the joint and ground it out beneath the heel of my sneaker. A thin trickle of smoke rose from the crushed remnants as I debated whether I should trust him enough to tell him what Adam had done.

"Want one?" Ambrose pulled a clear plastic bag filled with pills from his jacket pocket and said, "They'll help you calm down."

"Thanks," I said and plucked one from the assortment inside. Xanax. Probably the only thing that could help me relax right now. I didn't even hesitate before I swallowed it down dry. "He invited me to go with him into the forest on Friday. For a celebration. But he left me alone in a grove, and after that I don't really remember what happened."

"I know that place." Ambrose's mouth hardened. "He shouldn't have shown it to you."

"That's what Victoria said, too." I leaned back against the sun-warmed wall of the building and waited for the pill to hit me. To soften the world around me.

"You told her?" he asked as his eyes strayed to the gold ring on my finger. Decorated with the familiar engravings that marked it as Victoria's artwork.

"Yeah. I guess I ran to her house after he left me there—I don't remember that either."

"What did she say?" The bag of pills crinkled in Ambrose's fist. His throat twitched as he swallowed another one down.

"Not a lot. I think she was really worried," I said, remembering the relief on her face after I woke up on her floor that morning. "She told me that's the place all the stories are about. You know, that something will grant a wish if you leave a gift there in the forest. Adam said your family made a deal with it. Do you believe that?"

"I don't know." Ambrose's whole body tensed. As though his parents had coached him never to talk about it with anyone outside their inner circle.

"Then why did he leave me there—what was he trying to do?" I pressed.

"He fell apart after our father was committed." Ambrose chose each word slowly. "Now he's just so angry all the time. I think he needs a therapist or something, but Mom's afraid they'll lock him away, too."

"I'm sorry." I waited for him to continue.

"Adam's always believed the stories. He probably thought if he left a gift in the forest, it would fix everything," Ambrose said finally. Voice reluctant, like he'd told me too much already.

"But why me?" I asked, remembering the treasures left in the clearing. Coins, bracelets and rings. "Why not a piece of jewelry or something?"

"It doesn't work like that," Ambrose blurted. His hands startled up toward his mouth, as though he wanted to grab the words and shove them back. Almost comical, except for the horror spread across his face.

"Then how does it work?" I persisted.

"I can't tell you." Ambrose pushed his fists into the pockets of his jacket. His knuckles formed a ridge beneath the thin fabric as he said, "But let me know if he tries to hurt you again. I'll stop him."

"I can take care of myself. I don't need your help." My voice hardened. The final bell rang inside the building, the loud sound reverberating through the schoolyard.

"Well, you should still come to class," Ambrose said. He took a step toward the door before he turned around to face me again. "Trying to hide will just make things worse."

I followed Ambrose into the building, steps slow and hesitant. He waved as we separated to venture to different classrooms. Cradling my textbooks against my body, I hurried down the hallway and tried to ignore the whispers that surrounded me.

When I reached my first class, I claimed my usual seat behind Nathalie at the laboratory tables. The faint smell of cleaning chemicals still clung to their sterile surfaces. A fetal pig sat in a metal tray at the center of each table, and I wrinkled my nose at the pungent scent of formaldehyde. The dead animal stared up at me through black and sightless eyes.

After some moments had passed without Nathalie saying anything, I said, "Hey."

"Hey." Nathalie didn't turn around.

"How was your weekend?" I asked, desperate for a friend, ally or something—anything—as more whispers filled the room. My classmates peeked at me whenever they thought I couldn't see them. Stifled giggles between their hands.

"It was okay, I guess." Nathalie still didn't turn in her seat to look at me. Like she knew my reputation was ruined and didn't want to risk her own popularity by talking to me.

I would only drag her down, too.

"Hey." Victoria dropped her bookbag on the counter. She slid into her seat beside me and flashed a quick smile in my direction. "What's up?"

"Not much." The memory of her soft mouth pressed against mine surfaced in my mind. My skin flushed hot. I wanted her to kiss me again. But she couldn't. At least, not here in front of all our friends.

"Did you do the reading this weekend?" Nathalie turned around to smile at Victoria. "I thought it was really boring."

"No. We were busy," Victoria said. She tapped the scalpel resting on the table against the metal edge of the tray. The dead body of the pig shuddered, limbs pinned apart to expose its white stomach. Nathalie's expression changed. Her face fell when she realized she had made a mistake—I wasn't a complete outcast.

Victoria hadn't abandoned me yet.

"So, what really happened with Adam?" Nathalie twisted in her seat to throw the question at me. "I've heard all kinds of rumors."

"I don't want to talk about it." I slipped into the apron hanging from the back of my seat, tying the strings up tight.

"In case you don't know—they aren't saying very good things about you."

"What's that supposed to mean?" I asked. Fury stirred inside me. Intense enough to blot out the shame that had weighed down on me ever since I followed Adam into the forest on Friday night. Nathalie shrank back when I leaned forward, as though she were afraid that I would lunge at her from across the table.

"You should stop talking," Victoria pronounced each word like a warning. "You don't know everything."

"Okay. I'm sorry," Nathalie said, subdued. She turned back around as the teacher cleared his throat at the front of the room.

We spent the rest of the class dissecting the fetal pig in front of us. My hands shook as I cut a neat incision across its stomach, peeling back its skin to reveal the flesh and organs hidden beneath its surface. Squeamish, I glanced out the window, and my eyes settled on Reachwood Forest.

What other secrets might lie concealed within it?

CHAPTER 30

Victoria and I skipped our next class. We slipped out the door while the students milled through the halls, climbed into her car and drove until Reachwood High School vanished in the distance. As Victoria steered toward the outskirts of the suburb, my thoughts drifted back to what Ambrose had told me that morning.

What had he meant when he said the offerings to the grove don't "work like that"?

Victoria turned the car onto a disused road that cut through the forest a few miles outside of Reachwood. She drove for a few more minutes until she parked the car and killed the engine. I climbed outside and stretched before I followed her along the tree line, asking, "Where are we going?"

"There's an abandoned mine around here somewhere. Nobody will bother us there," Victoria looked back at me over her shoulder. Branches crackled and I froze—trying to reassure myself that it was just an animal, moving through the undergrowth. "We can turn back if you want. If it reminds you of—"

"I don't want to turn back," I said, eager to leave the school and the rumors far behind me. To be free, at least for a few hours.

My stiff muscles relaxed when Victoria touched my wrist. I held her hand as we walked beside the border of the forest. Leaves unfurled on the branches overhead. Wildflowers spread colorful petals toward the sun as we slipped underneath a chain link fence plastered with the logo of the Reachwood Mining Company and signs warning trespassers to keep out.

An abandoned mining site sat alone at the edge of the forest. Old, although the forest hadn't reclaimed it yet—dilapidated buildings untouched by the undergrowth. Dust-covered windows faced outside like lifeless eyes. We took a seat on one of the rocks beside the yawning maw of the mine. An iron gate blockaded its dark entrance. Victoria searched through her book bag as I lay back, basking in the sunlight.

"Here." Victoria offered a tightly wrapped joint and a lighter to me.

"Thanks." I placed it between my lips and lit it, inhaling until hot smoke filled my lungs. The bite mark on the hollow space between my neck and my collarbone stung. I reached up to touch it as I handed the joint back to Victoria. She took a deep drag before she lay down beside me, and warmth spread through my body.

"What's wrong with your neck?" she asked. Smoke trickled from her mouth as she spoke.

"Nothing." I let go of the injury quickly, not eager to talk any more about my trip into the forest with Adam. Or to think about what might have chased me through the trees after he took the photo and left me there alone.

"Are you sure?" she persisted, as if she knew I wasn't telling her everything. I accepted the joint when she passed it back to me again, taking another drag. My eyes watered.

"Something bit me," I admitted finally, pulling down the hem of my sweater and peeling back the bandage to reveal the scabbed laceration at the base of my neck. Victoria sucked in her breath. "I don't remember how it happened. It was there when I woke up at your place this weekend."

"Do you think Adam did it?" Victoria examined the half-healed wound.

"I don't know." The bite mark shone raw and red, oozing blood and clear liquid. "Maybe him, or some kind of animal."

"Has a doctor looked at it?" Victoria sat up and collected several stones from the ground. The gold rings that always decorated her fingers glinted as she cradled them in her hands.

"How would I explain what happened? It doesn't look like an accident," I said and smoothed the edges of the bandage back over my skin to hide the injury from sight.

"But what if it gets infected?"

"What if the nurse thinks someone hurt me? My parents would pull me out of school if they knew." I took another long drag from the joint. Light-headed already, eager for the weed to relax the nervous tension vibrating through my body. "And anyway, it seems to be healing."

"Really?" Victoria pitched a rock through a dust-covered window.

"Yeah, it doesn't feel like anything." I dropped the spent joint on the ground when Victoria offered me a stone to throw. Its weight felt like a reassurance in the palm of my hand. I curled my fingers around it and asked, "Won't we get in trouble if someone catches us?"

"My family owns everything here. I can do whatever I want," Victoria said. Voice certain and confident. I wondered what it was like to be born into a family—no, a dynasty, or an empire—surrounded by wealth and comfort. To be able to break any rules I wanted without consequences.

I hurled the rock through a window and it shattered. The sound echoed loudly in the silence. Victoria tossed another stone at the window and it clattered against the sill. The darkness spread out behind the gate that led down into the mine shaft. So deep it could conceal anything.

"So, you still really don't remember what happened?" Victoria asked after we had destroyed all the windows. Sharp points of glass glittered like cracked teeth in the tall grass.

"Not really. The last thing I remember is Adam leaving me in the clearing." My voice sounded soft and small. "Why do you think he took that photo and showed it to everybody? You know, if he was planning to leave me in the grove."

"To hurt you. He knew it would hurt me, too." Victoria's face darkened. "And if you disappeared out there somewhere, he could just say you left and he never saw you again. Pretend he had nothing to do with it."

"Is he really that mad at you?"

"He must be. I mean, he's made up this whole conspiracy that my family caused his father's breakdown to push the Albrights out of the company." Victoria laughed. "He probably thinks he's getting back at me."

"I talked to Ambrose this morning. You were right—he thought Adam left me in the grove so his father would come home." I studied Victoria's face, but her expression didn't give anything away. "He said something else I still don't understand though."

"Like what?"

"I asked him why Adam didn't leave something else instead. But he said the offerings to the forest don't work like that." I hesitated. "Do you know what he meant?"

"No. But I can guess," Victoria said. Her mouth twitched, as though she were deliberating over how much to tell me. "Some of our stories hint that a wish like that would need an equal gift to be granted. Gold or jewelry wouldn't be enough. Maybe he thought he needed to offer it something more than that."

"Do you think—" I bit my lip.

"What?"

"Do you think he did the same thing to Emily that he tried to do to me?" The words rushed in a jumble from my mouth. "Maybe he tried to make her into an offering and she got lost in the forest."

"Maybe." A frown crinkled the corners of Victoria's eyes. "That was around the same time all the trouble started with his family."

"He gave me something when he brought me to the grove. A bracelet," I said, remembering the delicate chain of gold he'd fastened around my wrist. "Does that mean anything to you?"

Brief unease flickered across Victoria's face. "You should put it back where you found it. My parents told me once you should never bring anything out of the forest—it doesn't like it when people take its offerings."

"I thought you didn't believe the stories."

"I don't. At least—not really." Victoria glanced away. "But it's best to be safe. In case there's any truth to it."

Before we left the abandoned mining site, I kissed her, pulling her close underneath the tall trees. When her mouth pressed against mine, I felt light enough to almost forget what had happened in the forest on Friday night.

"Why did you pick him instead of me?" Victoria asked after she pulled away.

I opened my mouth and closed it again, struggling to find the right words to say—to explain I didn't realize she felt the same way I did until it was already too late. It would have been easier to feel something for Adam instead. My parents would have been thrilled. We wouldn't have been forced to hide our relationship like some kind of unpleasant secret.

"I guess I just wanted to feel normal," I said and felt like a coward as soon as the words fell from my tongue.

Victoria said nothing as we left Reachwood Forest behind us.

CHAPTER 31

More obscene graffiti defaced my locker the next morning. I averted my eyes from the scribbled words as I twirled the combination until the lock popped open. Anger drummed against my temples—the early warning of a headache.

Another lovely day.

"What's that?" Victoria asked when I slammed my locker shut to reveal the words written against the metal. I jumped, startled by the sound of her voice.

"Someone probably thought they were being funny."

"I bet it was Adam." She frowned. The bell rang, almost loud enough to drown out her next question. "Have you told anyone about it?"

"Not yet." I couldn't say anything to the teachers. If I mentioned the graffiti, they might call my parents. Mother would demand to know what I did to deserve this, and if she found out about the photo . . .

My life would be over.

"I talked to my parents," Victoria said, interrupting my panic. Nobody so much as brushed against her as we walked down the hallway. Students parted to let her past, as though her family's wealth and power surrounded her with an untouchable aura everywhere she went.

"What did you tell them?" I raised my voice to be heard over the cacophony of teenage noises. Classroom doors slammed open and shut. Students swarmed through the narrow corridor.

"Just that he showed someone the grove in the forest. They'll make him pay for it."

"I hope so." I clutched my textbooks tightly. Their hard spines dug into my stomach as we headed toward our first class of the day. Biology again.

Adam and his friends were grouped at the top of the stairs, voices loud and raucous. The muscles in my shoulders tightened when they caught sight of me. One whistled as we drew closer, then another—until the sound echoed down the hallway.

"What are you looking at?" I snapped as we pushed past them.

"Nothing I haven't seen already," Adam said and grinned. Someone laughed, hidden in the crowd. A sudden rush of anger flooded my body like adrenaline.

"Fuck off." Victoria tossed the words over her shoulder.

"Hey—wait," Adam called as we hurried down the hall. "I want to ask you something."

"Like what?" I said. A furious blush heated my skin. When I turned back toward him, the soles of my shoes squeaked against the linoleum.

"Someone fucked up my car." Adam's expression darkened. "Was it you?"

"I mean, you deserved worse. After what you did," Victoria said. He took a step toward her as a group of curious students formed around us. Their hushed voices reminded me of leaves rustling on the trees.

"What's your problem, bitch? Mad I got what you wanted?" He spit out the words. Victoria didn't flinch, eyes black as storm clouds as she stared him down.

"What are you talking about?"

"You act like you're perfect, but I've seen the way you look at her. It's, like, the worst-kept secret ever," he said and took another step toward Victoria.

But she still didn't retreat, feet planted firm against the floor. "And I know you told your family what I did. Now my mom wants to talk to me."

"Afraid they're going to lock you away, too?" Victoria smirked.

"You don't control everything, you know." He loomed above her. "Even though your family might think so."

"Leave her alone." I grabbed the sleeve of his jacket.

"Fuck off." He tore his hand free.

"Did you do the same thing to Emily, too?" I blurted the words. The spectators around us fell silent for a moment.

"What?" Adam asked. His jaw clenched.

"Did you take her out there somewhere and leave her, too?" The question had barely left my mouth before he shoved me hard against the wall. My head smacked against the white-painted bricks. Dizzy, I blinked as the hallway blurred around me. But I kept going.

"You did, didn't you?" Fury surged through me like electricity as I pictured Emily lost inside the forest. Betrayed by someone she trusted—she didn't deserve that.

"Shut the fuck up. Don't you ever talk to me about her." Adam's lips curled back. "You have no idea what happened."

"You're a piece of shit." I stepped forward and pushed him as hard as I could. Adam stumbled back toward the stairwell. His friends grabbed him before he fell.

"Ava—" Victoria said, but Adam bared his teeth in a snarl and lunged toward me. He shoved me, and my head bounced against the wall again. Dark spots danced at the corners of my vision. I reached up to feel the sore spot at the base of my skull.

"Fuck you." I charged at Adam, slamming my full weight against his body as he stood on the edge of the stairs. He teetered for one uncertain moment before we both fell, bodies tumbling down the stairwell. My bones rattled every time I smacked another step. The world whirled fast around us.

We landed at the bottom of the stairs, the impact hard enough to knock the breath from my lungs. Pain radiated through my body. Adam groaned beside me, holding his head between his hands. A cut split his forehead, and blood masked his face in red. His eyes shone wild and furious.

Suddenly, he climbed on top of me and wrapped his hands around my throat.

"Let go of me!" I struggled underneath him. Blood ran down the back of my neck. His fingers slipped against my skin as I thrashed in his grasp. Darkness shimmered at the edges of my vision.

My sight fading, I reached up and clasped his face. He screamed as I shoved my thumbs into his eye sockets and the pressure on my throat eased for a moment. I gasped for air. The school snapped back into focus around me. Adam reared back and clutched at his face as pain sparked through my body.

I slipped free and stumbled to my feet. The hallway spun around me again. I coughed, ribs stinging as I leaned against the lockers. Dozens of cuts and bruises throbbed against my skin. Teachers rushed down the hall to break up the fight, pushing through groups of transfixed students. Their eyes shone bright at the sight of violence.

I smiled.

My body felt weightless for the first time since the weekend.

TODAY

CHAPTER 32

After I return home from the cemetery, I take a shower, standing beneath the hot water and waiting for it to wash away the memory of Adam's open coffin. Lost in thought, I trace the long-healed scars on my palm and at the base of my neck. The rough skin brushes against my fingertips. I swallow hard.

Who stole Adam's skull?

"Mom?" Marjorie knocks on the bathroom door. "Is something wrong?"

"What?" I step out of the shower. "No, nothing's wrong. Why?"

"You've been in there for a really long time." The fan stutters loud enough to muffle her voice. Concern undercuts her words. The same way it did when she checked on me after another vicious argument with my ex-husband.

"Well, I'm fine. Don't worry," I say as I towel my hair dry. Steam fogs the mirror and softens the edges of my reflection as I wrap another towel around my waist.

"Okay." Marjorie's footsteps fade away down the hallway.

I dress quickly and cross the hall to the guest room. My bedroom—for much longer than I'd wanted to stay here. Clothes clutter the floor. My phone rests on the nightstand, plugged into the wall to charge.

"Dinner is ready!" My father calls as I check my notifications. No missed calls from any unknown numbers. None from the repair shop, either. No response to the messages I've left since yesterday, asking when my car will be ready.

"That's okay." I raise my voice loud enough to carry through my closed door. "I'm not really hungry."

"You should try to eat something," he insists. The clatter of cutlery against ceramic plates carries from the kitchen. The painkiller I swallowed earlier muffles my senses and fills me with a pleasant kind of numbness. My stomach doesn't even rumble at the smell of food.

"I'll be there in a minute." I set my phone down before I venture into the kitchen, hair still damp from the shower. My family sits in a half-circle around the dinner table. I slide into the seat that has been mine ever since I was a child.

"Did you do something to my tablet?" Mother demands as I load my plate. Marjorie's eyes flit between our faces.

"No. Why?" I pick my meal apart with the tines of my fork. Mother glares at me until I take a reluctant bite. The food sticks tasteless against my tongue.

"It's stopped working," Mother says, and Marjorie hides a smirk behind her hand when she raises her fork again.

"Maybe the battery died." The words fall soft and slurred from my mouth.

"It was charging fine yesterday."

"You probably broke it—you break a lot of things." Marjorie leans back in her chair to stretch. Her arms reach above her head and small bones crack in her back.

"Aren't you going to finish that?" My father asks when I stand, carrying my half-empty plate over to the sink. "You've barely eaten anything."

"I told you I wasn't hungry." My eyelids flicker as I scrape my meal into the garbage.

"Are you sure you're okay?" Marjorie studies me closely.

"Yeah." I smooth the exasperation from my voice. "Why do you keep asking me that?"

"You can barely stay awake." Anxiety pinches the corners of her mouth.

"I'm just tired." I repeat the familiar lie. The same one I had used to excuse my exhaustion after another altercation with my ex-husband. To deflect Marjorie's questions and act like the violence had never happened.

Marjorie's expression doesn't change, so I can't tell if she believes me or not. She pushes her chair back from the table and retreats down the hallway. Her bedroom door slams shut as I help my father stack more plates in the dishwasher.

⚬━╋━⚬

"Can I talk to you for a moment?" Mother asks from the top of the basement stairs. I'd journeyed down there after dinner to sort through our belongings. Old clothes and unflattering photos, broken toys and dust-covered furniture.

"About what?" I straighten up.

"I'm worried—you've barely eaten since you arrived here."

"You've never cared before." Resentment lowers my voice. When I was still a teenager, she used to lecture me not to eat too much almost daily. Determined to keep my body thin and graceful for the ballet and gymnastics classes that she shuttled me to every day after school.

"You know that's not true." Her voice sharpens, although it was my father who had convinced her to send me to the treatment center after I passed out during practice. When it was almost too late. "And you should think about the example you're setting for Marjorie. She's always trying to be just like you. Do you want her to stop eating, too?"

I open my mouth but don't speak, as I remember how I had only really started to eat again after I realized I was pregnant. How much I had wanted Marjorie to be born healthy. I never wanted her to resent her own body.

Not the way I did.

"I'm just stressed about the divorce," I say, changing the subject.

"Have you heard anything from your lawyer?"

"They're still arguing in court." I pile everything I want to throw away on the far side of the room. "We need to decide what happens with Marjorie. I've petitioned for full custody. I don't want him to get any visitation."

"Do you really think that will happen?"

"I hope so—it's a good sign I was awarded it temporarily. Until the divorce is finalized, anyway." I remember the explosive fights I used to get into with my ex-husband. Infrequent at first, small outbursts followed by apologies and displays of affection. But it had escalated until things were getting violent almost every night. I fought back sometimes, hard enough to split his lip or bloody his nose. Maybe that could enable him to petition for custody to take my daughter away from me.

To hit me where he knows it will hurt the most.

"You need to talk to Marjorie. She's been angry ever since I broke your phone a few days ago," Mother says as I toss more of my old belongings into the garbage. Baby clothes and old stuffed animals, fur coated with dust.

"What are you talking about?"

"You must have noticed the way she's acting. It's like she hates me." Mother leans against the doorway. "And some more of my things have gone missing."

"Are you sure you didn't just forget where you put them?"

"I'm sure of it." Her acrylic nails click as she taps them against the brass railing and says, "You've been distracted ever since you came back from the cemetery this morning. I heard about what happened to Adam's tomb on the news—did you visit his grave, too?"

"Yeah, I made the call to the police when I saw someone had broken his coffin open."

"Why did you even go there?" Her voice tightens.

"I guess I just wanted some closure."

"Well, you won't get any if the Albright family finds out about this," she says, folding her arms across her chest. "They'll blame you for it. Just like they did before."

"Then I won't tell anybody," I say, picking up a box to carry upstairs. Ambrose's face materializes in my mind again. He could still be behind all of this. After all, I'd told him I was leaving. Maybe he sabotaged my car to keep me in Reachwood. Smashed Adam's tomb to force the police to reopen the case before I get away.

Mother moves out of the doorway to let me pass. Her eyes follow me as I set the box down with the others piled in the kitchen. Before I return downstairs, I twitch the curtains shut over the windows.

"Why do you do that?" Mother asks when I brush past her again.

"Do what?" I say as I sift through more artifacts in the basement, packing the objects I want to keep in moving boxes and discarding the rest into the pile destined for the landfill.

"Keep the curtains closed. It's like you're afraid to look outside."

"I don't feel safe leaving the windows open at night." My shoulders tense as she turns to leave. "And Marjorie thinks she hears things in the forest sometimes."

"Like what?" She pauses. Silence stretches out as deep and complete as all the years of things left unspoken between us.

"It's probably nothing," I say, although my voice wavers hard enough to betray me. "But I was wondering—have you ever heard anything out there?"

"You should tell her to stay out of the forest. It's dangerous." Mother never answers my question. "You don't want her to go missing like the other children."

"I know, I've told her. I just hope she listens."

"I hope so, too." Her eyes drift across the mess spread through the room as I shove more faded clothing into the garbage. "You don't want to keep anything?"

"Not really. Anyway, it's late—I'll work on this some more tomorrow morning."

The house is quiet when I return upstairs except for the faint music playing from Marjorie's bedroom. The sound floats down the long corridor. Light seeps out from beneath her door and pools against the floor.

"Good night," I tell Mother before I move toward my bedroom at the end of the hallway.

"I thought I heard something out there, once." A shadow flickers across Mother's face as I push open my bedroom door. "In the forest."

"Like what?" I hesitate, but Mother doesn't say anything more.

CHAPTER 33

"I'm so glad you could still make it." Nathalie leads me through the house she shares with Matthew. A spacious, two-story home located on the affluent side of Reachwood. They're wealthy enough to afford a house at the crest of the hill, although they've fallen short of making it through the gates of the historic neighborhood where Victoria lives. But it's still much nicer than my home below. "I thought you were leaving?"

"We decided to stay a little longer. My car broke down and we can't leave until they figure out what's wrong with it," I explain. *If* they figure out what's wrong with it. Days have passed since the engine grated to a stop in the middle of the ravine, and the mechanics still haven't given me a diagnosis.

"I'm sorry to hear that," Nathalie says as noise drifts from the kitchen. Voices and laughter. She invited me here tonight to attend their farewell party. One last chance to say goodbye before her family moves out of Reachwood forever. "It seems like everything has been falling apart lately."

"What do you mean?" I ask, remembering what Victoria told me when she drove me home after the Reachwood Festival. How Matthew's injury might not heal, even with surgery, and how Nathalie's tech start-up company might have to declare bankruptcy.

"Nothing." Nathalie brushes off my question as we walk through the house.

Cardboard boxes clutter the hallway, filled with evidence of the life Nathalie and Matthew have built together. Children's toys litter the floor. Framed jerseys still line the walls, emblazoned with the names of the teams Matthew has played for over the years.

People turn to stare at me when we enter the kitchen. I tilt my head down to evade their curious eyes, but a few smile as we move through tight-knit groups. Cautious, I smile back. Maybe some of them have forgotten the past. Or decided it happened so long ago it doesn't matter any more.

"Your place is lovely," I say as Nathalie hands me a glass of white wine. The party bustles around us, but I stick close to her side, like a shy child. More than a little bit surprised by all of the people who have arrived to wish Nathalie and Matthew well before they leave. Maybe their reputations had recovered after Adam's death—they never faced the same scrutiny I did.

Not after what had happened between me and him.

"Thanks." Nathalie smiles. A herd of children rush past, screaming with laughter. I catch a glimpse of her son and daughter before they turn the corner and disappear.

"So, why did you decide to move away?" I swish the wine inside my glass and pretend I don't already know the answer.

"Matthew tore a tendon in his knee," Nathalie explains. "His team has a good performance center in the city. He can get physiotherapy there after the surgery."

"I'm sorry." I feign surprise, as if Victoria hadn't already told me everything. Matthew waves at me across the room. He limps when he rises to his feet, gait unsteady as he walks over to the fridge to grab another beer.

"To be honest, we've wanted to move for a long time." Worry shadows Nathalie's eyes as she watches him.

"Why?" I sip more wine.

"Between the forest and the disappearances—it's not a good place to raise children." Nathalie takes a tiny bite of the food piled on her plate. "But every time we tried to leave, something stopped us."

"Like what?" I ask. A chill tickles the back of my neck.

"I can't really explain it. One of our parents would get sick, or something would break down and we'd need to spend a lot of money to fix it. It just seemed like everything conspired against us." Nathalie laughs. The humorless sound falls flat.

"I know what you mean. A few weird things have happened to me, too." I watch Nathalie's face closely, searching for any hint of recognition as I say, "Someone left a message on my door. Asking who left Adam in the forest."

"Is that why you wanted to leave?" Nathalie asks. Her voice cracks.

"Yeah. I think I made a huge mistake when I decided to come back here."

"Nothing that bad has ever happened to us." Nathalie's hand tightens around the stem of the wineglass. Her voice is terse enough to make me wonder if she is lying. If she had also received threatening calls from unlisted numbers, or gifts brought out of Reachwood Forest. "But some people never moved past his death. It's been—difficult, living here. Even after all these years."

"So you have no idea who might have done it?" I ask, picturing the coldness on Ambrose's face when I confronted him about the message on my doorstep.

"Not really," Nathalie says as she refills her glass. Wine splashes over the rim to glimmer against the countertop. "But I'm happy you decided to show up tonight. I never got a chance before, but I wanted to say I'm sorry."

"What? Why?" I stare at her, surprised.

"I just feel bad about the way everything happened, I guess." Nathalie takes another sip of wine and hesitates before she says, "I wasn't a great friend. I should have known you'd never let Adam take that photo of you."

"Don't worry about it." I touch her hand. "If I'd been in your place, I wouldn't have known what to believe either."

"I always wanted to be more like you," Nathalie continues. Words jumbled and rushed, as if she's held them in for a long time and is desperate now to get them out. Before her nerve fails her. "Everyone loved you at school. I don't think Victoria ever liked me the same way she liked you."

"I wanted to be like you, too. Your grades were perfect, and I was failing almost everything," I say, and the edges of her mouth tremble as she smiles at me. "Anyway, just forget about it. We were both pretty dumb when we were young."

"Tell me about it." Nathalie laughs as the crowd chatters around us. Matthew almost stumbles when he sits down on the couch again, and Nathalie's muscles twitch like she is ready to lunge across the room and catch him. He never winces, although the injury must hurt. Maybe he was prescribed some of the same painkillers my doctor had given me. "I was even jealous when you left. That you got away—it's so hard to leave this place."

"I don't think I ever escaped. Not really." I set my wineglass down on the counter as an idea materializes in my mind. "Is there a bathroom around here?"

"Yeah. Just over there." Nathalie waves a hand at the hallway. "You can use the one upstairs if it's busy."

"Thanks." I weave through tight groups of people until I reach the bathroom door. The lock holds firm when I twist the doorknob and I smile in relief. Just the excuse I need.

⚬—⟊—⚬

The sounds of the party fade away behind me as I climb the stairs to the second floor of the house. Still filled with Nathalie and Matthew's belongings. My eyes dart around the short hallway.

It's empty.

Hinges squeak as I push open each door until I find Nathalie and Matthew's bedroom. A king-size bed rests at its center, and a widescreen television takes up most of the wall across from it. Empty cardboard boxes litter the floor, ready to be packed tomorrow. My socks whisper against the carpet.

The door to the master bathroom swings open when I touch it. My eyes rest on the medicine cabinet. Nathalie and Matthew are moving soon—maybe they won't notice if a few painkillers go missing. I won't take many. Just enough to last until I can get out of Reachwood.

But shame still heats my face as I move across the floor toward the medicine cabinet. I shouldn't do this. But if I steal the pills here, I won't have to tell Ambrose I've changed my mind. If he takes the risk to get me the pills and I don't answer his questions about Adam or give him information about my friends in return, he'll want something else from me instead. I shiver at the memory of Ambrose's lips against my skin.

I don't want to give in to him.

But the door is locked. It won't budge no matter how hard I pull at it, although desperation strengthens my grip. I yank at it again. Pry at its edges with my hands. The hinges groan but the cabinet never opens.

Fuck.

Nathalie is drunk by the time I return downstairs. She wobbles slightly on her feet when she waves at me. I smooth the irritation from my face before I push through the party toward her. Strangers whisper in my wake.

"Where is Victoria, anyway?" I ask when I reach her side. "I thought she'd be here tonight to say goodbye."

"She couldn't make it." Nathalie picks at a chip of nail polish.

"Why not?"

"She said she wasn't feeling well. But you know what she's like." Nathalie stumbles over her words as she takes another sip of wine. "She hates saying goodbye. Cyril's not coming over either—he decided to stay with her until she feels better."

"How did they get together, anyway?" I ask the question Victoria never really answered.

"She fell apart after Adam's death. She was pretty much high or drunk all the time. I was actually scared she'd die next," Nathalie says. Her cheeks are red, eyes glassy. "They got together so fast. I think she wanted to forget what happened, and Cyril took advantage of that."

"You're probably right—I never thought she liked him."

"Me either. The way he followed her everywhere always creeped me out." Nathalie giggles. "But when she got pregnant, she had to marry him. Just like he always wanted. It really couldn't have gone any better for him—sometimes I wonder if he did something to her birth control. To keep her with him."

"Oh." A cold stone settles in the bottom of my stomach.

"She's changed a lot since you left, but I know she's happy to see you again," Nathalie says, voice almost hidden underneath the music playing from the speakers. "She might not show it, but I can tell."

"I'm happy to see her again, too." For maybe the first time, I wonder if Nathalie had ever guessed at the relationship between us. Her eyes focus on my face. A blush flushes hot against my cheeks and I turn away, saying, "I should go, though—it's getting late."

I wave at Matthew from across the room, reluctant to push through the crowd of people surrounding him. He waves back as Nathalie sets her wineglass down. She doesn't speak as we walk to the front door. I shrug into my jacket and lace up my boots on the mat. The night spreads black against the windows outside. I pause in the doorway, searching for something to say.

"Good luck," I say finally, as Nathalie wraps me up in a tight hug. "I hope everything works out for the both of you."

"Good luck to you, too." Her voice is muffled against the thick fabric of my jacket. "I hope you can get out of this place soon. Before anything else happens to you."

CHAPTER 34

I've changed my mind.

I give in and text Ambrose the next afternoon, while I wait for Marjorie outside of Reachwood High School. Parents compete for parking spots on the busy street as I stare at the blank screen. Defeat weighs heavily against my body as I hide my prescription bottle inside my purse. The last pill rattles inside.

I'll be completely out after I take it tonight.

More painkillers seem to vanish every time I count them. Faster than I can track. More than I can account for.

The bell rings, and children flee the school in a steady stream. They roam in packs across the lawn, talking and laughing. Some of their faces look familiar, like younger versions of the classmates I used to spend every day with when I still attended school here. They disappear into the vehicles parked on the street.

I unlock the car doors when I see Marjorie walk out of the building with a large group of students, deep in conversation. I recognize Catherine, Virgil and Aidan—and a few others whose names I don't remember. They mill around the entrance of the school. The same way I used to do with Victoria, Adam and Cyril.

Evidence that events only repeat themselves over and over again.

The sun catches in Marjorie's hair and lights it up like a golden halo around her head. Aidan slings an arm around her shoulders. She waves goodbye to her friends and rises on the balls of her feet to press a quick kiss against his mouth. My stomach lurches. I almost choke on my own breath.

Marjorie's face pales when she notices my borrowed car parked in front of the school. She hitches her backpack up farther on her shoulders before she hurries to the vehicle and opens the door. I say nothing as she slides into the passenger seat. The radio begins to play another sugar-sweet pop song.

"You're early," Marjorie says. The pungent smell of weed sticks to her clothes, the same way it had when I returned home from another long day of classes. She rolls down the window in an attempt to get rid of the incriminating scent when I steer away from the curb.

"I finished some errands sooner than I expected." I brake for a cluster of students.

"Oh." Marjorie types something on her phone as the air whistles through the open window. It pulls strands of hair free from the bun twisted at the crown of her head. Neither of us speaks as I steer through the suburban streets blanketed with autumn leaves.

"How long have you two been together?" My voice tightens.

"What?" she asks, expression innocent.

"You know exactly what I'm talking about. How long have you been dating Aidan?" I demand as I turn onto our street. Remembering how hard Marjorie had fought to stay in the suburb. Inexplicably reluctant to move back to Portland and see her friends again, although we've only been in Reachwood for just over six weeks. Nowhere near long enough to get this attached to the neighborhood. But her refusal would make sense if she had been dating Aidan in secret this whole time.

If she didn't want to leave him behind.

"I don't know." Marjorie clasps her hands in her lap. "Since the start of school, I guess."

"Why didn't you tell me?"

"Because I knew you wouldn't like it." Marjorie's mouth thins into a stubborn line.

"Why didn't you listen when I told you to stay away from him?" I ask as I park the car in the driveway. Marjorie plucks her backpack from where it rests between her feet on the floor.

"Why should I, though? You never told me."

"I still don't want to talk about it." The scar on my palm stings when I curl my fingers into fists.

"I'm so bored of you saying that." Marjorie rolls her eyes. Exasperation raises the pitch of her voice as she checks her phone again and says, "They all talk about you, you know."

"Who?" I ask. Nausea chews at my stomach.

"Everyone at school—all of their parents think you had something to do with that boy who died in the forest a long time ago." Marjorie types another message against the thin glass.

"That's not true." I climb out of the car.

"He was Aidan's uncle, right?" Marjorie persists as she follows me up the driveway. She stands close to me as I shuffle through my keys. "Is that why you don't like him—because he reminds you of him?"

I open my mouth and search for a way to convince Marjorie to stay away from him. How Adam left me in the grove alone to find my way back home. How he sent those photos of me to everyone in school. And something else.

Something I don't even know how to admit to her or myself.

"That's not the reason," I say and turn the key in the lock. She sighs loudly before she slips past me to disappear down the hallway.

"There's something else I need to talk to you about." I pursue Marjorie into the kitchen.

"What is it now?" She scowls and slams her backpack down on the table.

"Do you remember those pills the hospital gave me after they fixed my wrist?"

"I guess so." Her face turns unreadable.

"They've been going missing."

"What are you talking about?" Marjorie asks. The freckled skin on the bridge of her nose crinkles when she frowns again. She chooses an apple from the bowl on the counter and bites into it. Her teeth break it open to reveal the soft white flesh beneath its glossy red surface.

"I mean, I'm almost out already."

"So what, you think I've been taking them?" Marjorie bites the apple again and juice trickles down her chin. She wipes it away with the back of her hand.

"I hope you'd tell me if something's wrong. If anything's going on."

"I didn't steal anything," she insists. Her lower lip quivers.

"Well, they keep disappearing."

"You're probably taking more than you remember." She crosses her arms. "You're high pretty much all the fucking time."

I flinch. We stand in silence, facing each other across the kitchen. Marjorie's eyes shine like a cornered animal as I struggle to find the right words to say. To explain I need those pills—not only to erase the memory of my ex-husband but to numb the constant anxiety I've felt ever since I returned to Reachwood as well. To get away from myself.

"Marjorie—"

"I don't want to talk about it." She throws the same phrase I use to shut down every uncomfortable conversation back at me. "I need to go study."

"Marjorie—" I repeat as she pushes past me. I grab her wrist, and her lips pull back in a snarl. Her skin feels hot beneath my fingertips as she struggles in my grip.

"Let go of me." She shoves me just like my ex-husband did. So hard that my body bangs against the wall. My teeth click together inside my head. Fresh blood drips from my lip and trickles red and thick down my chin. We stare at each other, frozen, for a long moment.

"Mom—" Marjorie touches my shoulder, eyes wide.

"Don't. I'm fine." I shy away from her touch.

"I'm sorry." Marjorie's voice trembles.

"Just go to your room. We'll talk more about this later," I say and dab at the cut still dripping blood from my lip. Marjorie hesitates before she vanishes down the hallway. I wait for her bedroom door to click shut before I press my thumb against the new wound on my mouth to stanch the steady flow of blood.

CHAPTER 35

"I'm sorry," Marjorie says, pushing open my bedroom door in the morning. I sit up and blink as she perches on the edge of my bed. Dark circles purple the skin beneath her eyes, as if she didn't sleep at all last night.

"It's okay. Don't worry about it." I hold her tight, and she rests her chin on my shoulder. The sound of birdsong drifts through the windows. My parents' voices murmur in the kitchen. Marjorie slips out of my embrace and takes a quick breath, curling her hands in her lap. I stay quiet as the corners of her mouth twitch like she wants to say something.

"I don't want to be like him," she says finally.

"Like who?" I yawn.

"Like Dad. I don't want to hurt you like that." Marjorie's voice breaks. I wrap her up in another hug, and we hold each other close for several long moments.

"You aren't anything like him."

"I hope so." She pulls away and nibbles at her bottom lip with the tip of one pointed tooth. The cheap clock on my nightstand clicks. It counts down the minutes as I run my fingers through my sleep-tangled hair.

"Would you still love me even if I hurt somebody?" Marjorie asks as she rises to her feet.

"Did something happen at school?" My mouth dries as I remember the last time Marjorie got into a fight. How she had slammed the other girl's head into a table during the altercation, opening up a long cut across her cheek. Deep enough to leave a scar that won't ever fade away.

"No. But if I did hurt somebody again, would you still love me?" she asks. Voice innocent enough to make me wonder if she is planning something. But of course I would. Marjorie's the only good thing that's happened to me since I left Reachwood. I only made the decision to leave my ex-husband after Marjorie stepped between us one night. When I realized she deserved a better life than I could provide if I stayed with him.

I push away my misgivings. "Always."

Marjorie's face lights up when she smiles.

"Okay—I'm going to get ready for school," she says and crosses the room to my bedroom door. Her socks whisper across the carpeted floor. "See you outside?"

"Yeah, I'll be there in a few minutes." I stretch, flexing stiff muscles. Marjorie still stands in the doorway. "Is there something else you wanted to tell me?"

"Can I stay over at Catherine and Virgil's place tonight?" Marjorie's expression is open and hopeful. "They're having a party."

"What's happening at it?" I ask, picturing the parties Victoria had thrown when we were still in high school. The stolen liquor and smuggled pills that kept us awake all through the night. The twins look just like their mother.

Maybe they take after her in other ways, too.

"Nothing. We're hanging out and playing games and stuff." Marjorie struggles not to appear too excited as she waits for me to make a decision.

"Is Aidan going to be there, too?" I climb out of bed.

"No," she says, and I wonder if she's lying again. My stomach clenches at the thought of them spending time alone together. The drunken mistakes they could make.

"I don't want you going if he's there." I open my closet. Marjorie's eyes follow my every movement as I choose a loose sweater and denim jeans. Dead leaves pile on the windowsill. A chill creeps through the thin panel of glass.

"He won't be—I promise." A trace of annoyance surfaces in Marjorie's voice. "You talk to Virgil and Catherine's mom all the time. You can ask her, if you don't believe me."

"Okay." I give in and regret it immediately when a triumphant smile breaks across her face. "Now let me get dressed. I'll see you downstairs."

<hr />

As I slip into my clothes in the bathroom, Ambrose texts: *I've got them. But you still need to give me something in return.* Just over twelve hours since I took my last dose of painkillers, but my body craves the medication already. Hopeful, I open the medicine cabinet and check the prescription container.

It's still empty.

I will, I type back. Still not sure what I'll trade him for the pills. I can't tell him anything about Adam's death in the forest. But maybe I'll tell him something about Victoria and Cyril. Not much—not enough to hurt them. Just enough to satisfy him.

My reflection stares back at me in the mirror as I braid my hair. I don't meet my own gaze as I twist the long strands between my fingers. The new cut on my lip is red and swollen. Sweat beads on my forehead as a low ringing hums in my ears.

It will only grow worse.

"I'm dropping Marjorie off at school. See you later," I call to my parents as I walk down the hallway. Marjorie waits by the front door. Her backpack lies at her feet. Fog obscures the world outside the window, and frost blossoms against the glass. Another hint that winter will arrive soon.

"Drive safe." My father's voice drifts from the kitchen.

Marjorie hurries to the car, breath wreathing her face in white. I scrape a thin layer of ice from the windows while she huddles in the passenger seat. She cranks up the heat after I climb inside and back out of the driveway to navigate down the clouded street.

"Are you coming home tonight before you go to Catherine and Virgil's party?" I ask. The light ahead changes, and a cramp runs through my legs as I hit the brakes. The car jerks to a stop at the intersection, wipers swiping back and forth against the windshield. The sound grates inside the vehicle.

"I don't think so," Marjorie says. She glances up from her phone when we drive through the ravine. A few stubborn leaves still cling to the gnarled branches of the trees. Something nervous stirs beneath my ribs at the fervent intensity on her face as the forest passes by outside.

"Okay. Send me a text when you need me to pick you up." I steer onto the road leading to Reachwood High School. Relief washes over me when the trees recede in the rearview mirror.

"I will." Marjorie swipes cherry-pink lip gloss across her mouth before she asks, "Is it true there's a place in the forest that grants wishes if you leave something in it?"

"How did you know about that?" I ask. Immediately, I realize I've made a mistake when Marjorie's face brightens.

"I forget. Someone told me about it." Marjorie skips through the songs playing on the stereo until she finally settles on her current favorite. Loud rap music blasts through the speakers as the school appears in the distance. The sound ricochets inside my head until I lean forward and turn it off.

"I've told you already. Those are only stories." I repeat the words in the silence, like maybe Marjorie will believe them if I say them over and over again. What else does she know? Someone already told her the gifts had to be left in a specific place. Maybe they also told her how to follow the stacked stones to the grove.

"Some people don't think so." Marjorie shoves her phone back into her bookbag. "Do you think you'd win the divorce if I left something in there?"

"You need to stay out of the forest. I really mean it," I say and slow down because cars clog the road ahead. Like everyone forgot how to drive at the sight of the first few tendrils of fog on the road. Irritation rises inside me as the vehicles inch down the crowded street. I'd wanted to drop off Marjorie quickly this morning.

Pick up the pills as soon as possible.

Marjorie makes a face. She taps her feet against the plastic floor mats and says, "Have you heard anything more about the divorce yet?"

"No." My sweaty fingers slip against the steering wheel. "They're still sorting it out in court."

"Do you think they're going to make me go back to Dad?" Her voice quavers. "I don't want to—I want to stay with you."

"Don't worry. I won't let anyone take you away from me," I say and reach out to touch her hand. Marjorie turns away toward the window again, shoulders rigid as though she doesn't really believe me.

Someone honks when I swerve into an open parking spot right before they claim it. Marjorie laughs as they hit the brakes hard. They retreat to find another gap between the vehicles lining the street and Marjorie opens her door.

"Have fun tonight." I shiver in the sudden gust of wind. My teeth chatter together uncontrollably as my body aches for more pills.

"Yeah, see you tomorrow." Marjorie smiles. If she notices something is wrong with me, she never says anything. "Thanks for letting me go to the party."

"Be careful." The words blurt from my mouth before I even think about it. She pauses as she climbs out of the car, body framed by the half-open door—milky skin, freckled wrists and slim hips. Her eyes catch the light.

"I will be. Don't worry." She winks before she slams the car door shut.

My hands shake as she walks away.

CHAPTER 36

The ringing inside my head has grown even worse by the time I arrive at the Albright house. My stomach is churning as I hurry up the front steps and press the bell. Cramps grip my muscles. Sweat beads against my skin.

"You're late," Ambrose says as he opens the door. Dressed in an expensive suit like he might have an important meeting later. He steps aside to let me in, and I unbutton my jacket in the foyer. Still not sure what I should say to convince him to give me the pills. I'd tell him just about anything right now to stop the chills running through my body.

"Sorry—traffic was bad this morning. I didn't know you had any other plans," I explain as I follow him down the hallway. The mansion is busy today. A vacuum drones somewhere, and maids bustle back and forth with loads of laundry. A few cast quick glances at me as they hurry past. I fight back more shivers as my face flushes with heat, wondering what they must think of me.

"I got a call from the police." A vein in Ambrose's neck twitches as his back stiffens underneath the luxurious fabric of his suit jacket. "Somebody broke open Adam's tomb last weekend. They want to talk to me about it."

"I heard about that. Did they catch who did it?" I ask. Not eager to tell him that I had visited the cemetery that morning, or that I discovered the broken coffin and the scattered bones inside. Desperate just to get the pills and leave this house behind.

"Not yet. I think maybe they have a few leads," Ambrose says as he climbs the stairs to the second story of the house. The floorboards creak underneath his feet. "Maybe it's a good thing—it could get them to reopen his case. It's been cold for too long."

I say nothing, wondering again if this is what he wanted all along. If he broke open Adam's tomb to get the police involved. Sabotaged my vehicle to keep me from leaving Reachwood.

Silence sits between us, as heavy as the presence of Adam's memory. I picture the stained bones littering the inside of his casket. All that's left of him—ribs, spine and femurs mottled brown with age. His missing skull.

Where is it now?

We walk past several oak-paneled doors until Ambrose pushes open the last one at the end of the corridor. I hesitate before I follow him inside. Reluctant to be alone with him but at the same time eager to get this over with. The quicker I tell him what he wants to hear, the faster I can get out of here with the pills. Maybe the information will be enough.

Maybe he won't try to fuck me.

"It was a lot of trouble to get what you wanted." Ambrose closes the door. The same hunger I glimpsed before shines in his eyes again. "You better make this worth it for me."

"I know." Goosebumps break out across my skin as Ambrose moves in front of me. My gaze drifts past him to study the room as I struggle to find the right words to say.

It must be his bedroom—almost bare compared to the opulent spaces we passed through to get here. An unmade bed sits below gabled windows that look out over Reachwood. Fog covers the neighborhood outside and clouds the distant forest in white.

An open laptop rests on the desk in the corner. The only other piece of furniture in the room. Its screen displays an article about the vandalism to

Adam's grave. A photo of Adam sits beside it, taken sometime during the last school dance before we graduated. Adam grins at the camera, eighteen years old and still alive. Although not for much longer.

The photo was taken only hours before he died.

"So?" Ambrose prompts after a moment.

"Victoria and Cyril don't want you to build the monument for Adam." I blurt the first words that arrive in my mind. "They're going to vote to block it."

"I've already guessed that. They won't be happy until everybody forgets about him," Ambrose says. He walks over to the desk and searches through its drawers until he finds a plastic bag filled with white pills. My mouth grows dry as he waits for me to reply. My body trembles.

I need to tell him something else.

"Cyril thought I told somebody about Adam's body. He was really angry with me," I say finally. My gaze never wavers from the prize gripped tightly in Ambrose's fist. "Victoria doesn't like to talk about it much, but I think she's afraid of another investigation."

"They both knew he was there, too?" His eyes sharpen with interest.

"Yeah. We found him together," I say and wonder how Victoria would react if she found out about this. If she ever discovers that I told Ambrose one of our most closely guarded secrets in exchange for a few pills. She'd probably never speak to me again.

Cut me from her life completely.

"I still don't get why you didn't tell anybody about it," Ambrose says. A frown creases the thin skin on his forehead.

"We were scared." I repeat the same excuse I had given him before. Not a lie. Not quite. "I've told you everything I know. Just give me the pills now. Please."

"I don't believe you." Ambrose turns toward the window. His eyes rest on the mansion Victoria and Cyril built at the crest of the hill. Tall enough to throw its long shadow across the neighborhood their families built. "I don't think it's a coincidence that after Adam's body was found in the forest, you got everything you ever wanted. You all did."

"No, I didn't," I protest. Adam's death forced me out of Reachwood. Pushed me into a troubled relationship with my ex-husband in an attempt to forget about everything that happened.

I never wanted that.

"Yeah, you did." Ambrose's voice grows cold. "You got all that money from your grandparents. Victoria and Cyril got what they wanted, too—they took over the entire mining company."

"That doesn't mean anything," I say, although a small part of me wonders if it could be true. My grandparents' unexpected death left me with enough money to live happily for the rest of my life. If I don't lose everything in the divorce settlement.

"Sometimes I think all of the devils live at the top of this hill," Ambrose says, and I can't tell if he's talking to me or himself. He pushes the bag of painkillers inside the pocket of his suit jacket before he turns toward me again. "You've only told me things I already guessed. If you still want the pills, you're going to have to give me something else."

This time I don't turn away when he kisses me. Mouth hard and rough enough to remind me of Adam. His tongue slips past my lips, and I kiss him back as pins and needles tickle my skin. More tremors shiver through my fingers as I run my hands through his hair. I don't want to fuck him. I don't even trust him.

But I need those pills.

Ambrose shrugs out of his suit jacket before he pushes me down on the bed. His heavy body presses against mine when he climbs on top of me, the same way Adam's had. Sudden panic rushes through me and I struggle to breathe as he kisses me again. Instinctively, I bite down on his lower lip. So hard my teeth almost break his skin.

He jerks back. I slip out from underneath him quickly, picking his jacket up from the floor. The plastic bag of pills crinkles when I curl my fingers around it, the same way a child clasps a favorite toy close for comfort.

"What the fuck?" His eyes widen. Anger turns his expression feral as he climbs off the bed and steps toward me.

"I already told you everything. That was the deal—you owe me these," I say and back away. But he reaches out fast and grabs my wrist. The same one my ex-husband almost snapped in half during our last fight before I left him. The edges of my vision darken as pain ripples through my forearm. So intense that my knees grow weak for a moment.

"I still don't believe you," he repeats as I wrench free. I run to the door and dart into the hallway before he can catch me. Several startled maids stare at my smudged lipstick and tousled hair as they scurry past.

Ambrose hesitates when he notices them. Reluctant to make a scene where other people can see him. He stands in the doorway, tense enough that I can see the muscles in his jaw twitch. Then he draws a deep breath.

"Fine—I'll let you go this time," he says after a few seconds. "Get the fuck out of here. Don't ever let me see you again."

"Don't worry. I won't." I shove the pills inside my pocket and hurry toward the front door, eager to leave before he changes his mind. I barely breathe until I reach my borrowed car and climb inside. My wrist aches and I swallow one of the pills before I start to drive.

It tastes like nothing.

FIFTEEN YEARS EARLIER

CHAPTER 37

"What's wrong with you?" Mother demanded. She glowered over the steering wheel as I climbed into the vehicle. Fresh out of my lecture in the principal's office and a quick visit to the school nurse to patch up the worst of my injuries from the fight with Adam. "Have you lost your mind completely?"

"He deserved it." I cracked open the window and glanced at my reflection. Hair still clotted with blood. A bruise blossomed below my eye, swollen enough to blur my vision.

I squinted as Mother steered out of the parking lot. She said nothing, lips pressed together tightly. Her anger filled the space between us as I tugged at a loose thread on my jeans, threatening to unravel the seam. Maybe she planned to ground me. Or something even worse, like send me back to the treatment center permanently.

"Stop it," Mother spat.

"Stop what?" I asked and yanked at the denim thread again.

"You'll ruin your clothes." She slapped my hand away from the loose strand. I pouted as the neighborhood passed by outside. Rows of identical houses presided above manicured lawns, minivans parked straight in each driveway. A harried mother rushed after her toddlers as they screamed and chased each other in circles. A large dog squatted and lifted its tail in another white-fenced yard.

"They're already ruined," I said, rolling up my window. A rip split the neckline of my sweater. The torn knees of my jeans gaped open to expose the bruised skin below. Frayed threads sprung from the fabric.

"I still don't get why you did it," Mother said. She rubbed a hand across her forehead as she turned onto our street, lined with neat-trimmed trees. "I thought you two were friends."

"I thought so, too." I drummed my thumbs against the armrest. My scalp itched and flakes of red stuck underneath my fingernails when I scratched at it.

"I hope it was worth it—no one at school is going to want to talk to you now." Mother snapped. Already embarrassed by the rumors my fight with Adam would stir in the neighborhood. I had tarnished her image again. Humiliated her in front of her friends. Probably the parents of some of the same students who had teased me ever since Adam sent out the photo.

"I don't care about them."

"You should." She turned into our driveway and parked the car.

"Well, I don't," I repeated and unbuckled my seatbelt.

"Then you're stupid." Mother twisted in her seat to scowl at me. "What do you think his family is going to do? We don't have enough money to cover a lawsuit."

"They wouldn't do that." I clenched my hands in my lap, so tightly my nails bit into my skin. "He started it—I was just defending myself from him. There's no way they'd win."

"You can win anything with enough money. And they have a lot of it." She raised her voice, and I winced at the high-pitched sound. "I know you've been friends with him for awhile now. But you have to understand—his family crushes anything in their path."

"Victoria won't let them," I blurted.

"You really think that?" Mother laughed, fast and contemptuous. "She's just like the rest of them. She'll fall in line if they tell her to."

"That's not true." My voice wavered.

"Yes, it is." Conviction punctuated her every word. I cowered in the passenger seat while she spoke my worst fears out loud.

"You don't know that."

"I was friends with her father, when we were younger." Her hands clenched the steering wheel. Veins bulged beneath her thin skin as she said, "He faded out of my life when he realized how different we really were. He figured out I'd never have the same future as him."

"Victoria's not like that," I insisted. I needed to believe it. Victoria would never leave me, not after the way she had defended me at school—not after the way she had kissed me. She would never toss me aside just to please her family.

Would she?

"I've known those families much longer than you have. I've seen how they work." Her voice softened. "You might think she's different, but she isn't. They only care about their fortune. Gold is the only thing that matters to them."

"They're not all bad," I grasped for some sort of reassurance. "They can't be."

"Haven't you ever wondered why they don't just cut the forest down? They would be heroes if they stopped the disappearances. They could probably make a fortune all over again if they sold that land." Mother paused. "But they guard it instead. Like there's something in there they don't want found."

"Like what?" I frowned.

"I don't know. I just—" she hesitated. Her words tapered away before she continued, "The story goes that they only struck gold here after the first settlement disappeared. But maybe something else happened in there. Maybe they found the gold and decided they didn't want to share their claim with anyone else."

"So what? That happened a long time ago." I shook my head. "It doesn't have anything to do with Victoria."

"Is it true he took a photo of you?" She changed the subject. My stomach lurched like I was going to throw up. This was it—my life was over. She would never forgive me for this embarrassment. Never let me out of the house again.

"I've never been more ashamed," she said after several excruciating moments passed in silence. "I didn't raise you to be a slut. To take your clothes off for every boy who looks at you."

"I'm sorry." The words felt dirty. Tears welled at the corners of my eyes. I shouldn't have to apologize—I did nothing wrong. This was all Adam's fault, despite the way he tried to blame me during the long meeting in the principal's office. How he acted like nothing happened in the forest, as if nothing he did to me mattered.

He deserved much worse.

"We'll talk more about this later." Mother opened her door and swung her feet onto the concrete. "When your father comes home. You better hope he doesn't lose his job because of what you did today."

My bruises throbbed as I climbed out of the car. Mother grabbed my forearm and hustled me toward the house, away from the curious eyes of the neighbors. Eager to preserve the last shreds of her reputation.

She would never pick me over them.

"Let go." I winced as more pain shot up my shoulder.

"Go to your room. I don't want to look at you." She unlocked the door and dragged me into the foyer. I tore free from her grasp and retreated down the hallway to my bedroom.

The window lay open. The bracelet Adam had given me in the forest sparkled on my desk. A shiver crept through my body as I looked at the trees leaning over the white picket fence outside. It felt like I was being watched.

I slammed the window closed and drew the curtains to block out the sight of the branches that reached toward my bedroom. Almost as though the forest somehow knew I had brought home one of its offerings. Stolen it from the grove where it had lain for generations. My skin prickled as I remembered Victoria's earlier words.

Never bring anything out of Reachwood Forest, or touch any of the gold, coins or jewelry.

It might make something angry.

CHAPTER 38

woke with a start. Propped myself up on one elbow and blinked, eyes trying to adjust to the dark—not sure if I had really heard something, or if the sound was only the last fragment of a dream. My body tensed when the noise repeated. Three quick taps on the window pane.

My phone vibrated underneath my pillowcase. I jumped, heartbeat racing as I flipped it open. Half-expecting a threat from Adam—although he hadn't texted me since he left me in the grove, the fight at school might have enraged him enough to say something. But the message was from Victoria instead. I smiled as I read the words.

We're here. Meet us outside.

I crawled out of bed and picked up some clothes left discarded on the floor, dressing quietly while my parents slept upstairs. Careful not to make enough noise to wake them as I slid open the window and climbed outside.

My friends huddled together like shadows in the backyard. Victoria, Cyril, Nathalie and Matthew—all eager to see me. To confirm I had survived my fight with Adam earlier.

"You look terrible," Cyril said when I drew closer.

"Thanks," I snapped, tilting my head down. Embarrassed by the bruises and scrapes that still decorated my face. Our shoes drummed against the sidewalk as we walked toward the park where we usually met at night to drink and get high. "So, why are you here?"

"We just wanted to make sure you were okay." Nathalie studied my injuries. "Did you really get suspended?"

"Yeah." My voice flattened when I remembered how she had shunned me in class. "Not that you care, probably."

"I'm sorry." Her face fell. "It's just—I heard so many things about the photo. I didn't know what to believe."

"Did he send it to all of you?" Shame heated my face when they nodded. Adam must have shown it to absolutely everyone at our school. Even the kids nobody talked to.

Like he wanted to humiliate me as much as possible.

"He didn't even get suspended," Victoria revealed as we darted across the street. Lamps cast circles of light against the concrete.

"Fuck him," Matthew muttered. My friends all murmured in agreement—only Cyril remained quiet. He said nothing while we sat on the benches in the park and passed a flask back and forth. Hours rushed by, and the moon plunged toward the horizon.

When I stood to leave, Victoria began to walk back with me toward my house.

"Where are you going?" Cyril demanded.

"I want to talk more with Ava," Victoria said, and a thrill sparked through my body. Mother was wrong, she had to be. Victoria wanted to stay with me.

"Why?" A hint of suspicion shadowed Cyril's voice. His eyes drifted to the ring on my finger. The one Victoria had given me. Maybe he felt threatened by anyone else close to her. Or noticed the desire written across our faces whenever we looked at each other.

"Because I missed her." Victoria smiled at me. A shiver of happiness ran through me as I imagined kissing her again. Or something more—excitement and nervousness warred inside me. I'd never slept with a girl before. Never even allowed myself to consider it.

I'd always kept those wishes well-hidden.

"Really?" Cyril's tone turned disbelieving. "You just saw each other this morning."

"So what?" My words came out harsh. Razor sharp at the edges. "Is that a problem?"

"It's not safe out here in the dark," Cyril protested. Still hopeful Victoria would give in and walk home with him. I wondered if it ever bothered her that Cyril followed her everywhere. Desperate for her attention, always hopeful that she would notice him—as if he were convinced that she would give in and date him if he only persisted long enough.

"I'll walk back in the morning instead." Victoria dismissed him. She never even glanced in his direction as she stood beside me. So close it almost felt like we were alone.

As though I were the only person who mattered.

"Then I guess I'll see you later," Cyril relented. Disappointment darkened his face. Born into a life as wealthy and privileged as Victoria's, he had probably never had anything denied to him before.

"See you." Victoria waved. He strode away down the street, shoulders slumped underneath the weight of her rejection.

We both relaxed when he vanished around the corner.

⊶⊷

The flush of victory warmed my body on the journey home. Victoria's hand brushed mine as we hurried down the sidewalk. Excitement fluttered inside me as we crept across the dark yard and climbed through my open window—careful not to disturb my parents still fast asleep upstairs.

Victoria kissed me before I even drew the curtains. I pulled her closer as her tongue darted into my mouth and my teeth parted, eager to let her farther inside. My hands slid underneath her shirt to explore her skin. The smooth curve of her ribs. Not sure where her body ended and mine began, like our sharp edges had melted and merged together as we sank down into my bed.

But my whole body froze when her hands moved lower. The memory of Adam's skin against mine surfaced in my mind. Panic clutched like a heart attack inside my chest. Victoria pulled away and I drew an unsteady breath.

"What's wrong?" Victoria asked. Unease shadowed her face, as though she thought my reaction was her fault.

"It's not you. I'm sorry, I really want to." I blinked back tears. I had wanted this for so long—wished for it and hated myself for it. Suppressed my feelings and even tried to leave them behind in the forest. And now I'd choked at the perfect moment.

Couldn't go any further without picturing what happened with Adam.

"Don't be sorry." She brushed away my apology. "It's his fault, isn't it?"

"I can't stop thinking about it," I said and sat up, clutching a pillow against my stomach. My parents stirred upstairs. We both froze, holding perfectly still until silence enveloped the house again.

"Is that what he gave you?" Victoria's gaze strayed to the gold bracelet on my desk.

"Yeah." I sunk my fingers into the sunflower-patterned covers. "In the grove. Before—"

"We should get rid of it." She rose to her feet. "Give it back to the forest."

"Right now?" I swallowed. Reluctant to walk through Reachwood Forest in the dark. To return the piece of jewelry to the grove and lay it down between the gnarled roots of the hawthorn trees.

I still remembered the sensation of something in there following me.

"We don't actually have to go in there," Victoria said like she could guess my thoughts. "We'll just throw it over the fence."

"Okay." I relented and crawled out of bed. My body still ached for her touch as I said, "You know, ever since I brought it home, I've felt like the forest's been watching me."

"There's nothing out there." She dismissed my concerns. Face so serene that I couldn't read her thoughts. Maybe she didn't really believe there was any truth to the stories. Or maybe she was lying to me. I remembered Mother's words in the car earlier. How she had said Victoria's loyalty would always remain with her family.

If she knew the truth about the forest, would she tell me?

We climbed out the window and into the garden. The flowers sweetened the night air around us as we crept to the edge of the yard. I cradled the bracelet in the palm of my hand, gold cold against my skin. The forest stretched against the fence. When I threw the bracelet into the trees, it gleamed against the foliage.

A bitter reminder of what had happened to me on the weekend.

"I'm glad you hurt him." Victoria touched my wrist.

"Me too," I said, remembering the satisfaction I felt when his skin broke beneath my nails. "I just wish I made him pay for it more."

"You were perfect." Victoria smiled at me. Pride expanded inside my chest. She turned away toward the street like she planned to walk back home, but I grabbed her hand.

"Don't leave."

I kissed her again when we returned to my bedroom. She kissed me back until I couldn't speak—could barely breathe. We fell asleep holding each other close as faint moonlight filtered in through the blinds drawn across the windows. I felt safe in her embrace, for maybe the first time since Adam had left me in the grove.

Like nothing inside the forest could ever touch us here.

CHAPTER 39

Victoria stirred against me in the morning. Still half-asleep, I muffled a yawn behind my palm as the shower started to run upstairs. The low hum of my parents' voices carried through the house.

"You're leaving?" I asked when Victoria climbed out of bed.

"Yeah—my parents will be really mad if I skip school again." Victoria combed her fingers through her sleep-tousled hair. "They've been on my case about everything lately."

"Why?" I sat up and blinked in the early light.

"They don't like anything they can't control," she said. Her words betrayed a hint of bitterness as she sat down on the edge of the bed to lace up her sneakers. I fidgeted with the corners of my cotton sheets and wondered if this was all my fault. Maybe her campaign against Adam had set her against the rest of her family.

"How long are you suspended for?" Her voice caught, as if she would miss me every day while I stayed away.

"Not long—only three days. I'll be back on Monday for the last week of class," I said and swung my legs over the edge of the bed to set my feet down on the carpet. Crossing the floor to my closet, I searched through my clothes until I found an outfit I liked. "I can't believe they didn't suspend Adam, too. He started everything."

"They probably didn't want to make his family angry," Victoria said. Over the years, Reachwood High School had expanded through donations from the Albrights, Harts and Gallaghers—relying on their wealth to draw the best teachers and fund prestigious programs. Without their assistance, it would become just another unremarkable high school in the suburbs.

"I just wish they would have done something," I said as I dressed. Victoria watched me and a spark of lust flickered through me as her eyes drank in the sight of my body—eager and hungry.

"I know. I'm angry, too." She pushed open the window. "His family didn't do anything after my parents talked to them. But I'm sure they'll punish him now."

"You really believe that?" I asked as I pulled a sweater over my head to cover my bare skin. "If they didn't care what he did to me before, why would they care now?"

"Because he just keeps getting worse." Victoria leaned against the sill. "They'll want to put a stop to it. Before he does anything else."

"I hope so." I bit my lip. Adam was their golden child, the oldest son of the Albright family. It seemed unlikely that they would give him more than a slap on the wrist as punishment. And then maybe he'd lead another girl into the forest.

Just like me and Emily.

"Did he ever tell you what his father did?" Victoria asked. The familiar sounds of the neighborhood waking up drifted into the room. Suburban moms chatted as they pushed their strollers around the block. Babies wailed inside the oversized carriages.

"Not really."

"It all started when some chemicals from one of the mining sites he was supervising leaked into the forest, a few miles outside of Reachwood." Victoria spoke each word carefully. Maybe reluctant to reveal too much about the inner workings of the three powerful families who had founded the neighborhood. "It destroyed several acres before we cleaned it up. But afterward he was convinced that we had made something in the forest angry with us."

"So, what happened?" I asked and glanced outside. The trees still waited at the edges of the yard. I searched for the gleam of the bracelet among the leaves, but I didn't see anything.

Like maybe something had carried it away.

"He started to avoid the forest completely. I heard he got so stressed he stopped sleeping." Victoria interrupted my thoughts. "After a while, he couldn't even talk. Like he forgot how to speak."

"That's awful."

"It still doesn't make what Adam did to you okay," Victoria said as heavy footsteps traveled through the hallway upstairs. We didn't have much time left. My parents would head down to the kitchen soon for breakfast.

"I guess it could be worse." I changed the subject. "At least they're still letting me go to the dance on Friday. Even though I'm still technically suspended."

"Have you decided who you're going with yet?" Victoria climbed through the window. She stood among the flowers in the garden. Lovelier than any of them.

"I thought I would go with Adam. Before everything happened," I said. It felt almost embarrassing that I'd ever thought things would be so easy. That he'd ask me to go with him to the last dance of the school year and that everything would work out perfectly. "Now I don't even know if I really want to go."

"I could take you. We could go together."

"Aren't you going with Cyril? I thought he'd asked you already," I said, although I wanted nothing more than to go with Victoria. The last dance at Reachwood High School was organized each year by the Albright, Hart and Gallagher families. To celebrate the students who were graduating, but also to honor the contributions their families had made to the school.

All three of their oldest children were graduating this year. The whole event would revolve around their heirs. If Victoria went with me instead of

Cyril, it would prove Mother's prediction wrong, once and for all—Victoria really did care about me. Enough to resist the pressure from her entire family.

That had to mean something.

"I know he's definitely going to, but he hasn't yet." Victoria leaned through the open window. Her elbows rested against the sill.

"But won't he be upset—you know, if you don't go with him?" I asked, remembering the way Cyril's eyes had studied us last night. Anger had turned his entire body rigid when Victoria refused to return home with him.

"Who cares? I don't." The rising breeze blew loose strands of hair around her face, and she brushed them away. "I don't want to go with him, anyway. I want to go with you."

"I want to go with you, too." My voice caught when she smiled at me. "What should we tell everybody, though—do you want them to know?"

"Let's say we're going together because of what happened with Adam," Victoria suggested as the sun broke above the horizon and spread its light across the sky. "My parents will be mad enough already that I'm not going with Cyril. They'd lose their minds if they thought I was—well, if they found out I liked a girl. Like that."

"Yeah, my parents would probably kick me out of the house if they found out," I said. Pots and pans clanged together in the kitchen. "They're already mad at me over just about everything. Especially now that I've gotten suspended."

"Okay, it's a date." Happiness lit Victoria's face. "I should go, though. Before I'm late for school—I'll miss you."

"I'll miss you, too." I reached through the open window frame to wrap my arms around her shoulders. We stood close enough that I could feel the steady rhythm of her heartbeat beneath her skin.

Before she left, she kissed me again.

TODAY

CHAPTER 40

I spend the rest of the morning driving aimlessly through Reachwood, visiting half-remembered places from my childhood in an attempt to forget what I'd just told Ambrose. The movie theater where a boy kissed me for the first time, pressing his clumsy mouth against mine. The park where we used to hang out all night, talking and drinking until the sunrise sent us creeping back home like tired vampires.

But none of those places erase the memory of Ambrose's weight on top of my body. Or the unfettered rage on his face when I'd grabbed the pills and escaped. The last thing he'd said before I left still played through my mind.

I'll let you go this time.

Finally, I give in and turn toward the one place I want to be right now: Victoria's house. She lets me in without any questions when I ring the bell unannounced again. A hole yawns in the wall as she leads me down the hallway.

"Sorry—I would have called someone to clean this up if I knew you were coming," Victoria says when my eyes linger on the crater. About the size and shape of someone's fist. Photos lie facedown on the floor, knocked out of place by the impact. Carefully I step over the broken glass strewn across the carpet.

"What happened?" I ask. My tongue feels clumsy in my mouth—half-numb from the pill I swallowed this morning.

"I got into an argument with Cyril," Victoria says, as if this is normal.

"Oh." My stomach drops when I remember the fights with my ex-husband. The ruins left in the wake of each confrontation—broken doors and smashed phones. How it always escalated until at least one of us drew blood.

"So, what do you want?" Victoria asks. I wonder what she thinks of me showing up on her doorstep over and over again. If I represent a past she would rather forget, or if she still remembers the way she used to kiss me. We've never talked about it—not once. Although we've both danced around the subject, afraid to address the unspoken tension between us.

"I went to the cemetery this weekend," I say as we enter the kitchen. More fragments of glass and broken dishware lie scattered across the floor. "To visit Adam's grave."

"Why?" Victoria frowns.

"I thought if I could see the place where he's buried, I'd get some kind of closure." I follow her through the wreckage. The same way I used to follow her everywhere when we were still children. Out the window. Down the path. Through the forest and back again before the morning sun broke above the horizon. "Like I'd be able to accept it's over, you know?"

"No, I don't." Victoria skirts around the pieces of a shattered porcelain plate. "Why go picking at old wounds when you could leave them alone?"

"His tomb was open." My voice quivers. I take a seat at the counter while Victoria searches through the liquor cabinet. She splashes some vodka into a shot glass and passes it to me without a word. The bitter liquid stings against my throat when I throw it back. I cough as she pours a shot into another glass and swallows it all at once.

"I took a look inside his coffin." My fingers tingle. "His skull was missing."

"Did you tell anybody?" she asks. Voice tense, as if she is also afraid of another investigation. Of what secrets the detectives might unearth if they search hard enough. My stomach twists when I remember how I told Ambrose that Victoria and Cyril knew about Adam's body in the grove. The police could show up to ask her more questions.

She might guess that I had said something to him.

"I called it in," I admit, picturing the bones inside the broken tomb. All that's left of Adam. "But now I can't stop thinking you're right. Someone doesn't want us to forget what happened."

"Probably Ambrose. Or maybe Aidan." Victoria pours more alcohol into her glass and drinks it down fast. She doesn't even wince at the taste as she says, "But it could be anybody—everyone still talks about Adam. Even the kids."

"Yeah, Marjorie asked me about it," I say, picturing the way she stared out at the trees this morning when we drove through the ravine. Her questions keep getting more and more specific. About Adam's death and the grove in the forest. Things best left hidden. "She says they tell all kinds of stories about what happened to him."

"I've heard some of them. He's pretty much a local legend." Victoria laughs. "I actually think he would have liked that."

"Marjorie knows about the grove. She asked me today if there's a place in the forest that grants wishes when you leave a gift there." My body grows cold as I remember how Marjorie waited for me to react to her question. The way her face practically glowed when I confirmed her suspicions. "Someone must have told her."

"Well, it wasn't Virgil or Catherine. I haven't said anything about it to them." Victoria returns the half-empty bottle of vodka to the liquor cabinet. The decorative doors click as she closes them.

"She wanted to know if I would win the divorce settlement if she left an offering in the forest," I say. The harsh taste of vodka still flavors the inside of my mouth. "I'm worried she might try to search for it."

"How's the divorce going, anyway?" Victoria changes the subject. "Have you heard anything more about it?"

"Not yet." I draw an unsteady breath. "I'm still fighting to get full custody of Marjorie. I don't want him to get any visitation."

"Do you think she's—" Victoria says, and I guess her next question. I should have known I couldn't keep this secret from her either. Not when she's always had such an uncanny ability to piece things together.

"I don't really know." I ball my hands into fists in my lap before I relax them again. "I met my ex-husband early that summer. Only a few weeks afterward. It could have been him or Adam."

"She looks a lot like Adam, sometimes. When she smiles," Victoria says, and I remember how distant my ex-husband became after Marjorie was born. Almost as if he could sense she might not be his.

"I don't want to talk about it." My voice tightens. If Marjorie found out, it would destroy the veneer of normalcy I've struggled so hard to maintain ever since I fled my ex-husband. Her whole world would explode in her face. Destroy her all over again.

"Do you ever think about how different things would have been if you hadn't picked him?" Victoria asks, and I flinch at the hard edge in her voice. Surprised it still bothers her after all these years. That she even still thinks about it. But then again, she always hated being second best to anyone—especially Adam.

"I should go," I say and push my chair back from the counter. Eager to run away, like always. Still afraid to say anything about our past relationship out loud. To bring up what we've both so carefully avoided talking about.

The house is quiet as I walk toward the front door, careful to step around the broken glass on the floor. The hole in the wall gapes like an open mouth. Evidence of the violence before my unexpected arrival.

"Where's Cyril, anyway?" I ask as I pull my jacket from the closet.

"He stays out late in the forest after we fight, sometimes." Victoria fidgets with the gold rings on her fingers. "I don't know why."

"You've really never thought about leaving him?" My eyes drift across the wreckage.

"I can't—he would take everything from me." Her voice catches. Before I can stop myself, I reach out and touch her hand. Her skin is warm against my fingertips. My heartbeat lunges like a wild animal trapped inside my body.

"I'm sorry," I say and silence settles between us for a moment. Heavy with the words I left unspoken in the kitchen—the answer to her question. "I never should have chosen him. You were the only person I wanted, back then."

I hesitate when she moves closer. Not sure if we're making a mistake. But when her mouth presses against mine, I feel hungry in ways I thought I had forgotten. Like no time has passed between us and nothing has changed. She kisses me softly at first, then harder—until I forget all the years we spent apart. Until nothing else matters but the two of us here now.

Victoria says nothing when she pulls away. Just grabs my hand instead and leads me upstairs. We undress in her workshop—when she pulls off my shirt, she runs her fingertips across the scar that still marks the hollow of my neck. I shiver against her touch.

The light falling through the stained glass windows of her studio paints our faces with bright kaleidoscopes of color. It shimmers against the gilded skulls of animals and golden links of jewelry on her desk. She kisses me as her hands explore every inch of my exposed skin. I twist my fingers in her hair to pull her closer.

We slip out of the rest of our clothes, leaving them crumpled on the floor. A scar crosses her abdomen, where they must have cut the twins from her body over fourteen years ago. Another marks the palm of her hand.

She smiles when I kiss her again, dragging me down into her bed.

CHAPTER 41

"Where were you?" Mother demands as soon as I walk through the front door. Thick fog still blankets the street outside. Red lights flash beside a car crash at the edge of the road.

"At Victoria's place." I search for a lie. Some kind of excuse to hide why I had stayed over there so late. "I was hoping the weather would clear up."

"Why didn't you text me?" Skepticism tinges her question.

"I didn't know I had to tell you everything."

"What if we needed the car?" Frustration clips her words. "You can't just borrow it and bring it back whenever you want."

"I'm sorry, okay? I'll text you next time," I say and move toward my bedroom, eager to escape. Mother pursues me down the hallway, and I push my hands into the pockets of my jeans. My fingers close around the bag of pills I stole from Ambrose this morning. The plastic crinkles like the promise of relief.

"This isn't turning out the way we expected," Mother snaps, standing in the doorway when I enter my bedroom.

"What are you talking about?"

"We said you could stay here as long as you helped us move out." Resentment sharpens her tone. "But instead you've spent most of your time visiting with your friends."

"That's not true," I say. Not eager for yet another argument as I shuffle through the clothes in my closet. After I choose something warmer to wear, I push past Mother, but her frown follows me down the hall.

I lock the bathroom door before I pull the bag of pills from my pocket. The white caplets rattle against each other when I unlock the medicine cabinet, pop open my empty prescription container and pour them inside. The pills fill the plastic jar almost up to its brim. There's enough here to last over a month.

I shake one onto the countertop but falter as I remember Ambrose's mouth pressed against mine. Revulsion rises inside me. I can't go back to him again. Not after what happened. Once I run out, I'm done—maybe I should wait a little longer. Take smaller doses, spacing out the time between them.

Taper off until I don't need them anymore.

Mother knocks on the door. "Ava? I still want to talk to you."

"I'll be out in a minute." The first twinges of a headache press against my temples. I pick up the pill and turn it over in my fingers before I swallow it down with a sip of water from the faucet. One more can't hurt. I'll start to lower my dosage tomorrow.

"So, what do you want to talk about?" I ask after I exit the bathroom. Mother waits for me in the hallway.

"We're both really trying to help you." Her voice is earnest. Like she means it. "I know things have been difficult ever since you left your husband."

"I'll try to help out around here more."

"I just wish you'd be more grateful. We didn't have to take you in after you left him," she says. I wonder if she also expected me to be grateful every time she sacrificed my happiness to preserve her own reputation. Often enough that eventually I learned how to do it myself. Stopped eating to force my body to be perfect. Convinced myself that my feelings for Victoria meant nothing so I could pretend to be the daughter Mother always wanted.

"Don't worry. We'll leave as soon as they fix my car."

"I hope so—it's been difficult having the two of you back home." Her words turn cold and venomous. "Especially Marjorie—more of my things have gone missing around the house. You need to do something before she gets even worse."

"That's not her fault," I protest, although I remember the way Marjorie smirked when Mother's tablet stopped working. "You probably just forgot where you left them."

"Where is she, anyway?" Mother asks and peers down the hallway.

"She's staying over at Virgil and Catherine's place—they're having a party this weekend."

"I guess I should have known they'd be close." She sighs. A hint of judgment shadows her voice. "Especially with how much time you've been spending with Victoria."

"You say that like it's a bad thing." I say, pushing past her. My heels thud against the carpet-covered floorboards as I wonder if she ever suspected that the relationship between me and Victoria had been deeper than just friendship. Even if she had known about it, she never would have touched the subject. Better just to act as if it didn't exist.

"Aren't you worried Marjorie will turn out the same way you did?"

"What does that mean?" I ask and stop in my tracks. Hot anger surges through me.

"You know what I'm talking about. The drinking, the drugs—how you stopped eating." Her eyes never waver from mine. "And getting pregnant so early. Sometimes I think you never should have kept her. You were too young to really be a mother and your life would be so different now if you had just given her up."

"You don't know that," I say as sudden tears blur the edges of my vision. "And I'm her mother. I loved her from the first moment I knew I was going to have her—she's better off with me than anyone else."

Mother stays silent enough for me to imagine her next words.

Are you sure?

"I didn't mean to make you upset," she says finally when I open the base-ment door. But she suppresses a small smile, like she knows she hurt me. Attacked one of my worst insecurities. "But I still don't think it's a good decision to let Marjorie spend so much time around Virgil and Catherine. From what I hear, they're exactly like their mother."

"I think it's great she's making friends." The temperature drops as I retreat underground. "She needs them, after everything she's been through."

"Is she still seeing a therapist?"

"That's none of your business. But no—I had to cancel our insurance." My hand tightens on the railing. The smell of mildew grows stronger as I draw closer to the base of the stairs. When my feet touch down on the cement floor, I turn around to face her and say, "I still don't understand what Victoria did to make you hate her like this."

"I guess I've just never really liked the way she looks at you," Mother admits. I open my mouth before I close it again. The long years we have spent in silence stretch between us. A siren wails somewhere outside. The loud noise pierces the suburban quiet.

"Why do you always assume the worst of her?" I ask finally.

Mother says nothing as she walks away.

CHAPTER 42

pick Marjorie up from Catherine and Virgil's party early on Saturday morning. Face still numb from the autumn wind blowing outside while I wait for her in the foyer. The aftermath of Victoria and Cyril's fight yesterday has been completely erased. A painting hangs over the hole in the wall like a bandage. The shattered glass has been swept away.

"Marjorie should be down in a minute," Victoria says and glances at the stairs. Teenage chatter carries through the house—Catherine, Virgil, Marjorie and some other friends whose voices I don't recognize. My throat tightens when I wonder if Aidan stayed over last night. If Marjorie lied to me again. "Would you like something to drink? Coffee, or anything?"

"I'm okay. Thanks, though." I shiver. Victoria holds me close for a moment and heat flickers through my body. Warm enough to drive away the lingering cold.

"Mom, can you come up here for a minute?" Virgil calls from somewhere upstairs. We flinch away from each other.

"I'll be right there." Victoria shoots me an apologetic smile. I wonder if yesterday meant anything as she climbs the stairway, turns a corner and disappears from sight. If it was just a fling, or if she wants to kiss me again.

Sleep with me whenever the house is empty.

The door swings open, and I startle. Cyril steps inside the house—clothes rumpled, eyes tired, as though he had spent all night outside in the forest. The limp body of a stag hangs from his shoulders. Blood trickles from the hole in its head as he sets it down and stamps his boots against the mat.

"I'd heard you were leaving. I thought you'd be out of Reachwood already," he says as he shrugs out of his jacket. Splotches of blood stain the fabric. "What are you still doing here?"

"My car broke down," I say. A blush spreads as fast as a rash across my face as I remember the way his wife kissed me yesterday. "We're stuck here until they figure out what's wrong with it."

"I'm sorry to hear that." Disappointment darkens his words. He had probably hoped I'd be far away from Reachwood by now—we were never friends, not really. More like rivals locked in a bitter competition for Victoria's attention.

"At least Marjorie can finish the semester here," I say. Maybe it really is for the best. I won't have to pull Marjorie out of school nearly halfway through the semester and figure out how to enroll her somewhere else.

And it's a convenient excuse to stay close to Victoria.

"You should get out of here as soon as possible." Cyril moves toward me, and I take a quick step back. He has grown since we were teenagers, or at least is taller than I remember—now towering above me. Lean and muscled, skin stretched taut across his sharp cheekbones.

"What are you talking about?" I ask. Pain shivers through my wrist, intense enough to curl my fingers inward. I shouldn't have taken only half a painkiller this morning. Even though I need to stifle my growing need for the medication before I run out again. Before it becomes a problem. But it's the only thing that can muffle the anxiety that prickles across my skin.

"You must know about what happened to Adam's grave." He scrutinizes my face.

"That doesn't have anything to do with me." My eyes dart toward the staircase when more laughter floats through the hallway. Hopeful that

Marjorie will arrive and interrupt our conversation. But her voice is still distant, as if she hasn't even started to say goodbye to her friends yet.

"And I heard someone left a message on your door," he continues as if I'd never said anything. "All this shit only started when you came back. You should have stayed away completely—now it's like everybody can't stop thinking about the past."

"Cyril? What's going on?" Victoria appears at the top of the stairs. The memory of her body pressed against mine springs unbidden into my mind. I tilt my head down, desperate to hide anything on my face that could give me away. Maybe this is what Cyril meant when he said I'd brought the past back again.

Rekindled old feelings I'd thought were long since dead.

"I'm catching up with Ava. You never told me she was dropping by," Cyril says. The aggression drops from his voice all at once.

"I must have forgot." Victoria never looks at him, voice dismissive. I wonder if they have even spoken to each other since their argument. But then she notices the body of the stag left by the front door and she glances up to frown at him. "I thought I told you not to bring any more of those into the house."

"I'll take it to the workshop in a minute. I wanted to get started on it this morning," Cyril says, and Victoria's mouth tightens as if she's barely suppressing her anger. Her eyes linger on the drops of blood scattered across the otherwise spotless floor. Probably worth more than my parents have saved for their retirement. "If it bothers you so much, call someone to clean it up."

"You clean it up," she snaps as Marjorie and Catherine slip past her to hurry downstairs. Their footsteps beat against the floorboards like some kind of primal drum.

"I guess I'll see you around," I say and shuffle my feet, eager to leave. Marjorie retrieves her jacket from the closet and kneels to lace up her boots on the mat. Catherine pries at a chip of pink nail polish while she waits to say goodbye. They both dart quick looks at the body of the stag left on the floor. The corners of Marjorie's mouth twitch like she wants to comment on it, but she doesn't say anything. Thankfully.

"See you later." Catherine hugs Marjorie, the same way Victoria used to embrace me after sleepovers when we were younger. My breath catches in my throat. It almost feels like I'm watching our fourteen-year-old ghosts.

"Good luck with your car." Cyril opens the door. "I hope you get out of here soon."

"Thanks—I hope so, too," I say as I step outside. The words feel like a lie when Victoria smiles at me. I steal one last glance at her over my shoulder before Cyril closes the door tight behind us.

Marjorie sits quietly in the passenger seat on the way home. Her fingers dart across the screen of her phone. A tiny, star-shaped charm dangles from the chain attached to the phone's protective case. Delicate flowers pattern its clear shell.

"So? How was it?" I ask after a minute.

"It was fun. We stayed up all night—I'm still kind of tired."

"You should take a nap when we get back," I say as I steer onto the main road. Pain darts through my wrist and I grit my teeth. Fighting against the need to take another painkiller as soon as we get home.

"I know." Marjorie rests her forehead against the window pane when we cross the ravine. Reachwood Forest rushes by outside. Suddenly, she blurts, "Does Catherine's mom love you?"

"What? Why would you think that?" I stutter at the unexpected question.

"I guess there's just something in her eyes when she looks at you sometimes."

Is that what Mother meant when she said she hated the way Victoria looked at me?

Things are so different now, compared to when we were teenagers. Back then, all of our classmates would have shunned us if they found out. Our parents would have kicked us out of the house. There was no future for us—if we had stayed together, we wouldn't have been able to marry even if we wanted to. At least, not until a few years ago.

Now, it seems like nobody would even bat an eye.

"I never noticed," I lie, keeping my eyes fixed on the street in front of my vehicle. Fallen leaves clog the gutters. Barren branches reach toward the clouded sky.

"I've heard stories about the two of you." Marjorie turns to study my face.

"What kind of stories?" My voice tightens as we emerge into the suburb.

"You know—that you were close." Marjorie shrugs her shoulders. "And that you both were the prettiest girls in school."

"I don't think that's true." I laugh and shake my head.

"Anyway, Catherine thinks her parents are going to get divorced soon. She says they don't even sleep in the same room." Marjorie leans forward to crank up the volume of the song playing through the speakers. A fresh cut decorates her palm, skin ragged and broken. "I wouldn't care if you got together, you know. She's really beautiful."

"What happened to your hand?" I ask as I park the car in the driveway.

"What?" Marjorie's expression is guarded, as though she is trying to hide something.

"I saw that cut on your palm. How did you get it?"

"I don't remember. It was a pretty wild party." She brushes off the question and hops out of the car before I have the chance to ask her anything else.

Inside the house, Marjorie disappears into her bedroom without another word. I turn on the television in the living room to watch the local news, but my mind keeps drifting to the look on Cyril's face. The way his voice hardened when he warned me to leave the suburb.

He had always been ruthless—and had probably grown even more so when he took control of their mining business. If he found out about me and Victoria, he would lose his mind. Drive me out of Reachwood, the same way his family did to all of their competition.

My wrist aches. I grit my teeth as I flip through the channels, searching for a distraction. But nothing works. The pain only grows stronger—until I give in, turn off the television and walk down the hallway into the bathroom. I pause after I twist the cap off the prescription bottle, remembering how Marjorie accused me of being high all the time. But Cyril's words repeat again through my mind, as low and urgent as a threat.

You should have stayed away completely.

I shake a pill into the palm of my hand and swallow it down with a quick sip of water. For the first time, the medication tastes almost bitter.

CHAPTER 43

My cell phone rings late on Monday afternoon. The sound carries through the rooms of the house, shrill enough to startle me as I pack more of my parents' belongings away upstairs. I drop another pile of old clothes into the donation bin before following the noise down the hallway.

By the time I find where I left my phone in the kitchen, a message is waiting for me. The number for the auto body repair shop flashes across the screen. I press the button to listen to it—a mechanic called with a diagnosis for my broken car. Someone poured soda into the gas tank. Completely ruined the engine and the fuel system. He gives the cost to fix it, and I try not to think about my empty bank accounts or the debt piling up on my credit cards.

The phone beeps, signaling the end of the message. My hands tremble as I place it back onto the counter and wonder who sabotaged my vehicle. Maybe someone random—one of the same people who harassed me and my friends after Adam died. Or Ambrose, determined to prevent me from leaving Reachwood before he can make me pay for whatever he believes I did to his older brother. I still remember how his body tensed when I stole the pills from him. The same way an animal prepares to spring upon its prey. Ambrose said he'd let me go *that time*—but maybe he had already taken steps to ensure I didn't get away from him again.

Or maybe it's somebody else. Someone so close I would never suspect them.

The phone rings again before I can leave the kitchen. Still lost in thought, I pick it up without checking the number, press the button and say, "Hello?"

"Is this Ava Montgomery speaking?" An unfamiliar voice asks. My muscles stiffen as I wonder if it's the same stranger who called me in the middle of the night after Victoria's party. I shudder at the memory of the steady breathing on the other end of the line.

"Yes, this is Ava," I say finally.

"My name is Anthony Hernandez." He pauses like I should recognize the name. I say nothing as fog gathers outside.

"I'm the principal at Marjorie's school," he adds after a few moments pass.

"Oh—what's going on?" A hole opens in my stomach. Did Marjorie get into another fight? Or maybe she just decided not to show up to class today. Maybe it's nothing.

"I need to talk to you about an altercation your daughter got into." His words shatter my hopes. Another violent dispute, just like the one she got into at her old school. If she hurt the other student as badly as she did last time, there's no way I can cover another settlement. No way I can get her out of this.

"Is she okay?" I ask. My pulse races.

"She started a fight with another student—Aidan Albright." His voice crackles through the speaker. "They're both hurt. She's seeing the nurse right now."

"What happened?" My hand tightens on the phone and my fingers squeak against the shiny plastic. I never expected Marjorie to attack Aidan. Not when they were dating. The hole in my stomach grows deeper as I wonder what he did to provoke her. If he hurt her—the same way Adam hurt me so many years ago.

"We don't know yet. We need to interview both of them and figure out how it started."

"Is she going to be suspended?" I ask as I pace back and forth across the floor.

"We'll make a decision after we talk to the both of them." Exasperation sharpens his tone. "Do you have the time to talk about something else right now?"

"Like what?"

"We're concerned about your daughter's behavior. She's been caught bullying other students with some of her friends." He clears his throat. "She's also skipped class a few times this month. Sometimes when she shows up, she appears to be high or drunk."

"I'll talk to her about it," I say, remembering the pungent smell of weed that clings to Marjorie's hair and clothes sometimes when I pick her up from another day at school. How occasionally she turns away from me to speak, like she's afraid I'll catch the scent of alcohol on her breath. "Please don't be too hard on her—she went through a lot before we moved here. There must be a reason why she attacked Aidan. She's not a bad person."

"If she keeps acting out like this, she's going to be expelled." His voice is firm and unyielding. "I hope you can talk some sense into her before that happens."

After I hang up the phone, I lean against the counter and twirl a stray strand of hair around my finger. Thoughts rush through my head almost too fast to decipher as I twist it tighter and tighter. Until my finger turns white, tingles and goes completely numb. Finally, I give up and walk to Marjorie's bedroom to search for answers.

She's made my old room her own. The small space smells like a cloying mixture of perfume and other beauty products. Marjorie's bed lies unmade in the corner, worn clothes discarded in a pile on the floor. More posters decorate the lavender-painted walls. Glossy paper displaying the faces of rappers and boy bands alongside pictures of fuzzy baby sea otters. Her favorite animal. I smile as I remember how I used to take her to see them at the zoo in Portland when she was still a toddler. The way that she would beam and laugh as they swam behind the glass.

Guilt grips me as tight as a vice when I try to decide where to search first. I never wanted to do this—never wanted to smother Marjorie the same way my own mother did to me. But maybe I made a mistake. If I had watched her more closely, I might have noticed the warning signs before she hurt somebody again.

I check the desk first, opening the drawers to rummage through the mess of pens, pencils, and erasers Marjorie almost never uses, preferring to write everything on her tablet. It sits plugged into the wall and requests a password when I turn it on. I get the combination wrong. She must have changed it from the one we agreed on.

The nightstand beside her bed is empty, wooden drawers barren of anything that might reflect Marjorie's personality. Another cord to charge her phone. The clear retainer she refuses to wear when she sleeps at night because it makes her look like a loser. I feel like a traitor as I sift through her personal belongings, searching for—something. Drugs or empty bottles of alcohol. Anything to prove or disprove what her principal told me.

I check the bed after I shuffle through the contents of her closet and peer behind her bookshelves. My skin pinches when I shove my arm into the thin space between the mattress and the headboard. The same place I used to hide everything when I was a teenager.

My fingers close around something and I pull it into the light. A vape pen. The smooth metal shines obsidian as I turn it over in my hands. When I pull the liquid-filled pod from the machine, it smells crisp—like mint. I place it back into the pen and breathe in. My eyes water. I cough as thick vapor smacks against the back of my throat.

My body shakes as the nicotine rushes through my veins. I push my hand into the narrow space again and retrieve more things Marjorie wants to keep hidden from me—a clear bag filled with weed, sealed airtight. Several lighters, the pair of glasses Mother thought she lost several weeks ago and a small bottle filled with an assortment of pills.

I frown, recognizing some of the medication from my own prescription, remembering Marjorie's outraged reaction when I accused her of stealing them. But she did—they were here all along. Maybe this is some kind of attempt to self-medicate her own trauma. After all, I couldn't get her a therapist. She has no one to talk to about everything she witnessed before I finally left my ex-husband. This is all my fault.

I should have tried harder.

I slip the stolen pills into my pocket before I check beneath the bed. A thick layer of dust drifts up from the floor and I cough as my hand touches something. A large soda bottle. Empty, although it's the grape-flavored kind that Marjorie doesn't even like.

My mind flits to what the mechanic told me, that somebody had poured soda into the gas tank. Marjorie tried so hard to convince me to stay here—begged me not to move away. She had been overjoyed when the car broke down, forcing us to remain in Reachwood.

Mouth dry, I reach beneath the bed again and my fingers close around something else. Something cold and rough. My heart beats hard as I pull it out from where it sits hidden in the dark.

A skull.

CHAPTER 44

The skull stares up at me, eye sockets hollow and empty. Chipped teeth poke like cracked tombstones from its upper jaw. Grooves of bone rasp against my fingers when I turn it over in my hands. Adam's skull, it must be—hidden beneath my daughter's bed like a dirty memory or a bad dream.

My muscles weaken and I drop it. The skull rolls across the floor as my stomach heaves. I curl into a tight ball and swallow back the bile rising up the back of my throat. Vomit fills the inside of my mouth. It stings against my tongue as the front door opens. My parents must have returned home.

I stumble back to my feet and wipe my mouth clean with the back of my hand. Stomach acid still burns against the roof of my mouth. My parents' voices fill the house as I hide the skull away underneath Marjorie's bed.

My phone goes off in the kitchen. The familiar ringtone repeats over and over again, until my father calls, "Ava—are you here? Your phone's ringing."

"I'll be there in a minute." I raise my voice loud enough to carry down the hallway. Who could be calling me now? Maybe Ambrose, furious over Marjorie's fight with Aidan. Or maybe it's another number I won't recognize and I'll only hear someone breathing on the other end of the line.

Mother passes me the cell phone when I enter the kitchen. Her eyes focus on the name and number displayed in bold letters at the top of the screen. Another call from Reachwood High School.

"Is everything okay?" she asks. Her expression sharpens with interest when she notices my shaking hands. The same way it always does whenever she senses weakness.

"It's nothing." I brush off her question. Cradling the phone between my ear and my shoulder, I say, "Hello, this is Ava speaking."

"Hello, Mrs. Montgomery. I'm sorry to bother you again." The principal's voice carries to me from the other side of the line. Soft and hesitant this time, not filled with the righteous indignation from our last conversation.

"Why are you calling me—is Marjorie okay?"

"We made the decision to suspend her," he says. "She was supposed to wait in the office and fill out some paperwork. But she left instead."

"You just let her walk out?" My voice is high-pitched and frantic as I imagine the trouble Marjorie could get up to by herself. How she might walk into the forest to search for the grove.

"I was hoping she'd returned home." He sounds embarrassed. "She's not there yet?"

"No, she isn't." I take a shallow breath. "I haven't heard from her at all."

"I'll call the police. They'll put together a search party."

"It's fine—you've already done enough. I'll find her myself." Contempt fills my words like venom. I hang up before he can respond.

"Is something going on?" Mother asks. I open my mouth, almost ready to tell her everything. About the fight at school this afternoon and the stolen things I discovered underneath Marjorie's bed. Maybe she can help me.

But her eyes gleam as she watches me. If I tell her what's happened it will only confirm her suspicions. That I had Marjorie too young to be a good mother. That there's something wrong with my daughter.

"Don't worry about it," I say and hurry toward my bedroom, closing my door before I check my phone again. No missed messages. Not a single text from Marjorie to explain what happened at school today.

Where are you? I text Marjorie and wait for a response. But the message stays unread. Maybe she's out somewhere with her friends, afraid to tell me about her suspension. She might even be over at Catherine's place, working up the courage to return home.

Is Marjorie with you? I text Victoria next.

Her response comes a moment later. *No. Why?*

She hasn't come back from school yet. Can you ask Catherine if she knows where she went? I type back. My pulse throbs in my ears as I wait for a reply.

I cross the hall into the bathroom to search through the medicine cabinet. My fingers close around my prescription bottle and I turn it over in my hands. Still a few hours left before my next dose. But my body longs for the familiar comfort.

Catherine hasn't seen her. Is something wrong? Victoria responds.

No, I just need to ask her something. I send the message before I twist open the lid of the container and shake a pill onto my palm. My fingers tremble as I stare at it, remembering the expression on Marjorie's face when she said I was high all the time. And she's right—I keep taking them, desperate for something to deaden the persistent dread twisting inside me. Maybe I should wait. Keep a clear head, at least until Marjorie shows up again.

I place the pill back inside the container and hide it away in the medicine cabinet. When I check my text to Marjorie, I blink at the notification that it was never delivered to her phone. As if she's gone somewhere with no cell reception.

Into the forest, where the trees cluster too thick to carry a signal.

I hurry outside. The door slams behind me as I check my phone one last time, hoping for a text from Marjorie. But no new notifications appear on my screen except for a message from Ambrose that says: *Aidan didn't come home after school today. If Marjorie did anything else to him, you're going to pay.*

Panic grips my throat as I rush toward Reachwood Forest.

"Marjorie?" I hesitate at its border. Searching for any evidence that she returned home to sneak into the backyard and slip through the picket fence before she ventured down the overgrown path into the wilderness. Toward the grove.

"Marjorie?" I call again. My voice carries through the bare branches as I wrap my scarf tighter around my face to protect my skin from the frigid wind. No reply drifts back to me. I walk down the path until the trees close in around me.

The sun sets earlier with winter approaching, casting long shadows across the ground as it sinks beneath the horizon. Thick drifts of fog almost hide the path from sight, so I rely on memory to carry me through the forest. Warning signs rise from the earth, words nearly obscured by a thin sheen of frost. When the first pile of stones rises from the ground, I slip beneath the wire fence meant to prevent trespassers.

"Marjorie?" My voice cracks. Still no answer, so I push forward once more. My exposed skin becomes numb—cheekbones, eyelids and the bridge of my nose. Bark groans as the wood contracts in the cold. More stacked stones emerge from the earth to point the way forward.

Something moves ahead of me. Sweat beads between my shoulder blades and itches against my skin as I hurry toward it. Frayed ribbons flutter stiffly on the branches of the trees. The tattered fragments of a past search party. Maybe for Emily, maybe for Kristen. Or Adam.

So many children have disappeared here over the years.

"Marjorie?" I pull my scarf down and my hoarse voice carries through the wilderness. My breath billows in a white cloud in front of my face.

Something darts behind the trunk of a tree ahead of me. I stumble through the fog toward it.

Movement stirs ahead of me again. Maybe Marjorie, maybe something else. I remember the stories about the forest as I hurry forward. That something lives here. Something hungry for children. My skin prickles.

But when I circle around the trunk of the tree, Marjorie stands beneath it. Face pale, cheeks flushed red from the cold. I say her name again, and she smiles as she turns toward me—blue eyes bright.

Her teeth flash sharp and white in the fading light.

FIFTEEN YEARS EARLIER

CHAPTER 45

The moon rose strawberry-red in the sky on Friday night. It shone like a wide eye through my window while I made up my face in front of the mirror, getting ready for the last dance of the school year. The week-old bite mark on the hollow of my neck had almost healed over. The cuts and bruises from my fight with Adam had faded into faint scratches. I covered the imperfections underneath a thin layer of concealer and foundation. The silken fabric of my dress rustled when I slipped into it and struggled to do up the zipper.

"Are you leaving soon?" Mother pushed open my bedroom door.

"Yeah. Can you help me with this?" I said and gestured at the half-zipped back of my dress. She crossed the room to fasten it. The metal teeth pinched my skin.

"I don't know why you're bothering—you're not even going with anybody."

"Victoria's going with me." I drummed my fingers against the dresser over and over again, until the sound formed a nervous kind of rhythm.

"Well then, everybody's going to think you're a lesbian." She pronounced the word like something shameful. And I had been. So ashamed of my own feelings that I followed Adam into the forest, hopeful that they would disappear if I left a gift in the grove. "Do you want them to think that?"

"It's not a big deal. I mean, a lot of girls go together," I said as a blush spread across my face. "And anyway, I don't care."

"I wish you had gone with him." Mother retreated to the doorway. Her forehead creased like she wanted to say more but couldn't find the right words.

"With who?" I asked. She couldn't mean Adam. Couldn't possibly wish I had gone to the dance with him instead. Not after everything he'd done.

"With Adam. At least it would be normal," she said, confirming my worst suspicions. Anger stiffened my body as I remembered the way she had always pushed me to talk to the most popular kids ever since my first day of kindergarten. How she dressed me in the best clothes we could afford so I would fit in with everyone and make a lot of friends.

"You know about the photo." I almost choked on the words.

"Well, you should never have slept with him until he asked you to be his girlfriend."

"Fuck you," I said the words so soft and low that she had to lean close to hear me.

"What?" Mother's face flushed red. Her wrist twitched, as if she were about to lunge across the room and hit me. We stared at each other until my phone vibrated on my bed again. I flipped it open to check my messages.

"Victoria's here. I'm leaving," I said, but she didn't move from the doorway.

"Get out of my way." My voice sharpened. We stood face to face in silence for several long moments until she finally stepped aside. I pushed past her and hurried toward the front door, eager to leave the house—and her—behind.

Victoria smiled when I climbed inside the expensive car she had borrowed from her parents. I smiled back, although adrenaline still crackled like electricity through my body from my confrontation with Mother. My stomach fluttered.

"You look stunning," I said. She was beautiful enough to make me blush—dressed in white silk embroidered with golden flowers. Her hair fell in loose curls past her shoulders. A corsage of roses decorated her wrist. The ones I had carefully chosen for her earlier.

"You do, too." Victoria's face lit up as she backed the car out of the driveway. She drove through the familiar streets leading to Reachwood High School and I glanced through the tinted windows. Suburban houses rushed by outside.

Victoria parked the car on a secluded street and killed the engine.

"What are you doing?" I asked.

"We should get ready for the party." Victoria opened the dashboard to reveal a stash of pills and tightly wrapped joints hidden inside. I grinned as she rolled down her window. She lit a joint, took a deep drag and coughed before she passed it to me. The heat chapped my lips when I breathed in.

"Want one?" Victoria waved the clear plastic bag of pills at me. She swallowed one down dry before she handed the colorful assortment to me, saying, "You look like you need to relax—did something happen?"

"Not really." I selected one from the mixture. Bright green, identical to the ecstasy pills I shared with Victoria after Emily's vigil. Swallowing it, I settled back into my seat, leather soft against my skin. "I got into a fight with my mom before I left—she thinks I still should have gone to the dance with Adam. Even after what he did."

"Fuck her. I'm glad you're going with me instead." Victoria slid open the sunroof to reveal the night sky overhead. I leaned in to kiss her and she smiled again. My skin tingled as she twisted her fingers through my hair.

"Who else is going?" I asked after I pulled away.

"Nathalie and Matthew are going together—they said they'd meet us there." Victoria drew one last drag from the spent joint before she flicked it out the window. The lit tip smoldered against the asphalt, glowing like a red eye in the night. "I don't know about Cyril yet. He was pretty upset when I told him I was going with you instead."

"I'm sorry."

"It's not your fault—and anyway, he'll get over it eventually. We're still partying at his place after the dance is over." Victoria cranked the key, and the engine roared to life again. When she switched on the headlights, the beams illuminated the empty street in front of us.

"I wish Emily was here." My eyes rested on the forest at the end of the street. The place where she disappeared. "She would have loved this— the dresses, the dancing. All of it."

"I know," Victoria said, and I wondered how different things would have been if Emily had never vanished into Reachwood Forest. If she were here to celebrate tonight, ready to graduate with the rest of us. She had been so excited for college. And now her body lay out there somewhere, covered by the foliage. Maybe hidden well enough that nobody would ever find it.

"Have you heard if Adam's going to be there tonight?" I asked as Victoria steered away from the curb.

"Probably. He got nominated to be crowned king at the dance tonight." Victoria merged onto the main road. "He'll probably win, too. His parents just made a huge donation to the school."

"I hope he doesn't." The wind raised goosebumps on my skin—neck, shoulders and wrists.

"I hope so, too. They nominated me to be crowned queen, and I don't want to stand beside him all night," Victoria said, voice tight. "And he doesn't deserve it, not after what he did to you."

I said nothing. Victoria turned into the ravine and the trees reached toward us. She pushed her foot down hard on the accelerator, driving as quick and reckless as if we would live forever. The forest sped by fast.

I rolled down the window and laughed.

CHAPTER 46

A crown decorated Victoria's head when we left the dance several hours later, gleaming gold against her hair. She had stood stiff on stage as it was placed upon her brow, Adam posed beside her. He bowed his head to accept his own crown while cameras flashed around them. Before they each broke away, he leaned closer to whisper something into Victoria's ear. An unreadable expression flickered across her face.

Now we shivered in the fresh air as we hurried back to our vehicles. Nathalie and Matthew followed close at our heels, dressed in expensive clothes they would probably never wear again after tonight—bright-eyed, wide smiles painted across their faces.

"Are we still meeting at Cyril's place?" Nathalie asked. Headlights flashed when Victoria unlocked the car. Clouds swept overhead like the threat of an early summer storm.

"Yeah, see you there." Victoria waved as they walked away. She tossed her crown into the trees at the edges of the street before she climbed inside the vehicle. I slid in beside her and drew a deep breath, enjoying the rich scent of leather.

"You don't want to keep it?" I asked. The crown glittered on the ground.

"Fuck no." Victoria wrinkled her nose. She twisted in her seat to press her hand against my headrest as she backed out onto the street. "I wish

Cyril had come tonight, even if he just sulked the whole time. His parents just made a donation, too. Maybe he would have beaten Adam."

"I thought he said something to you on stage," I said, wondering if Adam was the reason she didn't want to hold on to the crown. It seemed strange she didn't keep it—not when she collected anything sentimental. The stuffed animal I stole from Emily's memorial and many other tokens of our friendship from years earlier. "What was it?"

"Nothing important." Victoria's voice tensed, like whatever Adam told her had really struck a nerve. I rolled down the window to let the crisp night air into the vehicle. The dark silhouette of the Hart house appeared at the crest of the hill. I glanced back over my shoulder at the forested ravine below. Victoria reached out to hold my hand, and I smiled. The trees receded behind us.

<hr />

"How did it go?" Cyril opened the door before we even stepped onto the porch. As though he had waited there all night, eager for Victoria to arrive. His eyes drank in the sight of her—beautiful in her expensive dress—as we hurried into the house.

"It was okay, I guess," Victoria said. Cyril never so much as looked over at me as he led us through the ornate hallways of the mansion. Probably still angry she had chosen to attend the dance with me instead.

"Did you win?" he asked. The sour scent of alcohol already flavored his breath. A half-empty bottle of whiskey sat on the counter when we entered the kitchen. Cyril poured the amber liquid into two shot glasses before he passed one to Victoria. Maybe he intended to shun me for the entire night as punishment for taking Victoria from him.

"Yeah, but so did Adam. I had to stand beside him pretty much the whole time." Victoria threw back the shot. The empty glass clicked when she set it down on the polished countertop.

"I told you we should have gone together." Bitterness crept into Cyril's voice. "You know we would have won."

"Really? I mean, he's always been more popular than you," I said and smiled when Cyril's eyes darkened. It was true—although Cyril's parents had bought him everything, their money couldn't buy him more friends at school. He would never possess the charisma that came so naturally to Adam.

"Anyway, everyone should be over soon." Cyril changed the subject as though I'd never said anything. "Where's Nathalie and Matthew?"

"They're probably fucking somewhere. They were all over each other on the dance floor," Victoria said, and Cyril laughed. I picked up the bottle and poured some into his empty shot glass when he still didn't offer me anything to drink. He scowled as I swallowed the harsh whiskey but didn't say anything. Of course he wouldn't.

Not in front of Victoria.

"Thanks." I grinned at him. The doorbell rang again, and Cyril left to let Nathalie and Matthew inside. Victoria poured two more shots and passed one to me. I drank it quickly. My eyes stung as the whiskey burned against my tongue.

"I'm going to go change." Victoria downed her own drink.

"Same," I said, eager to discard my dress in favor of a more comfortable outfit. We climbed the stairs to the second floor of the house. Empty, as if Cyril's parents had left him home alone for the weekend. I wouldn't be surprised if they did—they had always given him anything he asked for.

We separated to change out of our dresses in different rooms. I searched through my bag until I found the clothes folded at the bottom. After slipping into my new outfit, I adjusted the neckline of my shirt to cover the outline of the bite mark still marring my skin.

"So? What's the plan?" Nathalie asked when we returned downstairs. More people had arrived while were getting ready. Their raised voices filled the house. Someone had turned on the stereo and now deep bass vibrated through the walls, hard enough to shake the bones in my rib cage. I poured another drink and sipped it while I studied the faces of the people grouped around us. I knew most of them from school.

Some had laughed at me after Adam sent out the photo.

"We should check out some of the other parties," Matthew suggested, tossing his empty plastic cup into the garbage. "One of the guys on the team bought a few kegs. Another is hosting some kind of rave."

"Yeah, sure." Cyril finished his own drink. If anything were to get ruined while he left the party here unsupervised, his parents would just buy a replacement. They probably wouldn't even lecture him or ask any questions. Not like my own parents.

We all nodded in agreement as bottles crashed to the floor in another room. The party fell silent for a moment before everyone broke into raucous laughter. The song changed on the stereo, the beat heavy enough to rattle my teeth inside my skull.

We took mushrooms before we left, slipping outside to walk away into the night.

⊶

"I don't want to go back yet," Cyril said after we had visited every party. Stopped to drink hard alcohol, pop multicolored pills and snort thin lines of white powder on our way from place to place. "Let's go to the grove instead."

"Why?" My throat tightened. I teetered on my feet as we crossed the street, unsteady from all of the pills and liquor I had consumed throughout the course of the evening. Victoria reached out to catch me when I stumbled.

"I feel like wishing for something tonight." Cyril's eyes lingered on our intertwined fingers. Maybe he wanted to torment me. Pay me back for stealing Victoria's attention away from him by forcing me to revisit the place that still haunted my dreams. Filled with the memory of what Adam did to me.

"Let's not—the forest is really creepy in the dark," Nathalie said. A thin trickle of smoke rose from the joint clutched tight in her hand.

"Don't tell me you're scared." Cyril turned to face us, walking backward down the sidewalk. The leaves moved like illusions on the trees. The moon grew and shrank again in the sky as the mushrooms warped the world around us.

"Of course not." Nathalie protested. "But you remember what happened to Emily. I don't want to get lost like her, or worse."

"Don't be such a baby," Matthew laughed. Nathalie rolled her eyes and pushed him playfully. He slung an arm around her shoulders and held her close as we took a shortcut through a dimly lit park, moving through the rippling dark.

"I think it's a good idea." Victoria squeezed my hand. She smiled at Cyril and something cold slid like a knife between my ribs.

"Really—why?" I blinked at her.

"It can't hurt anything, right?" she asked. They all stared at my anxious face, waiting for me to say something. Pupils wide enough to cover their irises, turning their eyes as black as the night around us. Unease stirred in my stomach at the memory of the cracked tree that presided over the grove hidden deep inside Reachwood Forest. Of the offerings left there by desperate children, hopeful that their wish would be granted.

"Okay, fine." I gave in. Dread spread cold fingers down the back of my neck as we turned back toward the ravine at the end of the street.

CHAPTER 47

Cyril entered the grove first. Nothing stirred as we followed close behind him. A hush covered the clearing, silent except for the sound of the flower-laden boughs of the hawthorn trees whispering in the breeze. We huddled close together as the gifts piled between their roots gleamed in the dim light.

Something moved in the dark ahead of us.

"What was that?" I asked. Uneasy, I kicked at the ashes gathered at the bottom of one unlit fire pit. Grey specks scattered through the air. The still-healing bite mark tingled at the base of my neck, as if something here were watching us. Maybe the same thing that bit me after Adam left me in the forest—now lurking at the edges of the clearing, hidden by the night.

Just out of sight.

"It's nothing. Don't worry about it," Cyril said. We didn't speak as we moved through the grove, toward the tallest tree. It presided like a king over the countless offerings. The familiar fissure splintered its trunk wide enough to remind me of an open doorway.

Matthew unpinned one of the badges that decorated his varsity jacket. Nathalie drew several coins from her purse. Reluctantly I slid a ring from my finger—the one Victoria had given to me. The same piece of jewelry I planned to leave here when I followed Adam into the forest. It felt like a lifetime ago, although only a week had passed. Now, I had a different wish.

I wanted Adam to pay for what he did.

My legs shook when I knelt down in front of the crevice that split the trunk of the tree. The gold ring glimmered between my fingers. My skin prickled as if the grove were watching me, eager for another offering.

I set the ring down on the ground and whispered my wish. The shadows inside the dark space shifted as though something had heard me. I rose to my feet and stumbled away from the opening. My head whirled, still dizzy.

"Did you hear that?" Nathalie whispered the words loud enough to carry through the clearing. I scuffed my shoes against the dirt, hesitant to lean forward again and peer into the crack leading down into the earth. Afraid of what I might see looking back at me.

Suddenly, Adam sprang from the hollow inside the tree. We all leapt backward. My heartbeat lurched as I remembered his hands wrapped around my neck. So tightly I couldn't catch my breath. We faced each other in silence, muscles tense as we waited for something to happen.

As though some small part of us had always expected this confrontation.

"What are you doing here?" Adam's eyes rested on me. "Shouldn't you be getting fucked at some party?"

"Fuck off," I snapped. But when Adam stepped forward I took an instinctive step back, and he laughed. His sharp teeth shone white in the moonlight.

"I was hoping you'd be here, actually." Victoria moved between us. Offerings ground beneath Adam's feet as he walked toward her—tokens and trinkets left behind by the countless children who had made the pilgrimage through the forest.

"Why's that?" A smirk twitched the corners of his mouth upward. "Still mad I got what you wanted?"

"They never punished you for it, did they?" Victoria asked. Voice soft and measured, as if she were barely compressing her rage. "Even after I told them what you did. Your parents never did anything."

"I already told you—you don't own us." He spat the words. "You shouldn't even be here. This place belongs to my family."

"That's not true. It belongs to my family, too." Victoria didn't back down, not even when Adam drew himself up to his full height to tower above her. "I can go wherever I want."

"You think you can do anything because you're the favorite," Adam said. His lips curved back in a snarl. "But you won't be for much longer—not if I tell them how much you want to fuck her."

Victoria slapped him.

The sound echoed across the clearing. The rings that always decorated her fingers split his skin open. A thin trickle of blood dribbled from the cuts. Adam reached up and wiped it away with his sleeve as his eyes darkened.

"Fuck you." Adam lunged at Victoria. I stepped forward as he crashed into her, knocking her backward against the trunk of a tree. She twisted when he threw a punch. His fist collided with bark instead, leaving small cuts across his knuckles.

"Leave her alone!" I gripped Adam's shoulder, trying to pull him away. Distracted, he glanced back at me, and Victoria raked her nails across his face. Sharp enough to leave red traces across his skin. He roared and slammed her back into the tree again.

Cyril pushed between them and threw a punch. His fist connected with Adam's jaw, so hard that his head rocked back. Nathalie screamed as Adam charged at Cyril. Their bodies collided, and the momentum sent them both tumbling to the ground.

"You know what? Fuck you, too." Adam's hands closed around Cyril's throat. Cyril's fingers scrabbled against the dirt as he writhed underneath Adam. "I think you might be the worst of all of us. You do anything she asks you to just because she's pretty—but she's never going to want you, no matter what you do."

"Stop it!" Nathalie grabbed Adam's jacket. The thin fabric ripped as she attempted to pull him away from Cyril. Adam knocked her off with a quick twist of his shoulders. Cyril gasped as his face turned blue.

Matthew tackled Adam, the sudden impact knocking him off Cyril's chest. They wrestled until Matthew pinned him down and split his lip with several heavy blows. The folding knife Adam always carried with him fell from his pocket, and I knelt down to pick it up from the ground. The initials carved into the handle pressed against my skin as I flipped it open.

The silver blade shone as Adam thrashed, struggling to break free from Matthew's grasp. He slipped out of his jacket and scrambled out from beneath Matthew, eyes shining rabid and furious as they focused on Victoria again. He charged toward her and I stepped between them reflexively. Adam slammed into my body. The sudden collision knocked us both to the ground.

"Fuck." Adam touched his ribs as red spread across his shirt. The knife lay to one side, stained with his blood. I grabbed him when he lunged for the weapon. My fingers slid against his sweaty skin.

Matthew charged at Adam. They grappled against each other as Cyril stumbled back to his feet, breathing heavily. Matthew pinned Adam against a tree and forced his hands backward around its trunk. Victoria ripped a strip of fabric from Adam's discarded jacket and knotted it around his wrists.

"Let me go!" Adam struggled to break free of his bindings. Cyril pushed him back and dug his fingers into the stab wound on Adam's ribs. His shrill scream echoed through the grove.

"Where is she?" I asked as I climbed back to my feet again. The knife glistened against the dirt. I picked it up before I turned to face Adam.

"Who?" He glared up at me and spat out the broken tip of a tooth.

"Emily. You left her here, didn't you?" My head spun. If he told me, at least we'd be able to find her body. Her parents could lay her down in a grave. Reachwood Forest didn't have to become her final resting place.

"I don't know." Blood gurgled in the back of his throat. It dribbled in thin rivulets from his nose to stain his face crimson. "I only told her that the stories about the forest were true."

"I don't believe you," I said. My hand tightened on the knife as I moved closer.

"Her mom is sick. Cancer or something—I wanted to help." Desperation turned his words quick and high-pitched. "I knew Emily would come here to wish for her to get better. But I didn't think she'd disappear. I miss her."

"Whatever." I shook my head and turned away from him.

"I don't get it." His next words were almost too soft to hear.

I opened my mouth to respond, but froze when something moved through the darkness that pressed against the outskirts of the grove. Leaves crackled. Branches rustled against each other.

"My wish wasn't granted, even after I left you here." A frown furrowed Adam's forehead. "I was so sure she'd be found. I don't understand—why didn't the forest take you instead?"

"Did you hear that?" Matthew interrupted our conversation as something stirred again. We paused as it paced against the edges of the clearing, as if it were drawn to the fresh scent of Adam's blood. Like it was hungry.

"We need to leave." Cyril's voice trembled. But we all froze when something shrieked—shrill and unearthly. I dropped the knife and we took off running. The silver blade shone among the offerings piled at the base of the tree. We left Adam tied there like a sacrifice and his screams followed us as we sprinted out of the clearing.

CHAPTER 48

The moon had already started its descent toward the horizon by the time we returned to Cyril's house. We didn't speak as we tiptoed through the aftermath of the party—shattered bottles and crumpled cans, wet stains and broken things. A few stray partygoers lay passed out on the floor or curled up close together on the couches in the living room.

"We shouldn't leave Adam out there." I stopped on the staircase. "It's not right—we should go back for him."

"Right now?" Matthew asked. Unease dampened his expression. Nathalie shuffled her feet, reluctant to leave the warmth and safety of the house and make another journey through the forest. To maybe encounter the ravenous animal that had screamed unseen somewhere in the dark. If it really was an animal.

It sounded like nothing I'd ever heard before.

"We can go back later," Cyril said. He squinted as he spoke, the purple beginnings of a bruise mottling the soft skin beneath his eye. "In the morning."

"But what if he's—"

"He'll be fine, he'd stopped bleeding. Maybe it will even teach him a lesson." Victoria touched my shoulder. But she drew away when the gazes of our friends lingered on our faces. Suspicious, as if maybe they believed what Adam said about us in the grove.

"None of what he said back there about us was true," Victoria said after a few uncomfortable seconds passed in silence. "You saw him—he was crazy. He just said it because he knew it would embarrass me."

"We know. Don't worry about it." Nathalie pulled her into a hug. Victoria didn't look at me when she pulled away. Never even glanced in my direction. My stomach plummeted as she avoided my eyes, like maybe Mother had been right all along. Maybe Victoria would abandon me for her family's fortune.

We crept upstairs without another word and separated to sleep in different rooms. Matthew and Nathalie chose a door on the right and shut it tight behind them. Victoria followed me into an empty bedroom. Cyril's eyes scrutinized us before she closed the door.

"I'm sorry—I shouldn't have said that." Victoria spoke after a moment. Voice soft, as if she were afraid somebody might overhear us. She lit her last joint and blew a long stream of smoke out the window before she passed it to me. "I didn't mean it. I'm just not ready for anyone to find out about us yet."

"Don't worry about it." I wished I could believe her. The bruises and scrapes on my body ached when I sat down on the bed. Victoria settled in beside me as I inhaled the thick smoke and held it in the back of my throat. We passed the joint back and forth until it burnt down to nothing between our ash-smudged fingertips.

"What do you think we heard out there?" I ground out the joint on the windowsill and tossed it outside. Victoria said nothing as she pulled me down beside her on the bed. Her mouth met mine, and I smiled.

She kissed me hard enough to make me forget what had happened in the forest. Hard enough to steal my breath and push away the memory of what she had just said to our friends. Hot blood rushed through my body as hunger stirred inside me.

This time I didn't panic when we undressed and she kissed the soft skin at the base of my neck. When her hands slid lower, I came quickly under the rhythm of her fingers—shivering underneath the sheets.

Sometime later, we fell asleep.

⚬—⟊—⚬

The next morning, the bed lay empty beside me. I sat up and pulled the sheets over my bare chest. A chill breeze blew through the open window as the sun rose above the forest outside. Goosebumps spread across my skin.

"Victoria?" I called.

No answer. A dull ache grew at the base of my skull as I dressed in the clothes that I had discarded on the floor. The smell of smoke and spilled alcohol still clung to the fabric. Dirt stains and dead leaves mottled my jeans. A reminder—what had happened the previous night wasn't just a dream.

I opened the bedroom door and heard someone vomit in the bathroom at the end of the hall. They retched again and again. The shower started to run as I walked down the stairs to search for my friends.

Nathalie and Matthew were in the kitchen. They sat at the counter, eyes tired as they sipped glasses of water.

"Have either of you seen Victoria?" I asked.

"No. She's probably still sleeping or something." Nathalie yawned.

"She fell asleep with me, but she left before I woke up." I glanced away as they both studied me again. Like they still suspected there might be some truth to what Adam had said about us last night.

The other partygoers had left already, slipping out the door early in the morning to return home before their parents woke up. Shattered glass and crushed food lay strewn across the floor. The Hart family's housekeepers would probably clear it all away later, but I needed something to keep me busy and so I started to clean up the mess in silence. Nathalie and Matthew joined me after a few moments. They scrubbed the stone-tiled floors until they sparkled as I tossed leftover debris into black plastic garbage bags, piling them beside the door to the garage.

"Adam's been out there for a long time—we should go back for him," I said when Victoria and Cyril finally arrived downstairs. Victoria's hair glistened, still wet from the shower. My stomach twisted as I wondered why they'd spent so much time alone together. If Victoria had done something to convince him that Adam's words had meant nothing.

"Do you really think he's okay?" Nathalie asked, her voice soft. Everyone glanced at each other and then glanced away again, reluctant to speak first.

"We just left him there overnight." Matthew shrugged into the varsity jacket emblazoned with his name and number. "I'm sure he's fine. He has to be, right?"

"But what about the sound we heard?" Nathalie persisted. I remembered the screams that came from the darkness at the edges of the clearing. Guttural and hungry.

"We were all pretty high." Cyril laughed. "It was probably nothing."

"Yeah, probably." Nathalie echoed as we slipped out the door to journey back to the forest. We followed the path until the first stack of flat stones rose from the undergrowth. Nobody said a word as we pushed through the thick foliage. Storm clouds gathered overhead, dark enough to block out the sun. When we emerged into the grove, we walked between the offerings in silence until we reached the cracked tree at the center of the clearing.

Nathalie screamed.

Adam's body lay between the roots of the split tree. Stark naked, stripped of the clothes he'd worn the previous night. Blood stained the earth underneath him. A hole yawned in the center of his chest. Sinews and tendons gleamed red. My stomach heaved. Nathalie gagged somewhere behind me and dropped to her knees before she vomited into the leaves.

"What the fuck happened?" Matthew stared wide-eyed at Adam's corpse. The ground beneath his feet was churned into a torn mixture of grass, blood and dirt—like Adam had tried to fight off whatever had killed him.

"Maybe he was attacked by an animal," Cyril suggested as he ran unsteady fingers through his hair.

"If it was an animal, then where did his clothes go?" Nathalie asked, wiping the back of her hand across her mouth. No one said anything. Nausea swirled in the pit of my stomach as we formed a silent circle around the body.

"This doesn't look good." Cyril paced back and forth in front of the fissure that split open the trunk of the tree. "We were the last ones to see him alive. You stabbed him."

"It was an accident." The heat left my body as I remembered the struggle the previous night. How the knife had slid into Adam's skin, clutched tightly in my hands. "We didn't think anything bad would happen."

"Do you really think anyone will believe us?" Victoria asked, and we all fell silent again.

"What should we do?" The grove spun, dizziness threatening to overcome me.

"We won't tell anybody. Just leave him here—someone else will find him eventually." Victoria's eyes darted around the circle. Her gaze rested on each of our faces as she said, "No one even knows we were here last night. We don't have to tell them anything."

"We can't leave him here like this." Nathalie's voice dropped to a whisper, like she thought Adam still might hear us. I glanced back at his body. The corners of Adam's mouth curved upward like the beginning of a smile or a snarl. Teeth peeked between his rigid lips. The knife lay on the ground a few feet away, still smeared with his blood.

"Well, we can't tell anybody, either. If anyone knew, our lives would be ruined." Cyril knelt down to pick up the knife. It shone as he dug it into the palm of his hand, hard enough to tear open the skin. Blood bubbled up from the cut.

Cyril passed the weapon to Victoria next. Rain started to drizzle down from the sky above us as she drew it across her palm in an unspoken promise. A pact never to speak about it again, or to tell anybody what had happened.

Matthew cut his palm next, then Nathalie. I gritted my teeth as I drew the blade across my skin. Pain raced through my fingers. Blood dribbled down to stain the earth beneath our feet like a vow. The rain washed it away quickly. Hopefully the storm would erase any evidence of what had taken place in the clearing that night.

We wiped the knife clean and tossed it into the trees on the walk back home. None of us spoke as we followed the stacked stones away from the grove.

TODAY

CHAPTER 49

Marjorie smiles at me when I circle around the trunk of the tree. The waning sunlight sparkles across the newly formed frost on its branches. I squint against the sudden brightness as pebbles crunch beneath my feet, half-hidden by the thick layer of fallen leaves patterning the earth.

"What are you doing out here?" My eyes drift back to the piles of stones stacked against the dirt. The only way to navigate through the forest. Maybe someone told her how to follow the waypoints to the grove, or maybe it was a coincidence that I found her here.

Just how much does she know?

"I didn't feel like going home yet, so I went for a walk instead," Marjorie says. The cold paints her cheeks red. If she suspects how much trouble she's in, she doesn't say anything—face innocent as she waits for me to speak again.

"I found the things you were hiding in your room." Frigid wind chafes against my skin. The white puff of my breath punctuates each sentence.

"What are you talking about?"

"Don't play dumb with me." My voice sharpens. "You know exactly what I'm talking about—the drugs and other things you hid behind your mattress."

"Why were you looking through my room?" she asks. Anger flashes across her face as she kicks at a pile of leaves heaped between the roots of a tree. They scatter into the air, whirling around her.

"Your principal called me this afternoon. He said you were in a lot of trouble."

"So what? That doesn't mean you can go through my stuff!" Marjorie plants her hands on her hips. A scowl turns the corners of her mouth downward.

"Is it true?" I demand as Marjorie glowers at me. "Have you been going to class high? And bullying those other kids?"

"Only if they deserve it."

"Marjorie—" I raise my voice.

"I don't like some of the things they say about you." Marjorie shuffles her feet. Leaves crackle beneath her boots as she glances away from me.

"What?" Dread sinks deep into the pit of my stomach.

"You had something to do with the boy who died here, didn't you?" Her lower lip trembles. Tears well in the corners of her eyes when she moves toward me. "They said he hurt you—is that true?"

"Those are only rumors. I had nothing to do with it." I hold her close and repeat the familiar lie one more time. Marjorie buries her head in the hollow of my neck, the same way she did when she was a baby. When just being near me was enough to make her happy. I run my fingers through her wind-tangled hair as I search for the right thing to say—to explain everything. But when I open my mouth, no words come out.

"Let's go home." She pulls free from my embrace. "I'm cold."

"You're not going anywhere yet. Not until I talk to you about something else first." I grab her arm as she turns away. "The skull underneath your bed—where did you get it?"

Some kind of emotion flickers through her eyes. Maybe shock, surprise or anger. Maybe all three at once. Stubborn, she presses her mouth together and remains silent. Determined not to give up her secrets.

"I said, where did you get it?" My hand tightens on her shoulder. Her expression never changes as my fingers dig into the quilted fabric of her jacket.

"I don't know." Her lower lip sticks out, sullen.

"Marjorie, you need to tell me." My voice rises. She flinches and regret ripples through me as I remember the way she used to hide whenever my ex-husband raised his voice. The first sign of another fight.

I never wanted to scare her like that.

"Fine. I went to the cemetery one night with my friends." She rolls her eyes. "The tomb was already open. It was their idea to take it."

"Which friends?"

"Virgil, Catherine and Aidan," she says and slips out of my grasp. The forest lies still and tranquil around us. Like the rest of the world has vanished.

"But why did you take it with you?"

"I guess I wanted to impress them. To show I wasn't scared." Marjorie pulls up the hood of her jacket to protect her hair from the rising wind.

"You're not telling me everything. Why did you really take it?"

"I thought maybe I could find the right place to leave it here. As a gift." Her confession is so soft that I have to lean closer to hear the words. My body shivers at the thought of what could have happened if Marjorie left Adam's skull in the grove.

Of what might happen if she ventured into the forest alone.

"I've told you a thousand times—those stories are all lies. Who told you about that place, anyway?" I say and study her face. Hopeful I might discover the answer in her expression.

"Nobody." Marjorie avoids my gaze.

"You're not leaving here until you tell me." I grab her arm again when she pushes past me. Her body jerks to a halt. She struggles against my grasp but I hold on tight.

"Victoria told me. Now are you happy?" Marjorie spits the words at me. My grip weakens on her sleeve, and she tears free. Her eyes flash as she glares at me. My body hums with anger when I picture Victoria whispering stories about Reachwood Forest to my daughter.

What other things could Victoria have told her?

"You are never to go back to their house again," I say. My face flushes hot with rage at the unexpected betrayal. "Do you understand me?"

Marjorie stays silent. She lags behind me as we push through the trees. I fight the urge to look back at her over my shoulder. To make sure she hasn't disappeared somewhere in the fog as I follow the piles of stones through the undergrowth.

"I got a call from the repair shop today, too. They said somebody poured soda into the gas tank of my car," I say, remembering the empty plastic bottle hidden beneath Marjorie's bed. "Know anything about that?"

"What if I do?" She fidgets with the zipper of her jacket.

"Marjorie—"

"I don't want to leave. We're safer here than anywhere else," she whispers.

"No, we're not." Frustration crackles through my voice. I ball my hands into fists at my sides and resist the urge to shake her until her teeth rattle together. "It's not safe as long as you keep going into the forest."

"I'm sorry." She pronounces the words like she doesn't really mean them. My muscles relax when we step back onto the path. The early dark settles in around us.

"Who else knows you took his skull?" I demand as we hurry toward the border of the forest. If anyone found out about this, all of the suspicions about Adam's death would be kindled again. Not only that, but the Albrights would be livid. They'd probably accuse me of vandalizing his tomb. Maybe even do their best to lock me away for concealing his remains.

"No one—just Catherine, Virgil and Aidan."

"Where is Aidan, anyway? His father told me he didn't come home after school today."

The first suburban lights appear through the trees. They shine like signals to lead us through the deepening night as pinpricks of fear dance across my skin. Aidan must not have told Ambrose what happened at the cemetery yet. Kept it a secret. But now he's angry at Marjorie.

Maybe even furious enough to tell somebody.

"I have no idea. He probably went somewhere with his friends," Marjorie says with a shrug. "I didn't do anything else to him."

"What happened between you two?" The wind numbs my skin as I wonder again if Aidan hurt Marjorie. The same way Adam hurt me years ago when he took that photo before he left me in the grove.

"Nothing. I just decided I didn't like him," Marjorie says. She studies me from the corner of her eye as we walk down the path. If she is lying to me, she hides it well—her voice never changes. Like she had learned how to cover the truth seamlessly over years of watching me make excuses for my ex-husband. "What are you going to do?"

"About what?"

"Are you going to ground me, or tell somebody about the skull—am I going to be in trouble?" Marjorie asks, hiding her hands in the pockets of her jacket. The night sky stretches out above our heads when we emerge from the tree line. The moon slips through thin wisps of clouds to illuminate Marjorie's face. She really does look just like Adam, sometimes.

Especially when the light hits her eyes just right.

"I haven't decided yet," I say as we climb up the porch steps. My numb fingers struggle to turn the key in the lock. I finally push the door open and a gust of heat warms my face when we enter the house. My parents are nowhere to be found—probably upstairs in their bedroom, watching television. The house is quiet as I follow Marjorie to her room.

She says nothing when I retrieve the skull from its hiding place underneath her bed. I close her door behind me and tiptoe down the hall to the guest room. After I lock the skull away inside my suitcase, I hide it beneath the clothes piled at the bottom of my closet and conceal the key beneath some papers on my nightstand.

I get ready for bed early, exhausted from my search for Marjorie through the forest. Before I undress, I flick off the light. I climb into bed, pull the sheets up over my head and close my eyes.

All night, my dreams are restless and fleeting.

CHAPTER 50

The doorbell rings early the next morning. I hesitate as I pack more of my parents' belongings away in cardboard boxes. They never mentioned anything about somebody stopping by today before they drove away to see their friends in the city. It can't be Marjorie—she left early to study at the library while she serves out her suspension. She would have texted me if she had forgotten her key, and I'm not expecting a visit from anybody.

The bell rings again.

My muscles stiffen as the sound repeats over and over, as though whoever is outside won't leave until they get an answer. I tiptoe into the living room and peek through a gap in the blinds. Half-expecting to see my ex-husband outside.

But Ambrose stands there instead. He presses his finger against the doorbell again and again. Maybe he wants to confront me about what happened to Adam in the forest. Or decided to take back the pills I stole from him. The scar on my palm throbs as I wonder how he knows nobody else is home. Maybe he watched the house all morning.

Waited for a moment to catch me alone.

My hand closes around my cellphone when he slams his fist against the front door. A loud bang echoes through the house. I type the emergency number onto the screen as I walk toward the foyer. Ready to call at the first sign of trouble if I can't convince him to leave.

"It took you long enough," he says when I crack the door open.

"What do you want?" I ask, glancing past him. The suburb is quiet this morning, driveways empty after everybody has left for work. Blinds cover the windows. No cars drive down the road.

"I need to talk to you about Marjorie and Aidan." Ambrose steps forward but I block the doorway with my body.

"Did something else happen?" I ask. Marjorie told me she was going to study all day before she left after breakfast. But she could have lied to me again. Gone to hang out with her friends instead.

And if she ran into Aidan . . .

"No." Ambrose interrupts my thoughts. "But she broke his nose and gave him a black eye. Now he won't go back to class."

"Well, the school handled it. If you have a problem, go talk to them," I say and move to close the door in his face. But he reaches out and holds it open.

"I'm going to ask them to expel her." The muscles cord in his forearm. "She really scared him."

"Do whatever." I try to sound indifferent, but my voice trembles a little bit. It would be easy for Ambrose to get Marjorie expelled—Reachwood High School still relies on donations from the Albrights, Harts and Gallaghers to fund their prestigious programs. The school board would probably agree to anything to keep the Albright family happy.

A mark like that on Marjorie's record could ruin her future. Destroy any chances of her attending a reputable college. Maybe I should say something to Victoria—if she found out, she would never allow it. But I don't want to ask her for help. Don't even want to talk to her right now.

Not since I found out she told Marjorie all the stories about Reachwood Forest.

"Maybe I'll even see if we can charge her with assault," Ambrose says when I don't react to his first threat. "A stay in juvie might straighten her out."

"Aidan started it," I protest. A chill runs through my body at the thought of facing another lawsuit. I don't have enough money to win. Even if I get all of my assets back after the divorce, it's still nothing compared to the wealth of his family.

"Is that what she told you?" Ambrose laughs. The sound carries down the deserted street as he says, "Because Aidan said something completely different."

"Of course he did." I brush away his statement, determined not to give Ambrose the reaction he wants. To show any weakness he can pounce upon.

"He said she attacked him after he told her the truth about you," Ambrose continues. My throat closes at the thought of Aidan telling Marjorie about the photo Adam took of me a long time ago. Or any of the rumors that floated around school after he left me alone in the grove. Or maybe even what happened between me and Ambrose.

Would Ambrose have told him that? He must not have been happy about Aidan's relationship with Marjorie either. Something had to have changed between them. They dated for nearly two months—forever, in teenage years.

"What are you talking about?" I ask, although I don't really want to know the answer.

"He said you won't get away with what you did for much longer," Ambrose says. He must have whispered suspicions to his son until Aidan started to believe them. To blame me for Adam's death in the forest.

Just like everybody else.

"I didn't get away with anything," I snap. It's true—the rumors about Adam's death have shadowed me ever since I returned to Reachwood. I'll never escape them.

Not for as long as I stay here.

"I heard your divorce is still being settled." Ambrose changes the subject fast enough to make me blink. "I wonder what your husband's lawyers would say if they found out about your pill problem."

"You wouldn't do that." My voice finally shakes at the thought of losing Marjorie. It's my ex-husband's fault that I need the medication in the first place. I never would have begged Ambrose for more painkillers if my ex-husband hadn't almost snapped my wrist in half. Broken it badly enough for the pain to still linger after I ran out of my prescription. But he could use that as an excuse to petition for full custody. And then he would never let me see Marjorie again.

Another way to hurt me for finally leaving him.

"I could. But I wanted to give you a chance to fix things first." Ambrose moves closer.

"What do you mean?" I brace myself, half-expecting him to hit me or try to kiss me again. My eyes dart around the suburb, but the neighborhood still lies deserted. Fallen leaves coat the sidewalk. Wilted flowers litter carefully tended gardens.

"I still don't believe you've told me everything you know about what happened to Adam." Ambrose stands so close that his breath brushes my face. "If you do, then maybe I'll decide to make this all go away."

"I've already told you—I don't know anything." I don't step away, still not willing to back down first. "Why do you care, anyway? You were never really close with him."

"My parents blame me for what happened, you know," Ambrose says. The same feral expression I glimpsed once before emerges on his face. "They'll never let me forget about it."

"Why?" I ask, surprised.

"We fought pretty much all the time after I told him that he shouldn't have taken that photo of you." Ambrose laughs, and the sound catches in the back of his throat like a choke. "We had another fight on the night he died. If I hadn't been home, maybe he wouldn't have gone into the forest alone."

"You should go." I back away when he moves toward me. His hand still grasps the door, forcing it farther open.

"You know, something's been bothering me since the first time I saw Marjorie. She looks just like you, but she looks a lot like Adam, too,"

Ambrose says and pauses. "It's her eyes, I think. They're the same color as his. That would give you enough reason to hurt him."

"You should go," I repeat. "If you want to speak to me again, don't do it without a lawyer."

We stand face to face until he finally shakes his head and walks away. I step out onto the porch to watch him climb into his car and drive down the street, retreating back to his family's mansion on the crest of the hill. For now, at least. My eyes rest on the door when I turn back toward the house, and an uneasy thought crosses my mind.

It probably won't be much longer before a new message appears there.

CHAPTER 51

Another trophy skull decorates Cyril and Victoria's wall. It hangs over the hole punched through the plaster during their argument last week. A stag's skull, horns gilded gold. Maybe the same one Cyril had carried into the house while I waited for Marjorie after Catherine and Virgil's party.

The drone of a vacuum cuts through the afternoon quiet. The sound drifts from upstairs, like the cleaners must be up there somewhere. A half-full glass of wine rests on the coffee table when we enter the living room. Victoria picks it up and turns off the television. She doesn't speak as she opens the door and leads me outside, like she wants to talk somewhere private. She didn't seem surprised to see me when I showed up at her door earlier. Almost as if she expected me to return here again.

"Did you want anything?" she asks, gesturing at her wineglass as she leans against the railing overlooking the backyard. The forest spreads out beneath us, deep and mysterious. A quick spark of desire ripples through me when her eyes meet mine. I swallow down my need, reminding myself of what Marjorie admitted to me when I found her in the forest. How Victoria had told her all of its stories. But I can't confront her about that yet.

Not until I talk to her about something else first.

"No—that's okay." For once, I'm not eager to numb my senses and dull the sharp edges of my anger. "I just wanted to talk to you."

"About what?" she asks, and I wonder again if the time we spent in her bed meant anything to her, or if it was just a way to get back at Cyril for their argument.

"I got a call from Marjorie's principal yesterday," I say. The breeze teases strands of hair free from the bun twisted at the top of my head. "He said she was in trouble at school."

"I got a call from him, too." Victoria sips more wine. "He said the same thing to me about Virgil and Catherine."

"Do you think it's true they've been hurting those other kids?"

"I don't want to think so." Her expression is so innocent that I never would have guessed she told Marjorie about the grove in the forest. Never would have suspected her complete betrayal.

"I searched through Marjorie's room after he called me," I say and grip the edge of the railing tight. My fingertips turn white. "I found something you should know about."

"What?" Victoria turns to study my face. Eyes thoughtful, like maybe she's already figured out the real reason I'm here. Or maybe she wants to kiss me again. I fight the urge to move closer. To forget what Marjorie said to me and pretend everything is fine, for at least a little while longer.

"She hid a skull beneath her bed," I say instead.

"Was it—?" The rest of her question lies unspoken in the space between us. She waits for me to say something as the wind blows through the immaculately landscaped backyard. It tears the last stray leaves from the branches of the trees, whirling them high into the air.

"Of course it was his." I bite my lip. "Marjorie found it with Virgil and Catherine—she told me the tomb was already open when they went to the cemetery."

"That can't be true. Virgil and Catherine would never do that." Victoria's hands tremble when she takes another sip of wine. It stains the corners of her mouth dark red as she says, "Or at least if they did, I think they'd tell me about it."

"I used to think the same thing about Marjorie. She really surprised me."

"Why did she take it?" Victoria asks. Her gaze strays across the forest below us, as if she already knows the answer to her question. Hot anger seethes inside me again.

"She said she was showing off to her friends."

Distant cars rush across the street that cuts through the ravine. The faint rumble of wheels against asphalt floats up to us, and for a moment I imagine all of the separate people carried inside the metal vehicles. Different faces, traveling to different locations. Paths intersecting briefly before they continue on their journey. They're lucky.

They can leave this place.

"Does anyone else know about it?" Victoria startles me from my reverie.

"Not yet."

"What are you going to do?" Her voice shakes, as though she's afraid of what could happen if somebody else found out Marjorie stole Adam's skull. Scared of all the questions that might follow the discovery, and how the answers could lead the police back to the both of us.

"I'll probably put it back in Adam's tomb," I say. My tongue scrapes against the dry roof of my mouth. "I can't keep it in the house."

"You should get rid of it as soon as you can." Victoria touches the back of my hand. My skin tingles underneath her fingers. But fury drowns out my desire.

"Marjorie said a strange thing to me, the other day." My voice tightens. "She told me she wanted to offer his skull to the forest. Someone told her more about the grove and the offerings. Maybe she even knows how to find it, now."

"That doesn't surprise me." Victoria tilts her head upward. She fixes her eyes on the clouded sky, like she doesn't want to look at me. Probably afraid I'll read the lie on her face. "You know what it was like, back when we were in school. Everybody talked about it."

"Do you have any guesses about who might have told her?" I wait for her reaction. Part of me hopes Victoria will confess everything. That she'll apologize and explain why she told Marjorie. There has to be some kind of reason. If she admits it, maybe I can forgive her.

"I have no idea." Her expression never changes as she lies to me again. "But I'd bet it was Aidan. They dated, right?"

"That's funny—because she told me it was you, actually," I say. Shock spreads across her face. She says nothing, and silence falls between us, tense and electric.

"Why did you do it? You know how many people have gone missing in there." I almost choke on the words. "You remember what happened to Adam and to Emily. And another girl disappeared just when I moved back here."

"I didn't want you to leave again." Her voice catches.

"You didn't think she might vanish, too?" My voice rises as I turn toward the door. Blood rushes hotly through my body when I move toward it. Pressure hums in my ears. "It's true—you really don't look out for anybody but yourself."

"Where are you going?" Victoria reaches for me, but I twist free of her grasp. We stand face-to-face, so close I could lean in and kiss her quivering mouth. I swallow hard and step back.

"Home."

CHAPTER 52

almost hit Cyril as I speed away from the house. It happens so fast—he steps out of the forest and onto the street. My heartbeat skips and I hit the brakes. The wheels grate against the asphalt before the borrowed car skids to a stop. Cyril stands motionless in the middle of the road. My hands shake as he frowns at me through the windshield.

Fuck. I didn't even see him. He could have been killed. I could have . . .

Cyril's eyes glitter in the afternoon sunlight. He clutches a trio of dead rabbits in one fist as he strides toward my vehicle. He must have spent the entire day hunting in the forest again. Blood stains their white fur. The limp bodies tremble with each step forward he takes.

"Sorry. I didn't see you," I say as I roll down the window.

"What are you doing here?" He ignores my apology.

"Leaving. I was talking to Victoria."

"About what?" Distrust shadows his face.

"Marjorie." I glance away. Clouds cover the sun overhead as an autumn storm sweeps toward the neighborhood. "She's been getting into some trouble at school lately."

"So have Virgil and Catherine." His voice never indicates if he believes me, or if he suspects there is another reason why I visited his wife. "Maybe they should stay away from each other. She seems to bring out the worst in them."

I bristle at his accusation. "Or maybe they bring out the worst in her."

"You might be right." He laughs. The bodies of the dead animals sway back and forth in his grasp. Their eyes stare out at nothing, glazed and empty. For a moment, I wonder if he's really talking about Virgil, Catherine and Marjorie, or if he's thinking about me and Victoria. Maybe it's true, and we really do bring out the worst in each other.

"I should go. I have to pick Marjorie up from school," I say, searching for an excuse to escape. Another lie. Marjorie has probably walked back home from the library by now, bored of studying while she serves out her one-day suspension.

"Have you thought any more about what I said—are you leaving soon?" Cyril asks. He grabs the window frame with his free hand. I shrink back when he leans forward to scrutinize my face, and I wonder why he's so desperate for me to leave.

If there's something Victoria hasn't told me.

"Yeah—they finally figured out what was wrong with my car." I raise my voice over the first rumbles of thunder in the distance. Rain drizzles down from the clouds overhead. "I'm picking it up tomorrow and then we'll get out of here."

"I'm glad to hear that," he says as lightning darts across the sky. "It's like I already told you. You brought the past with you when you came back."

"I didn't mean to." I remember the feelings for Victoria I'd thought were long since buried. Tears well in my eyes as her face flickers through my mind. She'll probably never speak to me again. Not after the words I said today. The thought hurts, even though anger still burns in my chest.

"I need to leave." I repeat the words like a plea.

"Is that really all you talked to Victoria about?" Cyril leans closer.

"Yeah." I reach for a tissue and dab it against the corners of my eyes.

"I've never understood what she sees in you," Cyril says. Resentment darkens his tone. Blood drips from the heads of the dead animals clenched in his hand. It spatters red for a brief second against the pavement before the rain washes it away.

"I don't know either." A lump grows in my throat as I remember the way Victoria smiles when her eyes rest on my face. She'll never look at me like that again. Eager to leave, I shift the gear stick back to the drive position before I repeat the same lie that I gave him a few moments earlier. "I really need to go, though—Marjorie's waiting for me. I'm late picking her up already."

Cyril releases his hold on the vehicle. I roll up my window as the wipers swipe rapidly against the rain-blurred windshield. He stands still in the middle of the street, watching me leave, and I don't relax until I turn the corner and his figure vanishes from the rearview mirror.

⚬━┿━⚬

More words decorate the front door. Still fresh, like someone had only just sprayed the paint across its wooden surface and fled. They must have done it fast, before the neighbors returned from work and their children arrived back home from school. Maybe they watched the house all day as they waited for the right moment to vandalize it. My skin prickles at the thought.

Maybe they're still watching the house right now.

A gold piece of jewelry shines on the steps of the porch. My eyes settle on it as I walk up to the door. A ring. I turn it over in my fingers and suck in my breath when I recognize the engravings. It's the same one Victoria gave me. The ring I offered to the grove inside Reachwood Forest on the night Adam died.

The same one Ambrose said he couldn't find.

I hide it away in the pocket of my jacket before I open the front door. Wordlessly I hurry into the kitchen and kneel down on the floor to search for the cleaning supplies beneath the sink. The breeze nips at my skin when I return outside. I shiver as I scrub the words away, erasing them like a bad dream.

"What are you doing?" Mother walks around the side of the house. I jump at the unexpected sound of her voice.

"Fixing this," I say. The pungent odor of cleaning chemicals fills my nose and mouth. Her gaze falls upon the words painted across the wood. Too haphazard to read this time. Like whoever left it cared more about the message the damage would send.

"When did it happen?" she asks. Her voice cracks.

"Sometime after I left." I roll the sponge between my fingers. The paint leaves a red imprint against my skin as I wonder who wrote the words. Only a few people know about the ring I left in the forest. It has to be one of my friends.

Or maybe Ambrose had returned to the grove again and found it.

"You need to leave." Mother's mouth thins into a hard line. A car drives by on the street, and she moves in front of the door to block the graffiti from sight.

"And go where?"

"I don't care." Her voice flattens with anger. "We'll never sell the house. Not with you bringing all this—if this keeps happening."

"Don't worry, the car will be ready tomorrow. We'll be gone soon."

"Good." Her eyes drift back to the half-erased message. Marjorie peeks around the corner, drawn to the sound of our raised voices. "I'm sick of the both of you."

"Well, I'm sick of you, too," I snap.

Mother turns on her heel and disappears back into the house. Marjorie's gaze lingers on my face. Her lips twitch like she wants to say something. But then she presses them together again and returns to her bedroom without a word.

CHAPTER 53

I pick up my car the next afternoon. When I swipe my credit card to cover the repairs, I hold my breath while the machine processes the expensive charge. Several thousand dollars to replace the fuel system and repair the engine. My first card is declined. I murmur excuses to the clerk and try my second card.

It's declined, too.

I call my parents to persuade—more like beg—them to cover the cost. They give in after I promise to pay them back as soon as I receive my assets back from the divorce settlement. The keys chime together as I unlock the car and settle into the seat. The vehicle runs smoothly as I drive through the forested ravine to pick Marjorie up from her first day back at Reachwood High School since her fight with Aidan.

But Marjorie doesn't come outside when the bell rings and students swarm out of the building. They cluster on the lawn while they wait for their parents to pick them up or wave goodbye to their friends before they hurry away down the sidewalk.

Catherine and Virgil emerge from the school together. They laugh with their friends as they move across the pavement, headed toward the mall. The same place I had spent so much time with Victoria, Cyril, Adam and so many others each day after class.

More students trickle from the doors of the building, heads bent close together as they whisper the latest gossip. Some run to catch the last bus before it pulls away from the curb. Others trudge along, friendless, eyes cast down toward the ground as they shuffle along the sidewalk. My breath catches when I glimpse Aidan. A purple bruise shadows the skin beneath his eye—visible even from this distance.

A reminder of what Marjorie did to him.

I'm here. Where are you? I text Marjorie after the last stragglers leave the building. They walk alone down the street, shoulders slumped beneath the weight of their backpacks. The schoolyard lies empty. A few crumpled pieces of litter tumble across the lawn.

Are you still here? I text Marjorie again.

While I wait, I fidget with the bracelet Marjorie made for me back when she was still in third grade. I pinch the colorful beads between my fingertips and picture the radiant way she used to smile when she was a small child. How she used to follow me everywhere, as if she'd been scared I would disappear forever if I left her sight even for a moment. Our roles had been reversed now that she had grown older. Now it was my turn to worry she would vanish instead. That I'd never be able to find her again.

I unbuckle my seatbelt after ten more long minutes pass without a response. My phone stays silent as I climb out of the car and hurry across the lawn. The high school sits close to the edge of the forest—two stories of brick and mortar. I pause at its entrance, reluctant to revisit this place full of childhood memories. But Marjorie still hasn't replied to me, so I push open the doors to walk down the familiar hallways. Fluorescent lights shine down from the ceiling.

The school has changed, expanded and renovated through donations from the Albright, Hart and Gallagher families. But some of the hallways still lead to the same places. The heels of my shoes click against the tiles, grungy from the ceaseless parade of students that move through the building almost every day of the week. Voices float out from behind some of the closed doors as teachers prepare their materials for tomorrow. My stomach flutters like an intruder.

I climb the stairs to the second floor and hurry past familiar classrooms—the labs where we dissected animals for biology or mixed volatile liquids for chemistry. The room where the band used to practice lies silent. A smile flickers across my face at the memory of the discordant music we used to play in that space. Loud enough to reach any unfortunate passersby in the hallway.

"Excuse me—what are you doing here?" A voice asks. I freeze, shoulders stiff as I turn to face the source of the sound. A man frowns at me from the doorway of his classroom.

"I'm looking for my daughter. She never came outside after the bell rang."

"What's her name?" He studies my face like he's trying to decide if I'm lying.

"Marjorie Montgomery."

"I should have guessed." He laughs. "You look a lot like her—I teach her math class."

"Have you seen her today?" A hesitant smile twitches the corners of my mouth upward.

"She never came to my class this afternoon," he says and shakes his head. "I thought she was probably skipping again with her friends."

"I don't think she's with them."

"Do you want me to call somebody?" Worry creases his forehead.

"No, that's okay," I say as I retreat away from him, taking quick steps across the linoleum. My body tenses at the thought that Marjorie must have spent at least half the day away from school. The trouble she could have gotten into. "I'll check some other places she likes to go first."

"Okay—good luck with your daughter. I hope you find her."

I pass my old locker on my way back to the stairs. Thoughtful, I pause to run my fingertips across its scratched surface. The words are still there, carved deep into the metal. Covered up by a thick layer of paint that rubs rough against my skin. The smell of sweat and body spray wafts out of the gymnasium as I hurry down the stairwell.

Basketball players dribble the ball against the hardwood floor. The sound reverberates like a second heartbeat as I push open the doors and walk out onto the pavement. I follow a foot-worn path around the side of the building to check the place where the kids used to gather and smoke between classes. Stray teenagers look up at me, startled. They hide their contraband in the pockets of their jackets as I study their unfamiliar faces.

"I'm looking for my daughter—her name is Marjorie. Have any of you seen her?" I ask. They cast furtive glances at each other.

"No, she never came to class today."

I return to the car. After climbing inside the vehicle, I check my messages again just in case I've missed something. Still nothing—no reply from Marjorie.

This isn't funny. Why won't you say anything? I text Marjorie again, but my phone notifies me that the message can't be delivered. My eyes stray to the forest at the edge of the schoolyard.

I send another message to Marjorie and receive the same notification a moment later. A chill spreads through me as I remember the last time I couldn't reach her. When she ventured into Reachwood Forest, where the deep ravine and crowded trees deaden any signal. Marjorie must know this is her last chance to visit the grove before we move away.

Her last chance to make an offering.

CHAPTER 54

The forest stretches out below me as I follow the familiar road up to the crest of the hill. My headlights illuminate the way in front of me as I drive fast through the early dark. Deer graze at the edges of the street. They raise their heads when I speed past. Antlers gleam tall and proud at the crowns of their skulls.

Extravagant mansions lie caged behind wrought-iron gates when I reach the top of the steep ridge. My hands tighten on the wheel as I steer through the historic neighborhood, toward where Victoria's house waits at the end of the street. I drive through the open gate, park the car and step out into the yard. I never wanted to return here again.

But I need to ask Victoria one last question.

Gravel scatters beneath the soles of my shoes when I rush up the driveway to ring the bell beside the front door. Nothing moves inside the house so I ring the bell again. Footsteps hurry down the stairs, and then Victoria opens the door and freezes. Surprise widens her eyes.

"I need to know what you told her," I blurt before she can say anything.

"What are you talking about?" Victoria asks. She cradles a near-empty glass of wine between her fingers as she stands in the doorway.

"Marjorie didn't go to school today." My throat constricts so tightly I struggle to catch my breath. "I need to know if you told her how to find the grove in the forest."

"I thought you told her to never go in there again." Wine paints the edges of Victoria's mouth red. Her breath smells bittersweet. Unsteady, she leans against the doorframe as she frowns at me.

"I did. But she never listens."

"I told her to follow the stones," Victoria says after a moment. Her hand rests on the doorknob. The muscles and tendons in her wrist tense. "She was going to search for it anyway—whether I said anything or not. I thought at least if she knew about them, she wouldn't get lost."

"If she disappears, it's going to be all your fault." I press my palm against the door when she moves to close it. To slam it shut the same way I did when I left yesterday.

"Really?" Victoria laughs. The disbelieving sound echoes through the street. "You never talked to her about it at all, did you? You ran away from it, just like you did after Adam died. The same fucking way you run from everything that scares you."

"I—that's not true." My voice stutters.

"Anyway, you should probably hurry if you want to stop her," Victoria says. She finishes the last remnants of her drink and the crystal glass shimmers in her hand. "She had a good head start. She's probably almost there by now, if she hasn't found it already."

I walk back toward the car without another word. Eager to return home and follow the half-overgrown path behind my house through the forest, toward the grove. Goosebumps shiver across my skin. I don't hear the door close behind me, as if Victoria has decided to stand there and watch me leave. Retreat, just like always. The thought makes me stop in my tracks.

I can't run away again. Not now.

"I would have stayed if you'd asked me to." I turn back around to face Victoria. "Or I would have left with you. I would have followed you, no matter what you wanted to do."

"What?" She stares at me, silhouetted by the light spilling from the open door.

"But you stopped talking to me after they found his body." I force the words out before I lose my nerve. "I waited for days, but you never said anything. So yes, I left without telling you—I ran away, but you did, too."

Several long moments pass before Victoria steps out of the doorway. Shadows cover her face as she says, "None of this turned out like we thought it would, did it? When we made our wishes in the forest."

"No, I guess it didn't." I hesitate.

"What did you wish for, anyway?"

"I just wanted Adam to pay for what he did." My body feels light when I finally admit the secret. As though a heavy weight has lifted from my shoulders. "But I never thought it would turn out like this. Everything would be so different if he was still alive."

"I think maybe I made a mistake, too," Victoria says, twisting her wedding ring around her finger. The diamonds set into the gold band flash in the dim light. "I got everything I ever wished for, but it wasn't anything like I expected."

"What do you mean?" I ask as I walk back up the driveway toward her.

"The mine's exhausted. It's been that way for a long time—I don't know how much money we have left." Victoria looks away, like she's embarrassed to say the words out loud. "And I'm divorcing Cyril, too. I don't care if he takes everything. Not anymore, at least. My family only convinced me to stay with him because they thought it would be best for our children."

"I'm sorry." I touch her wrist.

"You shouldn't be—I was so happy when I saw you again. It made me realize I haven't felt like that for a long time." Victoria smiles, and the corners of her mouth tremble. I hold her close and catch a glimpse of the interior of her house over her shoulder. More holes puncture the walls. Broken furniture lies overturned on the floor.

"What happened?" I ask when she pulls away.

"I served Cyril with the divorce papers this morning," Victoria says as she turns to survey the damage. "He did the same thing he always does when he gets angry. Obviously."

"Did he—?" I leave the rest of my question unspoken, remembering the destruction left in the wake of my ex-husband's temper. Imprints on the walls the same shape as his fist. Doors torn from their hinges. Eventually he turned that same rage on me.

"No. He's never hurt me," Victoria says, and I wonder if she is lying.

The same way I did.

We fall quiet as clouds cluster in the sky overhead. Lightning flickers across the horizon, signaling the arrival of another storm. I picture Marjorie alone in the forest, determined to follow the stones to the grove. I shouldn't have stayed here so long.

Marjorie might already have made an offering.

"I should go." I clear my throat. "I need to find Marjorie and bring her home."

"Let me help you," Victoria offers. She sways when she sets her empty wineglass down on the table in the foyer, as if she's spent the entire day drinking after serving the divorce papers to Cyril.

"You should stay here." I place a hand on her shoulder to steady her. I've wasted too much time already, and Victoria will only slow me down. "I need to do this alone."

"I'm sorry for telling her about the forest." Victoria's voice shakes like she really means the apology. "She wanted more than anything to keep you safe."

"I know," I say and turn to walk away.

"Be careful." Victoria's voice follows me as I hurry down the driveway. The rising storm tears at the dying flowers in the garden. Withered petals swirl around me. The breeze muffles her voice, but I still hear her final warning.

"Cyril's out there too, somewhere. Hunting."

CHAPTER 55

Go down the path. Don't look back.

The words repeat themselves once more in my memory as I cross the border of the forest. Gravel grates beneath the soles of my shoes. I bend my head against the storm and walk fast down the path. When something moves unseen behind me, I freeze—as instinctively as prey catching the scent of a hidden predator on the breeze.

"Marjorie?"

Nothing stirs. My heartbeat batters against my ribs when I push forward again. Lightning flickers overhead as I wonder if Marjorie has reached the grove yet. If she's made an offering there already, or if something intercepted her before she could reach it. Maybe even the same thing that we heard fifteen years ago.

I'll never forget the way it screamed at the edges of the clearing.

"Marjorie, this isn't funny." My voice carries through the trees. Goosebumps mottle my skin. Nothing answers me, so I push through the forest again. Branches crackle as I hurry toward the first set of stones stacked against the dirt.

"Marjorie—are you in there somewhere?" I say and stand still to wait for an answer. Hopeful that Marjorie will call out to me. That we can return home together and leave this place forever in the morning. But no response carries back to me, and so I step off the path.

I never look back.

Reachwood Forest at night is another kind of quiet. Completely silent, broken only by the distant rumble of a storm. Twigs snap as I struggle through the dense foliage. Clouds cover the rising moon, leaving me with only dim light to navigate the forest. I jump back when a herd of startled deer bursts from the tall grass. Their white tails flash as they bound away.

Signs rise from the undergrowth, printed with warnings. I ignore them and slip underneath the fence. More lightning flickers overhead, and thunder roars close enough to rattle the ground beneath my feet. No sign of Marjorie, but she must be okay—she has to be.

If something were to happen to her, I would never forgive myself.

Rain is falling from the sky by the time I reach the grove. It drips from my chin and the tip of my nose as I take a hesitant step toward the thicket of hawthorn trees at the center of the clearing. Everything is still and silent around me. Offerings glisten gold beneath the roots of the trees—bracelets, necklaces and rusted rings.

"Marjorie?" I call her name again. The sound carries through the forest, but it remains quiet. I run my tongue across my wind-chapped lips as I take another step forward. The outline of the cracked tree rises in the distance, presiding over the grove like an idol. Its branches claw at the clouded sky as I linger by the edge of the forest.

Something moves behind me.

"Marjorie—are you there?" I turn so fast that I almost lose my balance. My muscles tense as I wait for an answer.

"Ava? Is that you?" Cyril steps into the grove a moment later, face half-hidden by the long shadows pooled beneath the trees. His eyes gleam as more lightning darts across the horizon.

"What are you doing here?" I struggle to catch my breath.

"The same thing as you—making an offering," he says and moves toward me. My skin prickles when I remember the warning Victoria gave me earlier.

Be careful. Cyril's out there too, somewhere. Hunting.

"I actually came here to look for Marjorie." I scratch at the scar on my palm. The long-healed injury itches as I wonder what gift he had intended to leave here. If he'd thought it would be enough to persuade Victoria to stay with him. "She didn't come home after school today."

"She knows about this place?" he asks. The night hides whatever expression might be written across his face. Rain soaks through my jacket, and I shiver.

"Yeah. Victoria told her how to get here," I say as the clearing stays quiet around us. Silence not even disturbed by the calls of wild animals. As though the whole forest is holding its breath in anticipation of what will happen next.

"I should have guessed." Cyril's voice hardens, almost drowned out by the storm overhead. He moves forward again, closing the distance between us rapidly, body rigid with anger. I take a quick step back.

"Aren't you scared?" I blurt.

"Of what?" Cyril hesitates.

"Being alone out here at night. You know, after what happened to Adam," I say. My eyes drift toward the split tree, barely visible at the center of the clearing. The place where Adam's body had lain in the forest for three days.

"There's nothing to be afraid of here," he says and steps toward me again as rain pounds against the earth. The downpour crushes dead leaves into the dirt. "This place has never hurt anybody in my family."

"Adam used to say that, too. And we both know how that worked out for him." I raise my voice over the wind as I back away from Cyril. "Anyway, I need to go. Marjorie isn't here—I need to find her."

"Don't go. I need to show you something." Cyril lunges forward and grabs my arm. His fingers dig into my skin as he drags me deeper into the clearing. I stumble over something and glance down to see the body of a half-eaten animal.

Its glazed eyes stare up at the storm-covered sky, small mouth open in a final scream.

CHAPTER 56

"Where are we going?" I ask, struggling against his grasp. Cyril says nothing as he drags me through the grove, and pain sparks through my wrist. The same limb my ex-husband broke during the last argument before I left him.

"What did you wish for?" he asks, ignoring my question. Bones, toys and old coins lie piled on the ground. Left in the hope that whatever dwells in this clearing would answer the prayers of the children who placed the gifts there.

"What?" I tear free from his grip. My skin tingles as blood rushes back into my fingers.

"When we left our offerings here, what did you wish for?" Cyril's body tenses, ready to spring forward at any moment. The same way my ex-husband's muscles tightened before another burst of violence.

"For the same thing you did, probably. Money, success and happiness," I lie.

"Yeah—I asked for that, too," he admits. A rueful smile tweaks at the corners of his lips.

"I guess we all got what we wished for," I say and step away. Anxious to leave—to follow the piles of flat stones through the wilderness until I find Marjorie.

"Not anymore." He laughs again. Quick and high-pitched, like the scream of a wounded beast. My eyes stray to the space where we found Adam's body beneath the tree. The open red hole in his chest, his sightless eyes pointed up toward the sky. "It's all gone now—the money, the success and everything else."

"I don't know what you're talking about," I say. The scar on my palm itches again, and I dig my nails into the long-healed ridge of skin. The sensation stops for a brief second, but returns as I retreat toward the edge of the forest.

"You lost your inheritance. If the mine stays exhausted, I'm going to lose the company—and now Victoria wants to leave me." He clenches his jaw so hard I can hear his teeth grind together.

"I'm sorry." The apology falls flat from my mouth.

"Why did you have to come back?" He exhales the words.

"I thought it was the only place we'd be safe." My voice breaks as I remember my ex-husband and his rages. The same animal expression now paints Cyril's face.

"Everything changed when Victoria saw you again." His voice grows low and furious. "I thought she would be different if she had children—that she would love them, and grow to love me, too. But I think she doesn't really care about anybody. Except maybe you."

"That's not true." I struggle when he grabs my arm again. "Stop it—you're scaring me."

"I thought I could make you go away if I wrote the messages. If I called you," Cyril says as his fingers slip against my rain-slicked skin. His grip tightens, hard enough to leave white imprints against my wrist. "I didn't think you'd stay after I found the offerings and brought them out of the forest."

"You did that?" A hollow pit opens in the middle of my stomach as I remember the objects left like a threat on my front doorstep. The knife, the ring, and the question scrawled like an accusation.

Who left Adam in the forest?

"I was so sure you'd run away after I broke open Adam's grave. It would have been best if you just left this place. Why did you stay?" he asks. The corners of his lips draw back into a snarl, illuminated by another flash of lightning. The brazen roar of thunder follows a moment later, loud enough that the offerings shudder across the ground.

"I had nowhere else to go," I protest as he drags me through the grove.

"And now Victoria's leaving—I would do anything to stop that from happening. To keep her with me." Cyril stumbles over the words as the tree looms before us. The crack in its trunk yawns as wide as a hungry mouth.

"What do you mean?" My voice shakes as I examine his dark silhouette for any sign of what he might have brought to hunt with in the forest. But I don't see anything. No outline of a weapon. Maybe he was so angry after Victoria served him with the divorce papers that he stormed out of the house before he could grab one.

"We all made a wish here once, and we got everything we wanted. Maybe if I make another sacrifice, it will bring everything back to me again," Cyril says. He doesn't look back when something stirs in the trees behind us. Like it is drawn to the scent of my fear on the breeze. Branches snap. Dry leaves crackle.

"Another sacrifice?" My half-asked question lies in the air between us.

"Didn't Victoria ever tell you what happened to Adam?"

"What are you talking about?" I ask as the wind tears against my body.

"I guess not. She always wanted you to think the best of her." He laughs. I flinch at the unexpected sound as he says, "I think maybe that's the only reason why she stayed with me—she knew I would tell everyone what happened here if she left. At least until she saw you again."

"She doesn't belong to you." I struggle in his grip.

"You always were her favorite, and I always hated it." He drags me toward the fissure that splits the trunk of the tree. "Was it true, what Adam said about the two of you?"

"Yes," I say, although I shouldn't admit it, especially not now. But it's almost a relief to say the words out loud. To finally confess the secret that I've kept hidden for so long.

"I never understood why Adam's wish didn't come true when he left you here," Cyril continues like he didn't hear me. "But I think I've figured it out. It's not enough just to leave something in the grove. The forest doesn't always claim it. I think the only guarantee is to leave it a body."

"Let go of me." I twist my wrist and break free of his grasp. He yells something after me as I sprint toward the edge of the clearing. My foot catches the edge of a dead bonfire and I stumble, tumbling down onto the ground. I hit the dirt hard enough to knock the breath out of my chest. Dazed, I cough and crawl back to my feet—hair tangled with dirt and leaves. My heart pounds hard enough to drown out the storm overhead as I take off running again, plunging into Reachwood Forest.

Cyril screams, loud and angry, as the trees close in around me.

CHAPTER 57

The wilderness stretches out to swallow me whole. Branches tear at my face and clothes as I crash through the undergrowth. I trip over a gnarled root and topple headfirst into the trunk of a tree. Pain explodes inside my skull. Black dots shimmer at the edges of my vision as blood runs from a scrape on my forehead. I wipe a hand across my face and crawl back to my feet. The world spins around me.

"Get the fuck back here!" Cyril bellows, and I flinch like startled prey. My shoes churn against the dirt as I struggle through a thicket of brambles. Leaves crackle behind me. My breath rasps in my chest as I follow the piles of stones back toward the path.

Cyril lunges out of the shadows, and I shriek. He slams into me and we both tumble to the ground. The weight of his body holds me down. My nails scrabble against the earth as he pins me beneath him. His hands reach toward my throat.

My fingers close around a rock. I slam it into his head again and again, sound echoing through the forest around us. The stone cracks against his skull until it splits open his skin. Blood dribbles down his face as he jerks away.

"You bitch, you fucking bitch—" Cyril clutches at the wound. I slip free and sprint through the forest, glancing back once to see him stagger to his feet in pursuit. Lightning flashes overhead. Black spots float in front of my eyes as the earth shudders. Thunder crashes loud and deafening around us.

Cyril tackles me as I pass another stack of flat rocks. We smash into it and the stones scatter across the ground. His hands press hard against my neck and I gasp for air as a familiar darkness shines at the corners of my eyes. The world turns indistinct and white.

Someone screams, and the pressure on my throat eases for a moment. The forest blurs back into focus. Marjorie charges into Cyril, scratching at him as he struggles to defend himself from the unexpected attack. Feebly I roll out from underneath him and dig half-blindly through the dirt for something—anything—I can use as a weapon against him.

"Leave her alone!" Marjorie yells. Her pale eyes shine bright and wild. She rakes her nails across his face hard enough to break his skin. Cyril roars at the unexpected pain and hurls her to the ground. Marjorie curls on her side as she gasps for air.

My fingers close around a fallen branch. Marjorie rises to her feet, teeth bared in a feral snarl as she charges at Cyril again. He grabs her wrist and his thick fingers bite into her skin as she twists in his grip. A bone in her forearm snaps, and she cries out. The high, thin sound carries through the trees.

"Don't fucking touch her!" I stumble to my feet and run toward them as Marjorie plunges her other hand into her jacket pocket. Something silver glitters in the moonlight, and Cyril makes a garbled noise that sounds almost like a scream as he clutches at his chest.

Marjorie twists the knife deeper between Cyril's ribs. Her knuckles turn white as she clenches its handle tight in her fist. He throws her to the ground again, and the knife skids away into the foliage. I dart toward it as he rushes to pick up the weapon. My hand wraps around its hilt and I raise the knife instinctively as I spin to face him, bringing the blade across his throat.

Cyril chokes.

I step back as blood sprays from the wound on his neck to stain his shirt dark red. His mouth moves like he is trying to speak. Mute as more blood sputters from the deep cut. Cyril's knees buckle, and he collapses to the ground. His body shudders until he falls still.

I drop the knife. "You shouldn't have done that—why did you do that?"

I'm not sure if I'm asking the question to Marjorie or myself as the knife tumbles onto the forest floor. Thick blood slicks the silver blade. It gleams almost black in the dim light before the downpour washes it away.

"I didn't want him to hurt you. I don't want anyone to hurt you," Marjorie says as she climbs to her feet, face white in the dark night. Drops of red blotch her clothes. Blood flecks her wet hair. Tears run from the corners of her eyes, mingling with the rain falling down from the sky as I embrace her, the same way I did when she was younger. When I could still protect her.

"Are you okay?" I ask as she hides her face against my shoulder.

"I think something's wrong with my wrist." Marjorie pulls away, grimacing as she flexes her fingers. Movements stiff and clumsy, the same way mine had been when my ex-husband broke my wrist just over two months earlier. My chest tightens.

I'd hoped nobody would ever hurt her like that.

"Where did you find that?" I ask, pushing away my worries as I point at the knife on the ground. A folding knife, familiar initials carved into its wooden handle. The same knife Adam carried with him all the time, back when he was still alive.

The same one I buried in the grove weeks ago.

"I found it out here earlier." Marjorie's throat twitches when she swallows. "Is he dead?"

"I think so." I kneel down beside Cyril's body and wait for something. The rise and fall of his chest as he draws a breath. The tremor of a muscle. But he doesn't move, lips drawn back to expose his teeth.

"What are you going to do?" Marjorie asks as the storm flashes overhead. I pull my phone from my pocket before I remember there's no reception in the forest. And if I tell anybody, they might take Marjorie away from me. Send her back to my ex-husband and lock me in prison for decades. They might even lock her away, too.

I can't stand the idea of never seeing her again.

"You should go home and change out of those clothes," I say finally. "Leave them in my bedroom—I'll wash them in the morning, and we can figure everything out."

"Where are you going?" Her lower lip trembles.

"I'm going to take care of this." I turn back toward Cyril's body. Marjorie hugs me again, and I rest my chin on the crown of her head. Nothing moves around us.

"We could leave him there." Marjorie's eyes light up as she pulls away. She glances over her shoulder in the direction of the grove as she suggests:

"We could offer him to the forest."

CHAPTER 58

Cyril's body has grown cold by the time we reach the grove. My muscles strain as we pull his dead weight into the clearing. The hawthorn trees sway in the wind. The storm still flickers in the distance as sweat trickles between my shoulder blades.

Marjorie leads the way toward the cracked tree that rises at the center of the grove like a forgotten icon. Blood stains her clothes and smudges her pale face. Her quick breaths rasp as we drag his heavy body through the clearing. When her foot catches on the edge of an unlit fire pit, she stumbles over it before regaining her balance.

We set Cyril's body down in the long shadow cast by the tree, and I collapse beside it. My lungs heave as my breath whistles in the back of my bruised throat. Marjorie sits down beside me and draws her knees up to her chest. She wraps her arms around them as she favors her right hand, wincing every time she moves her fingers.

"I think it's broken." Her mouth twists when she touches her wrist.

"I'll drive you to the hospital in the morning," I say. The wounds on my body throb as the rain slows to a thin drizzle. It whispers through the barren branches like words spoken in a language we will never understand.

"What should I tell them, though?" she asks. Worry creases her forehead. "Won't they want to know what happened?"

"Just tell them you fell down." My stomach clenches when I repeat the lie I always told after another fight with my ex-husband. But it always worked for me. The doctors and nurses never pushed any further. I curl an arm around Marjorie's shoulders and pull her close as the wind dies down around us. She leans against me, eager for comfort. Her eyes rest on Cyril's unmoving body lying between the roots of the tree.

"What are we going to do now?" She digs her fingers into the dirt.

"We'll leave him here," I say. Every bone and muscle in my body aches when I rise to my feet. I brush dirt and debris from my jeans before I take a step toward the fissure that splits open the base of the tree.

Marjorie helps me drag Cyril's body toward the crevice. Darkness swallows us when we cross its threshold, like some kind of doorway down into the underworld. To the land of the dead, where the sun never rises and never sets. We conceal him beneath dirt and fallen leaves, snapping boughs from the trees to cover his body like a shroud.

By the time we return outside, the clouds have dissipated. Stars shine in the dark above us. Reachwood Forest lies silent, nothing stirring in the quiet, as if nothing had ever really lived here. As though all of the legends about this place are only stories made up by bored children to frighten one another at night.

"Are you going to tell anybody what happened?" Marjorie asks and glances back at the hollow where we left Cyril buried underground. A shiver ripples down my spine when I wonder if there was any truth to what he told me. If the forest really does need a body to grant a wish.

Another sacrifice.

"No. They would take you away from me, if they knew."

"I didn't mean for any of it to happen—for you to hurt him. I just wanted to keep you safe." Marjorie's voice breaks as we retreat from the clearing. I turn around to pull her into another hug. Her hair smells like fresh rain, mixed with the faint scent of the vanilla shampoo she always uses.

"I know," I say. My eyes rest on the place where Adam's body lay alone for three days before it was discovered in the forest. Left like an offering to something that granted us everything we asked for and more.

"Do you think our luck will change now?" Marjorie asks, question muffled against my jacket. Shallow cuts smart against my wrists and fingertips as she pulls out of my embrace and puts on a brave face. "Maybe the forest will grant our wish. Since we've left his body here."

I say nothing.

We never look back as we leave the grove to return home.

"Get changed and take a shower," I say after I close the front door. The rain hadn't fully erased the evidence of what had just happened in the forest—traces of blood still smudge Marjorie's clothes like paint. I run a hand through my hair, and dirt and dead leaves fall to the floor. The house is quiet as we unbutton our jackets in the foyer. Empty, except for the two of us—my parents left to spend the night in the city after closing on their new home.

Marjorie disappears down the dark corridor without a word, and I hear the bathroom door click shut. The shower starts to run after I walk into my bedroom. Water rushes through the pipes as I sit down on the edge of my bed and wait for my legs to stop shaking.

I draw the blinds across the windows before I change out of my ruined clothes and return to the hallway. Marjorie left her bloody sweater and jeans rolled into a bundle outside the bathroom door. I cradle our stained garments close as I carry them to the laundry room, adding detergent and a cup of bleach before I turn on the machine. It hums as it rinses the fabric clean.

I shower after Marjorie, pausing when I catch a glimpse of my face in the mirror before I step underneath the warm water. My heartbeat quickens at the sight of the blood still speckled against my skin. Cyril's blood. His words play over and over again in my head as my eyes drift to the medicine cabinet.

The prescription container waits on the shelf when I open the door. Pushing down on the lid until it pops open, I hesitate after I shake one of the white pills onto the countertop. I've tried so hard to taper off of them. To prevent the dependency from becoming one final way that my ex-husband hurts me. But I need something to soothe the new cuts and bruises across my body. To blunt the memory of what happened in the forest tonight and erase Cyril's dead gaze from my mind.

I swallow the pill before I step into the shower. The water runs hot enough to turn my skin red. I wince as I scrub away dirt and crusted blood. Cuts and scrapes smart underneath my touch. Dark purple bruises spread across my shoulders.

I dress again and return to my bedroom. Marjorie climbs in beside me when I finally crawl beneath my sheets. She doesn't say anything as she curls up close against the warmth of my body. The same way she used to when she was still small enough to believe the only monsters in the world lived hidden just beneath her bed.

CHAPTER 59

"What if they don't believe me?" Marjorie is curled in her seat the next morning. She still favors her right hand, fingers stiff as she fidgets with the beaded friendship bracelet on her wrist. I park the car in the first open space in front of the hospital.

"They will," I say and unbuckle my seatbelt. The doctors had never asked too many questions when I arrived in the emergency room after another battle with my ex-husband. Overworked and tired from the long hours they spent on shift. Or maybe I was just a good liar.

"But what if they don't—what if they think you hurt me?" Marjorie asks. Her lower lip sticks out in a pout. The wind rises as we step out of the car. Clouds cover the sky. Maybe the oncoming storm will wipe away any remaining traces of what had happened to Cyril last night. Erase the blood and any other signs of our struggle, the same way the rain had washed away any evidence of what happened to Adam fifteen years ago.

"It's going to be fine. Trust me, alright?"

"Okay," Marjorie says. Her feet scrape against the concrete as she follows me toward the building. Shadows darken the thin skin beneath her eyes.

She sticks close to my side when we enter the hospital. People bustle around us as we follow the signs through the white corridors. After Marjorie registers her name at the front desk in the emergency room, we sit down on one of the hard benches and wait for the nurse to call her name. I flip through the slick pages of a magazine. Marjorie fidgets in her seat as the local news plays across the televisions mounted to the walls. I hold my breath, half-expecting Cyril's face to flash across the screen. But he never appears.

Maybe nobody knows he's missing.

"Marjorie Montgomery?" A nurse smiles at us from the doorway. Marjorie rises to her feet. We walk down a sterile hallway into a cramped room where we wait together in silence. My stomach flutters. Maybe this time the doctor will become suspicious. Realize we're lying.

"How did it happen?" The doctor asks when she enters the room. She closes the door behind her and rests her pen against her clipboard.

"I fell during gym class," Marjorie says. Her innocent expression never wavers as she tells the lie. The same as mine when I evaded the doctor's questions at the hospital back home. Marjorie had sat beside me countless times while I made up stories about my bruises and broken bones, and her voice never stumbles as she answers more questions until the doctor nods in satisfaction.

A cast wraps Marjorie's wrist in white plaster when we walk outside. Not badly broken—an incomplete fracture that should heal in only a few weeks. The doctor had stabilized it and advised me to give her some aspirin for the pain. When we climb into the car, she slams the door shut hard. The sound echoes across the busy lot. Slouching in her seat, she picks at the edges of the cast encasing her right hand as I back out of the parking spot.

My hands clench against the wheel when I catch sight of the posters on the drive home. They plaster the streets, the same way they had after Adam, Emily, Kristen and so many other children had disappeared. Paper now printed with Cyril's face, name and date of birth instead. Victoria must have called the police when he didn't return to their house last night.

After he stormed out during their fight.

"Do you think they'll find him?" Marjorie asks. She turns away from the window as we pass another poster taped across a picket fence. The bruises across my throat ache with every breath, hidden beneath a high turtleneck sweater.

"No—I don't," I say as I turn into the ravine. The trees reach toward the street.

"How do you know, though?" Marjorie persists, eyes dark with worry.

She waits for an answer as I search for the right words to reassure her. I don't know—not really. It didn't take long for Ambrose to discover Adam's body there fifteen years ago. But the grove is hidden well enough that the search party might miss it as they comb through the forest. If nobody visits it, Cyril's body could lie out there for years. Reduced to skin and bone, scavenged by animals. Sometimes they find the bodies of the children who go missing, but sometimes they vanish without a trace. Emily's body still hasn't been found, although it's been over a decade since she disappeared now.

Silence falls between us like a wall. We don't speak after we emerge from the ravine to steer through the familiar suburban streets.

A moving van blocks the driveway when we return home. Men haul heavy boxes from the house. All of my parents' belongings, packed away for their move to the city. We wait for an opening before we slip through the front door without a word.

"You should go out," I say as Marjorie retreats toward her bedroom. "Your friends should be out of class by now—go spend some time with them."

"I don't want to," she protests, folding her arms across her chest. "I just want to be alone right now."

"It's going to look weird if you disappear," I argue. We have to act normal. There's not much time left before they open an investigation into Cyril's disappearance. Nobody knows we went into the forest last night. Nobody but Victoria. If she suspects what happened, would she tell anybody—or would she stay silent to protect me?

The edges of Marjorie's mouth tremble as my father follows another pair of movers down the stairs. They walk slowly, muscles tense as they carry the dresser from my parents' bedroom between them. Wrapped underneath a layer of plastic to protect it from damage during the move to their new home. We step back to let them through, but my father stops when he catches sight of us.

"Where were you?" he asks. His face furrows with worry as he notices the cast on Marjorie's wrist. "What happened—are you okay?"

"I'm fine." She brushes aside his question.

"She fell down," I explain as he opens his mouth again. "We went to the hospital this morning. It's broken, but it should heal pretty quickly."

"Yeah, it just cracked a little bit. Don't worry about it." Marjorie smiles, and I wonder if she feels the same guilt I do for lying to him. If she's concealing it just beneath a thin veneer of cheerfulness.

"Well I'm glad it's nothing serious," he says as another pair of movers lumber past us, balancing the pieces of my parents' bedframe between them. "Are you going out again?"

"I'm walking over to the mall," she says as they maneuver the iron frame through the front door. "Some of my friends are there right now. They're having a party tonight, so I might be back late."

"Okay. Just be careful," he says, and I wonder if he's heard that Cyril hadn't returned home last night. "Don't go near the forest."

"I won't. Don't worry." Marjorie flashes a quick smile at him as she heads toward the door. "See you. Good luck with the move."

"Call me if you need me to pick you up," I say and wave as she walks through the doorway. Hopeful that she won't say anything to give us away. That she'll be able to pretend everything is okay.

I retreat to the guest room until my parents leave to supervise the move into their new home. After the moving van pulls out of the driveway, I wander through the vacant rooms of the house. No pictures remain on the walls. Most of the furniture is already gone. I search through the bare cupboards in the kitchen until I find a spare glass and pour some water from the tap. The cold liquid soothes my sore throat as I return to my bedroom.

I flinch when the front door slams open again. Heavy footsteps travel down the hall. Maybe Cyril survived the injuries he sustained last night and dragged himself back out of the trees to look for me. Or maybe my parents just forgot something. I hold still, barely breathing as the sound moves closer.

My father pushes open my bedroom door and says, "I wanted to talk to you about something else. Are you busy right now?"

"Not really." I exhale. My shoulders relax as the tension leaves my body.

"Did you hear Cyril went missing?" he asks as a crisp breeze blows through the open window, raising goosebumps on my skin.

"No. When did it happen?" I feign surprise. Cyril's dead eyes surface in my mind again, covered by leaves inside the hollow tree. Maybe insects have already started to eat the soft parts of his body.

"Last night sometime," my father says, voice low with worry. Silver streaks the thin hair at his temples. Wrinkles line his broad face, and I wonder how much I've also changed in the years I've spent away. Although I've only been back in Reachwood for just over two months, it feels like decades. "He went into the forest alone and never came back. They're sending a search party out to look for him tomorrow."

"I hope they find him." My mouth turns dry as I realize I need to return to the grove. To journey back through the trees and make sure his body is concealed well enough that no one will ever discover it.

"You should keep a close eye on Marjorie. I don't want her to get lost somewhere out there, too." He pauses in the doorway and asks, "Have you heard anything from your lawyer?"

"No. Nothing." I shake my head.

"We haven't sold the house yet." He clears his throat. "You can stay here until we find a buyer. I know your mother thinks it would be best if you leave. But I don't agree with her."

"Thanks," I say. Grateful tears blur my vision as I embrace him.

After my father exits the room, I retrieve Adam's skull from the closet. Bone scrapes rough against my skin as I turn it over in my hands.

What did Cyril mean when he asked if Victoria had ever told me what happened to him?

CHAPTER 60

I join the search party the next morning. After I answer a few questions from the police and sign my name on the sheet, I fall in line with the rest of the volunteers spread out through the forest. A chorus of voices shout Cyril's name into the trees.

I slip away from the grid formation when we reach a mound of stones gathered at the edge of the path, hurrying away as the volunteers continue to comb through the wilderness. Dead leaves tapestry the earth. The sun shines bright enough to drive back the shadows while I walk through the undergrowth.

Everything falls quiet when I reach the grove. The rhythmic hum of insects fades away to silence as I linger at the edge of the clearing, reluctant to enter the ring of hawthorn trees at its center.

I take a shallow breath before I move forward again. The bruises on my body ache as I head toward the cracked tree that presides over the heart of the grove. The hole in its trunk waits like an open invitation. I hesitate on the threshold and stare into the dark below. Not eager to climb inside to view Cyril's body. Confront the memory of what happened a few days ago in the forest.

What I did to him.

But Cyril's body is missing when I finally slip into the hidden space. Gone just like all the other children who have vanished out here—disappeared without a trace, without leaving so much as a sign behind. As if they had never existed before this place claimed them.

My skin prickles as I stand still in the darkness. Maybe some kind of animal dragged his remains out from beneath the tree to feast on his bones and flesh somewhere else. Or maybe the forest decided to keep him and hid his body away.

Accepted it as an offering.

The clearing lies empty when I climb back out of the fissure inside the tree. This place looks almost beautiful in the daylight—gold shines beneath my feet. I admire my surroundings for a moment before I leave the grove. My body feels weightless as I follow the stacked stones through the foliage.

❦

"Ava? I didn't expect to see you here," Victoria says as she falls into step beside me sometime later. After I slip back into the line of volunteers combing through another section of the undergrowth. She's already dressed in black. Like she knows Cyril isn't coming back.

"I heard Cyril went missing." My voice croaks. I pluck at the turtleneck covering the bruises on my throat. "I wanted to help look for him."

"What happened to your voice?"

"Nothing. I'm just coming down with a cold." I turn away to conceal the guilt on my face when I remember how the knife sliced across the soft skin on Cyril's neck. The way his limbs turned stiff and rigid before we left him inside the hollow tree.

And how something out there stole his body.

"I'm glad you still decided to help. Even though you aren't feeling well." Victoria drops the subject. Her eyes drift to her children as they search through the thick foliage ahead of us. They shout for their dad, panicked voices dampened by the breeze. "I hope we find some sign of him today. Virgil and Catherine have been devastated."

"I hope so, too." I almost stutter over the words. Victoria says nothing, and I wonder how much she suspects. If she has already guessed what happened to Cyril in the forest.

"How's Marjorie doing?" Victoria asks and touches my hand. Sparks of heat flicker across my skin—the last thing I should be feeling right now. Not with Cyril's body missing.

"She's fine," I say and push my hands into the pockets of my jacket. "I found her at home. Turns out she caught the bus into Portland to hang out with her old friends for the day."

"I'm happy she's okay." Victoria's voice doesn't give her thoughts away. "I'm relieved to see you, too—I was so worried. After you went into the forest."

Silence settles between us, heavy with secrets. Reachwood Forest stretches out before us, as deep and complete as a dream. We spend the rest of the morning following the voices of the volunteers through the trees. I push through the undergrowth as the crisp breeze rises.

Radios crackle as different members of the search party relay messages through the channel. Sweat sticks to the back of my neck. My muscles stiffen every time one of the volunteers shouts or points at something, fearful that they might have discovered Cyril.

But it always turns out to be nothing.

"Are you okay?" Victoria asks when we follow the path back to the edge of the forest. Police vehicles line the street. Red and blue lights flash as another group of volunteers scouts through the foliage. More white ribbons knot the limbs of the trees, the same way they did after Adam went missing.

Before they found his body.

"I feel great," I say. Not quite a lie—my body feels light for the first time in a long while. But an ache grows in my chest when I glimpse Virgil and Catherine ahead of us. Their frantic voices echo through the forest as they call out for their father. Raw pain written across their delicate faces, like maybe they already suspect Cyril will never come home again.

"Are you sure?" Victoria touches my hand. "You're crying."

"I'm fine." I brush at the tears running down my cheeks.

"He's not coming back, is he?" Victoria asks, and I say nothing.

When I turn in her direction, she is smiling.

CHAPTER 61

The house is vacant when I return from the search party late in the afternoon. I pace alone through its empty rooms while I wait for Marjorie to return home from school. Almost nostalgic for the time I spent here. For the years I shared with my friends, before Adam's death tore us apart.

I open Marjorie's bedroom door, leaning against the wooden frame to survey the empty space. It looks much the same as when I grew up here—bed freshly made, sunflower-patterned sheets smooth and neat. Walls plastered with posters. Her notebooks lie open, scribbled pages scattered across the desk.

Reachwood Forest waits at the border of our yard outside when my eyes stray over to the window. Trees wrap around the edge of our property like a protective wall—thick and impenetrable. Cyril's body is still out there somewhere. Maybe the forest will protect us.

Hide his body well enough that nobody will ever find it.

My phone rings. I pull it out of my pocket, and my lawyer's number flashes across the screen. My fingers tremble as I push the button to accept the call. Maybe I've won the settlement and gained full custody of Marjorie. Or maybe I've lost everything.

"Hello?" I say and sit down cross-legged on the bedroom floor.

"Ava? I have some good news for you," my lawyer says. A smile spreads across my face as she speaks.

After I hang up the phone, I retrieve our clothes from the laundry. The stains on Marjorie's sweater and jeans have washed away, leaving the fabric clean and immaculate. I return to her bedroom to hang the garments up in her closet, but pause as I remember the blood smeared across them. I can almost still picture the smudges of red now.

I hesitate before I cross Marjorie's bedroom floor and push my hand into the narrow space between her mattress and headboard. Nothing is concealed there—no lighters, weed or pills I can steal. Disappointment grows like a hole in my stomach as I exit the room, closing the door with a soft click behind me.

Marjorie returns home in the evening. She slips through the door and disappears into her bedroom before I can ask where she has been for the last few hours. After I cook dinner, she sits quietly at the kitchen table and picks at her meal. Face clouded, as if she's still thinking about what happened to Cyril in the forest.

"Are you okay?" I ask. My voice rasps, still hoarse.

"What?" She glances up. "Oh, yeah—I'm fine."

"Do you want to talk about what happened?"

"Not really." Her eyes narrow like she expects some kind of confrontation.

"I meant it, when I said I'm not going to tell anybody." I reach across the table and touch her wrist. "You just wanted to keep me safe—none of this is your fault."

"Every time I close my eyes, I see his face."

"It will go away, eventually," I say, remembering the guilt that threatened to swallow me after we discovered Adam's body in the grove. How it drove me out of Reachwood, desperate to escape my memories. I'll never forget it completely, but it's lost the sharp teeth it possessed when his death was still fresh. Grown gentler over time.

"Do you know that because of what happened to Adam?" Marjorie asks, like she can read my mind. My tongue sits mute and clumsy in the back of my mouth as I search for the right words to say. To finally tell her everything.

"It was an accident," I admit finally. "I didn't mean for anything bad to happen to him. Just like you never planned to hurt Cyril when you went into the forest."

"Did you hear they're already looking for him?" Marjorie changes the subject. Eyes thoughtful, like she's still processing what I just told her. The wooden legs of her chair scrape against the floor when she rises to her feet. She picks up her plate and scrapes the untouched food into the garbage bin beneath the sink.

"Yeah. I joined the search party this morning."

"What?" Marjorie frowns as she leans against the countertop. "Why?"

"Because I wanted to know if they found anything," I say and stand to carry my own uneaten meal over to the kitchen counter.

"Did they?"

"No—nothing yet," I say as I rinse the dishes clean in the sink. "I went back to the grove to make sure his body was still hidden. It was missing."

"What?" Marjorie stutters. The color drains from her face.

"Some kind of animal probably dragged it away. Hid it somewhere else in the forest." After I place the plates in the dishwasher, Marjorie wraps her arms around me.

"Thank you." She holds me tight.

"I really mean it. I won't let anything bad happen to you, alright?" I say. Warmth blossoms inside me as I run my fingers through her hair, the same way I used to do when she was younger.

"I know." Marjorie flashes an unsteady smile at me when she pulls away.

"I also have some good news. My lawyer called today." My voice lightens. "The judge granted me full custody, so you won't ever have to see your father again. They've given me almost all of our assets back too, so we won't have to worry about anything anymore."

"That's great." She beams.

"Yeah, it looks like our luck has finally changed."

"Does that mean we're leaving?" Marjorie asks. She fidgets with the plaster cast encasing her right wrist while she waits for me to speak. Her eyes stray to the forest outside the window. Cyril's body is still out there somewhere, along with the bodies of all the other children who disappeared over the years. But the forest didn't take Marjorie. It didn't take me.

It gave me exactly what I wanted.

"No—I've decided to stay."

CHAPTER 62

When weeks pass and Cyril still hasn't been found, I help Victoria pack his belongings away inside their vault. Virgil and Catherine help us haul heavy boxes filled with his possessions through the circular door. Faces sullen, as if they expect their father to return at any moment.

Marjorie watches from her seat in the living room. A cast still wraps her forearm. The broken bone heals beneath white plaster, almost hidden under all of the signatures from her friends at school. If she feels any guilt while we carry Cyril's belongings through the room, her expression never betrays what she might be thinking.

I hope mine does the same.

"Is that everything?" I ask. My fading bruises throb as I stack the last heavy box on top of the pile in the vault. Shelves line the walls. Bright lights shine down from the ceiling. Gold statues and jewelry sparkle inside locked glass cases.

"Not quite. There's still some other things I want to get rid of," Victoria says as she turns away from the crates. Filled with belongings Cyril won't need any longer—clothes, hunting rifles and the polished bones of trophy animals.

Catherine and Virgil disappear from the doorway. Resentment shadows their eyes, like they can't understand why Victoria wants to forget their father so quickly. They join Marjorie in the living room, and their subdued voices float through the long hallways of the house as I follow Victoria upstairs.

The holes Cyril punched through the walls have all been repaired. The scent of fresh paint still remains in the air. The broken furniture has been removed, replaced by new models. As though Victoria wants to erase every trace of her husband.

"You're redecorating?" I ask as we weave between more cardboard boxes stacked in the hallway.

"Yeah. I don't want to keep anything that reminds me of him."

"What are you going to do—you know, now that he's gone?" I glance at the smooth animal skulls still lining the walls. Horns decorated with swirls of gold. Eye sockets hollow and empty.

"I don't know. We struck a new vein of gold in the mine a few days ago, so at least I won't have to worry about having enough money." Victoria's face lights up when she smiles.

"That's great." I smile back, saying, "I have good news too, actually—my divorce is finally over. I got all of my assets back, and the judge granted me full custody of Marjorie."

"I'm so glad to hear that." Victoria wraps me in an embrace. I rest my head against her shoulder and close my eyes for a moment. Her hair smells sweet. A flash of heat darts through my body.

"Yeah—it feels like I've been given a chance to start over again."

"Me too." Victoria fidgets with the gold rings adorning her fingers when she pulls away. "I wanted to say I'm sorry for everything that happened. I'd like to start over again with you, if you want to."

"I'd like that, too," I say and smile again when she presses a quick kiss against the corner of my mouth. I follow her to the stack of boxes piled at the end of the hallway and pick one up, cradling it in my arms.

The contents rattle inside as she asks, "Do you mind bringing these downstairs? I just sold a piece of jewelry to a new client—I need to get it ready to send to them."

"Sure." I carry the boxes to the vault one by one. After I set the last one down, I pause in the doorway to admire the golden jewelry displayed behind glass cases. Probably worth a fortune, crafted by generations of Victoria's family.

Her hope chest sits in the corner of the room, wooden surface carved with roses. The same one that always rested at the foot of her bed when we were teenagers. Victoria used to hide all of her contraband away inside—pills that turned the whole world bright.

Maybe a few are still left behind.

I hesitate before I cross the floor toward it. I shouldn't look inside, but I only have a few painkillers left before I run out completely. The only thing that can block out my thoughts about what happened in the forest. I need to stop taking them. To keep Cyril's death from pushing me over an edge I can never come back from again.

But I still long for that comforting numbness.

The lid creaks when I push it open to search through its contents. Victoria's wedding dress, gold-threaded sheets and other valuable things from her dowry. Something glitters at the bottom of the chest. I pick it up and suck in my breath.

A heart, cast in gold like a trophy. Anatomically correct, it's an intricate masterpiece—one that should be displayed proudly alongside the other works created by Victoria's family. So why would she hide it in here like a secret?

The chambers, arteries and veins look incredibly realistic. Detailed enough that I can feel the texture of the tissue. Victoria could have preserved the exact shape in silicone from the heart of some animal Cyril brought home from the forest. Cast it first in wax, and then later in gold. But it's about the size of my fist—large enough to be human.

I turn it over in my hands as I remember the hole carved into Adam's chest, deep enough to expose the flesh and bone below. How his heart was missing when his body was discovered in the grove fifteen years ago. And how Victoria concealed her finest piece of artwork here like a souvenir instead of putting it on display.

Hid it away like something she wanted to keep safe.

"Ava, are you still in there?" Victoria's voice carries down the hallway.

"Yeah, I'm here." I flinch and grip the heart tight as it almost slips from my hands. After I return it to its hiding place at the bottom of the chest, I fasten the latches on the lid and step away quickly.

"Catherine and Virgil asked me if Marjorie could stay over tonight," Victoria says when she appears in the doorway. "They don't really like spending time alone here since Cyril disappeared."

"Sure—I think she'd like that." I turn away as my voice shakes. Victoria studies my face, and I hope my expression doesn't betray me.

Later, after our children disappear outside to spend some time with their friends, I follow Victoria into the bedroom she used to share with Cyril. We undress, and she kisses the faint scar at the base of my neck before we fall into bed. My body tenses when I remember how Cyril wrapped his fingers around my throat in the forest and choked the breath from my lungs. The way his glazed eyes stared up at me before we left his body in the grove.

"Hurt me," I whisper. Victoria hesitates before she bites down on my shoulder, so hard that her sharp teeth almost break my skin. The sudden pain is intense enough to make me forget what happened in the forest. To drive those thoughts away, until there is nothing left. I barely have a chance to catch my breath before Victoria kisses me again. Later, we fall asleep curled up close together beneath the sheets.

I close my eyes and drift into oblivion as Victoria breathes beside me, soft and steady.

I startle awake in the middle of the night. My heartbeat races as my dreams about the forest fade from my mind. Victoria lies fast asleep beside me. She never stirs when I slip out of her embrace, the same way she must have slipped out of mine fifteen years ago. To journey through the forest and confront Adam in the grove.

Maybe she had always intended to put a final end to their rivalry—to silence him before he could reveal her secret to their families. Or maybe it was an accident and she hadn't meant for it to happen. But maybe she had been compelled by something else. The wish I whispered in the grove earlier.

To make Adam pay for what he did.

Cyril must have followed her out there and witnessed what happened. The same way he always trailed in her footsteps, hopeful she would notice him. Maybe he participated in Adam's murder, or just stumbled upon the aftermath—but later, he must have used that secret to bind them together.

So that if she left, he could threaten to take everything from her.

Thoughts rush through my head as I dress and splash water on my face in the bathroom. The outline of the bite Victoria gave me earlier still lingers against my shoulder. I lean closer to study my reflection in the mirror. The teeth marks look familiar—about the same size and shape as the long-healed scar at the hollow of my neck.

What really happened on the night Adam led me into the forest? Maybe Victoria found me after Adam left me in the grove and bit me as payback for picking him instead. For trying to leave my feelings for her there.

Or maybe something else did.

I climb back into Victoria's bed again, and she stirs in her sleep. I don't say anything, hopeful that some new kind of future can rise from the secrets between us. I curl up beside her and hold her close. I still don't want to let her go.

Despite everything I know.

I lie there for a long time before I slip out of bed again to check on Marjorie. Virgil and Catherine's rooms are both vacant—windows open wide to reveal the forest outside. A breeze blows through the empty space, crisp enough to raise goosebumps across my skin. I stay awake for the rest of the night as I pace through the silent rooms.

In the morning, our children sneak back inside like wild animals as the sun rises over Reachwood Forest. I catch a quick glimpse of Marjorie, and she smiles at me before she disappears down the hallway.

Autumn leaves decorate her hair, wreathing her brow like a crown.

EPILOGUE

One night, we venture back into Reachwood Forest. We stride down the path as the darkness presses in around us. The moon shines in the sky, bright enough to reduce the stars to small pinpricks of light. A strong breeze shakes the barren boughs of the trees, carrying the crisp scent of winter.

Dead foliage crackles beneath our feet as we follow the stacks of stones through the undergrowth. Branches weave together above our heads, tight enough to block the sky from sight. We stand still in the silence for one long moment after we emerge in the grove of hawthorn trees. Our breath drifts like smoke in front of us, made visible by the cold.

We bury our last offerings underneath the tree where they found Adam's body. Things we no longer need—a skull, our wedding rings, gleaming like broken promises in the dim light.

Stars shine through gaps in the forest canopy as we leave the grove to follow the landmarks back home. When we reach the tree line, we pause and look back.

Nothing moves in the shadows gathered deep and dark at the edges of the path.

ACKNOWLEDGMENTS

Thank you to my agent, Penelope Burns, for championing this story and for your encouragement and support throughout every step of this process. It has been a joy to work with you to bring *Vicious Creatures* into the world and I am deeply grateful to have shared this journey with you.

I would like to thank my editor, Luisa Cruz Smith, for her belief in this story and for taking a chance on a debut author. Your knowledge and guidance have been invaluable, and your suggestions have helped shape this book into something I am truly proud of. Thank you to the entire team at Scarlet for your support bringing this book into the world.

I would like to thank my mum and dad for reading to me every day when I was young and kickstarting my interest in books and writing. Thank you to my sister, who had to endure some of my first attempts at storytelling. Thank you to Margaret, Karen, Douglas and the rest of my family for supporting my love of reading and for your interest in my stories.

I would also like to thank the friends I made at the Imaginative Fiction Writers Association (IFWA) for your encouragement throughout the years. Your feedback and suggestions have helped me grow immensely as a writer, and I would never have made it this far without your support.

Thank you to Pitch Wars and the team of volunteers who help organize the program. The chance to take part in Pitch Wars is something that I am grateful for, and I am very happy that I was able to share this experience with the class of 2019.

And finally, I would like to thank my Pitch Wars mentors, P. J. Vernon and Kelly J. Ford, for believing in this book from the very beginning. It was an honor to be chosen as your mentee, and I am deeply grateful for the knowledge and experience that you shared with me throughout the Pitch Wars program and afterward. This story developed and grew so much through your feedback, mentorship and encouragement. Thank you for your kindness, guidance and support as I brought this story out of the forest.